WINTER FLIGHT

K-9 SEARCH AND RESCUE BOOK 5

LINDA J. WHITE

WINDY BAY BOOKS

Cover Design, June Padgett, Bright Eye Designs.

First printing, June 2023

Scripture quotations are from the ESV Bible (The Holy Bible, English Standard Version), copyright 2001 by Crossway, a publishing ministry of Good News Publishing. Used by permission. All rights reserved.

White, Linda J. 1949-

ISBN 978-7-7372356-4-4 (paperback)

ISBN 978-1-7372356-5-1 (ebook)

For my children,
Matt, Becky, and Sarah,
with much love

Pray that your flight may not be in winter or on a Sabbath.

— MATTHEW 24:20

1

I STOOD at the whiteboard breathing in a set pattern to ease my anxiety, a diverse class of twenty adults spread out before me—men and women, ranging in age from twenty- to fifty-something, all properly social-distancing, well-trained by two years of pandemic. They were deputies, search-and-rescue volunteer hopefuls, and old hands hoping to refresh their skills, all looking to me for information, insights, and inspiration. *How in the world did I get here?* I thought.

The door at the back of the room opened and in walked the answer. Nate. Nathan Tanner, my teacher, mentor, friend, and advocate. Nearing fifty, his dark, curly hair and beard were speckled with gray, but his eyes—those searchlight-blue eyes—were shining as brightly as ever. He taught me search and rescue; he encouraged me to begin consulting with police departments; and he pitched the idea of organizing a series of seminars to raise search-and-rescue proficiency across a broad spectrum of first responders to the Virginia Department of Emergency Management. The smarter the search, the sooner a lost person would be found.

Which is why I was here. I cleared my throat and began.

"You're called out in late afternoon on a beautiful fall day. A child is missing from a campground. Where do you begin to look?" I let that rhetorical question hang in the air, then continued.

"What's the difference between a lost person and a missing person? How do people react once they realize they're lost? Do they tend to stay put? Turn left or right? Go uphill? Downhill? Follow a stream? Does age make a difference? Or mental state? As a searcher, you can thrash around the woods all day," I said, "or you can search intelligently, based on documented probabilities and using proven techniques."

I held up a blue, spiral-bound book. "*Lost Person Behavior* by Robert J. Koester is the bible on this subject, and much of what I will go over today is from this book. I highly recommend you get it. Koester's been studying the subject for decades. In the heat of the moment, when you are called out and a life is on the line, you want to search smart. There is no better guide than this book.

"In search and rescue, you have to think on your feet and ask the right questions about the person who is missing. You need to know that a lost two-year-old will act differently than a four-year-old and a teenager will likely be found in a different place altogether. Dementia patients will present challenges that are different from the ones despondent people present. You need to be able to analyze the maps to see the hazards and note the places a person might be likely to miss a turn. There's a lot more to SAR than good boots and wind direction, though there's that too."

For the next three hours I kept my students' attention, going over the basics of lost-person behavior and peppering my talk with stories of actual searches I'd been on, some successful, some not. My German shepherd, Luke, lay on his side nearby, his ear twitching occasionally.

"Your first job," I said, "is to profile the lost person. What is their age, their fitness level, their mental state? What were they doing outside? Hiking? Fishing? Working? Skiing? How much experience in the outdoors do they have?

"After that, what's the area like that you're searching in? The topography, weather, and visibility? What trails are available, how well are they marked, and what turns might be missed? How about animal tracks, deer trails that a person might try to follow? Or features like streams, drainages, power lines, or fences?

"In general, when a person gets lost, at first they can't believe it. They're shocked, maybe embarrassed. They know what they're seeing doesn't match with what they should be seeing, but they'll convince themselves they're going the right way and keep moving. Reality has not quite set in. They don't believe they're lost, so they don't believe anyone's looking for them. They may ignore the helicopter circling overhead.

"Then, when they realize they truly are lost, it's flight, fight, or freeze, Koester says. Some will move faster to 'get somewhere,' some will strategize, some may stay put and wait for help."

We talked about dementia patients, a frequent reason for call-outs, and I told them about the elderly man we'd found trapped in the mud in a swampy area near Williamsburg. We discussed other cognitive cases, like people with autism or folks with intellectual disabilities who may not realize you're there to help, or despondent people, like the boy Nate literally talked off a ledge. Then there are those with medical issues, like the diabetic who'd passed out from low blood sugar.

We talked about every kind of case I could think of except criminal cases, although Luke and I had stumbled into our fair share of those. Searching for murder victims or worse, criminals on the run, was a specialized field, one for the professionals.

I saved a half hour for questions, fielding them like solid infield hits. The last one came from a dark-haired SAR volunteer I'd not met before. "What about Geraldine Largay?" he asked. "Didn't they use all this stuff and still couldn't find her?"

I saw Nate put his empty pipe in his mouth.

I took a deep breath. "Geraldine Largay," I began, "was an Appalachian Trail thru-hiker in her sixties. She was solo hiking in Maine in July 2013. She left the trail to relieve herself and became disoriented. Lost. She couldn't find her way back to the trail through the thick woods. Despite the best efforts of searchers, including the Maine Warden Service, she was not found. Two years later, surveyors stumbled on the remains of her tent, and, sadly of Ms. Largay. She was about seven hundred yards off the Appalachian Trail. According to the diary she left, Ms. Largay survived twenty-six days before dying in her tent."

I straightened my back. "SAR will never be 100 percent successful. Proper techniques, including understanding lost-person behavior, will increase your chances of a successful search but ...," I hesitated, "... but be prepared to give yourself grace." I paused and restated it. "Cut yourself some slack when a search ends without finding the person." I glanced at Nate, who stared forward impassively.

AFTERWARDS, throwing the ball for Luke outside the high school where my talk had taken place, I said to Nate, "Why is it mentioning Geraldine Largay makes me want to take off and hike the AT? I mean, what is it, twenty-two hundred miles? Five or six months? Scott wouldn't notice, would he?"

Nate laughed. "Girl, what are you running from now?" He shook his head, the corners of his eyes crinkling in amusement. "What's your husband doing today?"

"Scott and Ethan are reroofing the barn."

"That boy's still hanging around?"

Ethan was Scott's daughter's ex-boyfriend. "He loves working with Scott, and Scott appreciates the help." I picked up the ball and threw it again. "He pays him, of course, but I think Ethan would do it for free." Luke galloped after the ball, his black-and-gold coat glistening in the warm September sun. "It makes

Amanda mad, but oh well." Scott's daughter wasn't around much anymore now that she was a student at the University of Virginia.

"She's enjoying college?"

"Too much. She's drinking. Partying." I picked up the ball and threw it again. "Dating one guy after another and none of them the kind Scott would like her to be with."

"Lost-person behavior," Nate said, grinning.

I blinked. Once again Nate nailed it.

Our phones went off simultaneously. I didn't recognize the number on my screen. "Hello?"

"Ms. Cooper?"

"Yes."

"This is Ty Carson. Deputy from Rockbridge County? I was in your class this morning?"

"Okay..."

"Tall, sandy blond hair, black backpack, blue shirt. I sat to your left."

Ah, yes. He asked good questions. "I remember."

"I'm still driving back home, but I got a call. The sheriff's little boy is missing. They've been looking for over two hours. Can't find him anywhere. Everybody's been looking."

"How old is he?"

"Four. Anyway, could you come help us?"

I glanced at my watch. "Where does he live? How far are we talking about?"

"He's near Lexington about an hour from Charlottesville."

"Has he called it in to VDEM?" The Virginia Department of Emergency Management was the go-to for calling out search teams.

"Yes, ma'am. My buddy told me he hated doing that, but they can't find the little guy. Trouble is, there's old wells and a creek near the sheriff's home. Thick woods. His wife's got cancer, and the stress is getting to both of them."

I glanced over at Nate, who was still bent over his own call, his brow furrowed.

"He's a good guy," Ty said. "A good sheriff."

"Okay, look. Text me an address. I'll head that way. In the meantime, organize another hasty search of trails and structures near the house. Remember, kids his age tend to hide in sheds or outbuildings, cars, things like that. And they may not respond to searchers' calls. You have to look."

"Yes, ma'am. Thank you!"

"Call me if you find him before I get there." I clicked off my phone. Nate was sliding his into his pocket. I told him about the missing boy. "Want to come?"

"Cain't. Laura needs me. I gotta get home."

"Okay, I'm going to go. They'll probably find him before I get there."

"Hope so. Let me know."

THE DRIVE over to Lexington was beautiful, but I took it too fast to let the early leaf changes in the mountains nudge their beauty into my soul. My mind was elsewhere—on the boy that was missing; on the house Scott and I had bought two years ago and the work we were doing on it; on Scott's job and his daughter; on Nate and his crazy idea of doing SAR on horseback; and on my two-year-old nephew, my sister Brooke's son. At the last minute, Brooke had decided not to marry her son's father. I worried about the kid growing up without a dad. I know it's none of my business, but still.

I'd been consulting a lot with local sheriffs in Virginia over the past two years. COVID seemed to make everybody a little crazy, and the rash of runaways, despondent persons, wandering dementia patients, and inexperienced hikers getting lost had not abated even as the pandemic wound down. My skills as a SAR volunteer, a private investigator, and a former police detective remained much in demand.

Lexington, home of Washington and Lee University, is a small town in the Blue Ridge mountains. I remembered it as being hilly, full of trees and green lawns, pretty old houses, little shops, and, of course, the university.

Some newer developments had sprung up around the town, and that's where my GPS took me, to a street called Cherokee Lane. The houses were set back off the road and wide apart, separated by trees. My guess was each lot had four or five acres of land, with just enough cleared for a drain field.

I knew I was approaching the sheriff's house when the lane became lined with parked cars and pickups. I edged forward and double-parked near the end of his driveway. I was blocking the road, but I wasn't going to leave Luke in my Jeep half a mile away, and I didn't want to take him out until I'd scoped out the situation.

Ty found me right away as I approached the house. "Thank you for coming, ma'am."

"Still haven't found him?"

"No, ma'am."

"Okay. First, where can I park? I don't want to leave my dog down the road while I interview the sheriff and study the maps."

"I saved a space right here for you." Ty gestured toward a spot angling off the driveway, marked by traffic cones. "Give me your keys and I'll park it for you. The sheriff is up at the house. He's expecting you."

I handed over my keys. "It's the white Jeep at the end of the driveway. Park it, then leave the back gate open to give my dog some air."

"Yes, ma'am."

I walked up toward the house, still dressed in what I'd worn to do my lecture—black pants, a burgundy collared shirt, khaki blazer, and short leather boots. That morning I'd gathered my

honey-blonde, highlighted hair in a neat chignon for a professional look. I was glad of that as I approached the cluster of men
surrounding the man my gut knew was the sheriff.

He was short, not more than five foot nine, broad-shouldered,
and fit. His arms were ropey with muscle, his chest broad and
tight under his uniform shirt. He had a no-nonsense buzz cut,
and the scar on his neck said he had a story to tell.

He saw me and moved to greet me.

"Sheriff, I'm Jessica Cooper." I extended my hand.

"Skip Ward. Thank you for coming."

His eyes captured me. They were dark, almost black, and I
wondered if he might have some Native American blood in him.
"Is there some place we can talk?"

He took me around to the back of the house to a screened-in
porch overlooking the woods. Through a large picture window I
could see woman half-reclining on a couch, covered by a quilt,
her face pale. Another woman sat nearby in a chair, a book in
her lap.

"Have a seat." The sheriff gestured toward a patio table.

I pulled out a chair, retrieved the small black notebook I
always carried, and said, "Tell me about your son."

"Brody, he's like me. Stubborn. Active. Loves to be outside.
Weather don't faze him. Loves animals. More energy than we can
keep up with." His voice caught. "My wife, she's got cancer, and
it's been hard on her. She can't watch him every second."

I nodded. "You have a picture?" He showed me one on his
phone. I gave him my number and asked him to text it to me,
then I continued. "When and where was he last seen?"

"Around nine this morning, he asked her if he could collect the
eggs from the chicken house down there." He nodded toward the
coop about twenty yards downhill. "Right after that, she felt real sick.
That chemo is kicking her hard. She was in the bathroom throwing
up for about fifteen minutes. When she came out, she called for him.

The eggs, they were on the kitchen table. But she couldn't find Brody. She yelled, she walked around the house, she blew the whistle, but he didn't come. Around 9:45, she called me, crying, scared. She was upset that she couldn't find him and was too weak to search further."

Ty had joined us while the sheriff was speaking. He gave me topographic maps and a bottle of water, which I immediately cracked open.

"I came right home," the sheriff said, "ready to give that boy a talking to for scaring his mom, but then, I couldn't find him either. I called some neighbors, got them searching, and then my deputies. We been at it all morning. Nothing." His voice caught again.

"Has he ever done this before? Disappeared?"

"He knows the boundaries. He's not allowed to go in the woods by himself. We have allowed him to explore over there." He gestured toward a small patch of woods between his house and his neighbor's, not more than a hundred yards away, a patch so small you could see straight through the trees.

"Does he have a dog?"

The sheriff shook his head. "He wants one, but with my wife ..."

"I get that," I said. "I only asked because it's not unusual for a kid to follow a dog into the woods and get lost. When did he have breakfast?"

"Probably about seven. I was gone by then."

I moved into my reassuring mode. "Sheriff, the vast majority of kids are found within twenty-four hours. A lot of kids Brody's age get lost and curl up somewhere and go to sleep. But they can be really hard to find. They may fail to respond to searchers' calls. You've been in touch with VDEM?"

Ty answered. "Yes, ma'am. They're calling out the SAR people."

"Good. What's the ETA?"

Ty checked his watch. "About ninety minutes. There's not a group close out here."

I nodded. Then I looked down and studied the map. "Show me where you've searched." I listened as both the sheriff and Ty showed me on the map where they'd looked. "All right. You've got a command center set up in the garage, right?" They nodded. "Here's what I want you to do: Send searchers again to all the high-hazard features. Have them recheck all the wells you know of, the creek, any vehicles that are around, sheds, and so on. Extend the door-to-door area. Tell them to assume Brody won't respond to their calls.

"I will search with my dog, at least until the SAR people show up. If we haven't found him by then, I have another plan." I rose. "Do you have a place where I can change? And would it be possible to speak briefly with your wife?"

"Yes," the sheriff said.

I turned to Ty. "Would you get my go bag from behind the driver's seat in my Jeep?"

"Yes, ma'am!"

Sheriff Ward opened the French door to the house. "Come on in."

I hesitated. "Wait. One more thing. Is there any chance this is an abduction?" I asked in a low voice.

He frowned. "I mean, people get mad at me all the time, but take my kid? No. I really don't think so."

I hoped he was right.

2

AMY WARD OPENED her eyes as the sheriff and I walked into the house.

"Honey," the sheriff said, "this is Jessica Cooper. She's an expert in finding people. She's come to help us and would like to talk to you."

Tears formed in Amy's eyes. "Thank you." She was thin and pale, her skin slightly gray. A pink-and-blue paisley scarf covered her bald head.

I felt fear tighten my gut as I sat down in the chair the sheriff pulled up. Cancer was one reality I had not faced. I took a deep breath and began. I asked her all the normal questions, when had she last seen Brody, what was his mood, where did he like to play, was he in trouble for anything? Had there been an argument?

On my way in, I'd noticed the eggs in a wire basket on the table. One was broken. I could see it leaking out. Was the boy avoiding punishment for a broken egg?

I kept on, asking what shows he liked to watch, what toys were his favorites, where his playmates lived, and were there older kids in the neighborhood who were not in school.

"His best friend used to live next door," Amy said, gesturing toward the house to the east. "They've moved, and the new neighbors don't have kids. The older kids on our road are all in school. So Brody is pretty isolated. I want to put him in preschool but...I can't drive every day."

"Understandable," I said. Then I asked about the broken egg.

"No, he wouldn't have been punished for that," Amy said. "Maybe if he'd left the door to the coop open. We have foxes around here," she explained. "He knows the chickens need to be penned up. Still, I don't see him running away over that."

We kept talking until Ty came in with my go bag. The sheriff suggested I change in a second-floor bathroom. "Up the stairs to the left," he said.

As I climbed the stairs, I couldn't help but glance around this neat-as-a-pin house looking for places Brody could hide. The access to the attic, the blanket chest, a small closet in the hallway. As I changed into my SAR gear, my blue cargo pants and long-sleeved shirt, I thought about Sheriff Ward and Amy, teetering on the edge of an emotional cliff with their son missing.

This is why I do SAR, I thought. *I want to help these people. I want to find their son.* I couldn't do anything about the cancer, but I could help find their kid.

And right there in that upstairs bathroom, I prayed.

When I arrived back downstairs, the sheriff was sitting next to his wife, holding her hand in both of his, his eyes fixed on her face. When he heard me, he kissed her cheek, stood, and turned toward me.

"I have a plan," I said. "First, let me ask whether the house has been thoroughly searched. Closets, attic, basement? Under the beds?"

"Twice," he said. "First by me, then by my men."

"And Jill," his wife said. "Jill's my close friend. She knows Brody well. She went through the house too."

I looked at the sheriff. "Let's go outside. I have some questions about the map. Then I'll get my dog, and we'll search until the other SAR teams get here."

"Okay—"

"Wait, Skip ... help me." Amy struggled to get off the couch. "I'm going to throw up."

The sheriff rushed to help her, the tension in his face raw.

I WENT OUTSIDE and found Ty. "Can you go over this map with me? And find me a walker to help while Luke and I search?"

"Sure."

"Show me again where you all have searched so far," I asked.

He pointed to some places on the map: the neighborhood, the paths back into the woods, and several drainages. He marked houses, sheds, and parked vehicles they'd covered. "We have three groups searching here, here, and here." He indicated places on the map.

"What's this?" I asked, pointing to a red line about three-quarters of a mile back in the woods, running northwest.

"That's heavy-duty cattle fencing, square wire with three strands of barbed wire. We made that the edge of our search area."

"What's beyond it?"

"More woods and then a pasture. The sheriff told me the guy who owns it raises Angus cattle. I didn't see how a four-year-old could climb that fence, or any reason he'd want to." He pulled out his phone and showed me a picture of the fence.

I nodded. "All right. I'll get my dog. You get me a walker."

LUKE LEAPED out of the crate when I opened the door, excited by the sight of his SAR vest in my hand. I put the vest on him, leashed him up, and walked him around to the back of the house. Well, he kind of danced.

Since Brody was used to playing in the backyard, it was logical he'd have wandered into the woods beyond. But the search plan I'd worked out in my head started with the area around the house. I wanted Luke to get a good whiff of the smells there.

My walker was a deputy named Sam Smith. He was young, probably twenty-five, and slim, sharp-faced, with dark hair. He'd never done search and rescue before, but he was comfortable with dogs, and he volunteered to go with me while Ty continued to direct the other searchers. He didn't know how to use a GPS but was willing to learn. I showed him the basics, then said, "You play with it for a minute, and the map, while I take Luke around the house. Then we'll start."

I walked Luke counter-clockwise around the perimeter of the house on a loose leash, letting him sniff the smells in the yard. I knew Brody's had to be in there. His toys were scattered around.

On the east side of the house, I heard a dog barking. "Who's that?" I asked Sheriff Ward, who had just emerged from the house.

"I don't know. They moved in like two days ago."

Ty lifted binoculars to his face. "Looks like a golden retriever. He's in the screened-in porch, looking our direction. Probably smelled or saw your dog. You want us to go ask them to put him inside?"

I shook my head. "No. If he's contained he won't bother us."

I HAD ALREADY DECIDED to start by going down the path that led to the compost pile—the place where Ward dumped his lawn clippings and leaves. "Mark this spot on the GPS," I told Sam.

"Yes, ma'am."

In the meantime, I turned on my Garmin InReach, the hand-held satellite tracker Scott bought me after I'd scared him to death by getting lost overnight after a search. I'd promised Scott

I'd use the InReach anytime I was on a search or running in the woods. I thought that was a little obsessive, but if it made him happy, I'd do it.

I slipped the Garmin into the cargo pocket on my right leg and checked the wind. It was coming from the southeast, which could mean rain was on the way. I started down the path but then angled to the right so Luke would have the full benefit of the wind.

Fall had arrived. Every year, the leaves of golden-yellow poplars, red dogwoods, and russet oaks floated through the air like invitations, beckoning me to forget my worries and run—run through the woods until my muscles were tired and my bones were happy.

Today, though, I had to focus on a lost kid and a dog who was quartering ahead of me, searching for a scent, working hard for his play reward.

The land we were searching was hilly, rocky, with some shallow drainages and minor drop-offs. Typical for the Blue Ridge. Oaks, birches, beeches, and maples populated the forest, with dogwoods and redbuds providing the underlayment. Mountain laurel grew in thick patches. I'd tangled with that on many occasions.

Half an hour into our search, we reached the fence line, and I told Luke to turn north. Sam stayed about ten yards behind me, quietly keeping up, which is all I cared about. I thought I'd go a little way along the fence before checking the map and deciding which angle to take going back. The woods were as thick on one side of the fence as the other.

I checked my watch. We'd been searching for forty-five minutes. The others had been deployed for several hours before we got here and were continuing to look. It was time for Plan B, so I starting thinking ahead about how to organize the SAR teams once they arrived, and about the remote possibility Brody had been abducted.

Luke, who had been ranging ahead of me, came back toward me, staying close to the fence line, his head up, sniffing the air. I saw him stop right at the place a clump of mountain laurel intersected the fence. Then he kept going, retracing our steps. Why? What was he sensing? I dutifully followed him, shrugging at the question on Sam's face.

At one point along the fence, there was a small drainage. Barely perceptible. It looked to me like a place where a tree had been uprooted, leaving a depression now filled with brambles and mountain laurel. Luke was very interested in that place, and I wondered if he smelled a wild animal. When I looked closely, though, I saw that the depression provided a spot someone or something could wiggle under the fence. And on the fence I saw a tuft of gold-and-white fur, quite plausibly hair from a golden retriever.

The new neighbors' dog? Could Brody have followed the dog all the way out here?

The sheriff had said Brody wanted a dog. His playmate, the former resident of the dog's house, had moved away. Brody would have been comfortable with that backyard. Could he have gone over there to play and then followed the dog?

I asked Sam to radio Ty and ask him to check with the neighbors to see if the dog had been loose in the yard that morning. When I turned back, I saw Luke wasn't waiting for me to get my questions answered. He was wiggling under the fence.

I almost called him back but then I thought, no, I trust my dog. I slipped off my pack, threw it over the fence, and followed him, scooting under that fence like a mutt. "Come on," I said to Sam, who was looking at me with a mix of disdain and concern.

"They have cows. Maybe a bull."

"I'm following my dog. Come on."

Luke took over, swinging left and right in small arches, but heading through these woods. I could see we were approaching a clearing. The cow pasture. Was there a bull? Should I call Luke back?

I broke into a run. I wanted to get a look at the herd before they saw us. But I stopped when I saw Luke racing toward me. He grabbed the tug on my belt and took off again. Had he found him? Found Brody?

Adrenaline surged through my body. "Come on!" I yelled to Sam. I ran, emerging from the woods into the sunny pasture. I saw a dozen black cows grazing and more beyond them. I saw a pond, a farm pond, sparkling in the sun. And Luke stood next to it, barking.

Oh, no. Fear gripped my chest. Luke turned and ran toward me. I put on more speed. And that's when horror hit me.

A boy lay in the pond, his body submerged, head back, his face barely visible, his eyes wide with fear.

Was he alive?

"Call it in!" I yelled to Sam. "Get help!"

Farm ponds are dangerous. Cows wading in and out break down the banks, forming thick muck. They can get through it but for people and dogs it can be like quicksand. "Don't ever swim in a farm pond," Nate told me once. "It'll suck you down."

Plus, can you imagine the bacteria from the cow poop?

I did not want to go in that water.

"I'm coming, Brody!" I yelled as I dropped my pack and unlaced my boots. I didn't want to go in, but I could not leave that boy.

My plan was this: I'd try to swim, keeping my feet off the bottom so I didn't get sucked down. I'd support him, keeping his face above the water, until more help came.

I for sure didn't want Luke following me.

"Luke!" I said, grabbing his collar for attention. I looked straight into his deep-brown eyes. "Down! Stay!"

He dropped. "Stay!" I reiterated. And then I launched myself into the pond.

It wasn't that deep. Not deep enough to support me. I floundered immediately, my left foot finding the muck at the bottom. I reacted, slightly panicked, by crying out as I jerked my foot back. I heard a splash. Luke! He thought I was in trouble. "Luke, no. Go back!" I yelled, but he wasn't leaving me.

I had to refocus. I had a kid to save. I managed to work my way over to Brody. He was knee deep in mud. The pond at this point was slightly over waist-deep on me. "Brody, my name is Jess. I'm going to help you," I said. "My dog found you!"

Brody was too exhausted to give me anything but a look. I wrapped my arms around him and tried pulling him up. Nothing. My movements sloshed water in his face, and he sputtered and coughed. My mind went back to the elderly man stuck in mud near Williamsburg. I thought, *I have to break the suction.* To do that, I had no choice but to plant my feet at the bottom.

So I did. My feet sunk in, and I found something that resembled a firm bottom. I gently wiggled Brody as I pulled upward. I felt the muck give a little, so his head was above water. I sunk in further.

Brody's lips were blue. The sun was warm on my head, but this must have been a spring-fed pond because the water was cold. I held him to my chest. He put his head on my shoulder. "You're going to be okay. Help is coming. Your dad is coming for you."

I hoped that was the case. I couldn't see Sam anywhere. I tried not to think about the snapping turtles and snakes that inhabit farm ponds. I willed the warmth in my body into his as I gripped him. I jiggled him upward. My left foot sank some more.

Luke paddled to my left. At least he was above the mud. I thought about him getting swept downstream in a flood two years ago. About losing him. About not knowing where he was or even if he was alive for over a month. At least the pond didn't have a current.

I heard sirens. "Listen, Brody. Listen! Sirens." I got no reaction. *Please, God. Keep him alive. Don't let him die in my arms.*

Three black cows moved over to the pond. They stood chewing their cud, staring at us with their big brown eyes. The sirens grew louder. Then I heard another noise. I saw a pickup truck, bouncing over the pasture toward us, a sheriff's car right behind him.

Sheriff Ward jumped out of the passenger seat before the car came to a complete stop. He shed his gun and his shoes and headed toward the pond.

"Throw me a rope!" I cried out.

He didn't stop. He waded into the water. He was taller than me, and no doubt stronger, and he took his son out of my arms. "Come here boy!" he said. He fought his way back to the side of the pond, some of his officers helping him navigate the last six feet of muck.

I tried to move but sank deeper. By that time, I was up to my knees, too tired and too cold to make progress. I was afraid of being sucked in further. The farmer knew what to do. He threw me a rope, and he and a deputy pulled me out while Luke barked encouragement. Freed from the muck, I collapsed, falling hard on the grassy pasture. I turned and sat up, my arms draped over my bent knees, my head down, my breath coming in gasps. Luke, muddy to his belly, licked my ear.

3

LUKE and I rode in the back of the farmer's pickup to the sheriff's house, where I used the hose in the backyard to squirt as much mud off me and Luke as I could. The sheriff had gone straight to the hospital with his little guy, and the rest of the searchers had disbanded. I didn't want to bother Amy Ward, so I put a towel in Luke's crate and a towel in my seat and we drove home wet. I tried not to think of the germs we'd been exposed to.

A mixture of elation and exhaustion filled me. My arms were heavy, my legs weak, and I wondered if I should be driving. My mind kept going back to that pale oval in the pond, Brody's face, lifted skyward as he tried to breathe. How long would he have lasted? I was so glad Luke found him! Now all I wanted to do was sleep. Well, shower, then sleep.

I called Nate as I drove to update him on the search and keep myself awake. "You sound like you're on the move," I said as he answered.

"I am that. You find the boy?"

I told him the story.

"Mmm-um," he responded. "That's grit."

"What?" I knew exactly what he meant. I just wanted to hear it again.

"You do what you're scared to do. You got grit, girl."

I laughed. "Where're you headed?"

"Me and Laura, we're headed up to Clear Springs. She cain't raise her mom, and the neighbors say she ain't in the house."

Clear Springs was up in the mountains near Monterey. Etta, who was eighty-something, had experienced episodes of confusion lately, and I knew Laura was worried about her. To complicate things, cell service was spotty up there. "Do you have Ember with you?"

"Ember cut her foot t'other day. She's home resting. I got Sprite here."

I heard Laura saying something in the background.

Nate laughed. "Laura says if we need Sprite we're really in trouble." Sprite, a sweet old springer spaniel, was a human remains detection dog, now retired.

"Can I help you all?"

"I don't think so. If we get hung up, Scott said he'd come over and let Ember out and feed the horses."

We talked a little more, and then I said, "Let me know when you find her," and clicked off my phone.

TWENTY MINUTES LATER, I turned off the two-lane road at the large, hanging sign that read "Dark Horse Farm," a gift I'd had made for my husband. The name was both a joke and a reality. The joke was that we said we were both "dark horses" to get married, yet here we were. The reality was Scott's black horse, Ace. Scott had bought out Nate's share and brought him to our place. He was soon joined by a sorrel gelding named Beau. My Christmas present last year.

Two horses. I had a feeling it was only the beginning.

To replace Ace, Scott helped Nate buy a chestnut quarter

horse, a sure-footed little gelding Nate hoped to use for SAR. I still had my doubts about that, but in some ways it did make sense. The loss of Nate's leg in a terrible fire had put a crimp in his ability to continue with SAR, especially since most of our searches were in the mountains or foothills. He missed it. Meanwhile Ember, the black German shepherd he'd adopted two years ago, turned out to be a really good air-scent dog. Riding Chief on searches would let Nate work with her.

The house Scott and I had bought was a big, square, old country home with a broad front porch and a lot of land. Gradually, we were updating it. Scott, of course, wanted to start with the stable, although I did talk him into paying someone to modernize our bathroom first.

As I drove up, I could see him and Ethan, Amanda's former boyfriend, up on the roof. They looked like they were finished working, standing there talking. Scott waved and immediately moved toward the ladder. By the time I'd parked and let Luke out, he was wrapping his arms around me.

"You're wet!" he said, his eyebrows raised as he pulled back.

"Damp. Damp is more like it," I said, and I grabbed him and pulled him close. "Huh! Look at that. So are you," I teased.

"You feel good anyway." Scott held me and kissed my cheek.

We separated as Ethan walked up. "Miss Jessica! Mr. Scott said you found the boy?" Ethan was a true Southern boy. Couldn't bring himself to call us by our first names alone.

"Luke did. Luke's the hero."

"You jumped in a farm pond to save him?"

"And I probably still stink." I laughed and looked at Scott. "I need to give Luke a good bath and then shower. Then I may crash for a bit. Are you guys done for the day?" The sun was edging down toward the foothill behind Scott.

"Yep. We were talking about trying to get in a ride. Tell you what," Scott said. "I'll wash Luke. Ethan, you saddle up the horses. We can ride once the dog is clean. Jess, you go take your shower and relax."

What a sweet offer. I grabbed my go bag from the car, leashed up Luke, and told him to stay with Scott. "Don't let him roll afterward!" I said as I went inside.

Within minutes I was standing under the hot shower, tension streaming off me and down the drain along with the water. After that, I crawled into bed and immediately fell asleep.

SCOTT WOKE me up sometime later, jostling me gently. "Jess, Jess!" I opened my eyes. "You left your phone in the Jeep. Nate's trying to get ahold of you."

Nate? What? I raised myself up on one elbow and took the phone. "Nate? Did you find her?"

"We could use you, Jess. You and Luke. If you can come up."

I sat up and looked straight at my husband sitting on the edge of the bed. "Right. I'll text you when I'm on the way." I clicked off the phone. "It's Laura's mother. She's missing."

Scott nodded. "You feel okay to go?"

"I need to."

"Let me get you some food. After you leave, I'll go take care of Nate's horses. And I'll bring his dog back here."

I had about four sets of SAR clothes—shirts, pants, and gaiters—plus two pairs of boots, a couple of rain jackets, two parkas, and lots of hats. It was a good thing, too, because I needed the extras now.

I got dressed, repacked my SAR go bag with a clean backup shirt, pants, and underwear, loaded my dog, and was ready to go in twenty minutes. Scott handed me a cooler of food and water, plus a thermos of freshly brewed coffee. "You have the Garmin?" he asked.

Oops. I ran back inside, retrieved the Garmin InReach from my other pants, and stuffed it in my pocket. I ran back to the Jeep and kissed Scott goodbye again, holding him extra long. In three years of marriage, I'd learned it was hard for him when I left, although he'd never admit that. "Got it. Thanks for everything! I love you."

"Be careful."

CLEAR SPRINGS IS in the Alleghany Mountains of western Virginia in Highland County. I felt my ears popping as the altitude changed. Two hours after I left home, I pulled up to a white rambler set in a hillside off a two-lane road. Nate's new Tahoe and a sheriff's car were parked on the side of the fifty-foot driveway. My headlights caught the shine of a big silver propane tank near the back of the house. But that was all I could see in the dark. The normal glut of SAR vehicles was MIA.

When I stepped out of my Jeep, the chilly air hit me hard. Nate came out as soon as my headlights lit up the house. "Thank you for comin', Jess."

"So what's up?"

"She's eighty-three, you know. Lived up here her whole life. Been alone since her husband died. And mostly she does all right. People up here take care of gettin' her to town. But lately Laura says she's been gettin' forgetful. Now, she ain't been seen for two, three days. It's gettin' cold at night. Laura's worried."

"Did the sheriff call it in? Are other teams coming?"

Nate's jaw shifted. That usually meant he was trying to temper his language. "Tomorra," he said. "Too far and too dark tonight."

"Well, I'm here and Luke's here. We're ready to go."

"Come on inside. Bring the dog. Let's talk."

"Thanks, Jess," Laura said as I stepped into her mother's cramped living room and looked around. A TV took up half the room. Doilies covered the arms of the brown couch and the recliner. A brown-and-tan, hand-crocheted, zigzag afghan lay on the back of the couch. Laura, Nate, Sprite, Luke, and I filled that room to overflowing.

"I'm glad I could come," I said.

Luke and Sprite immediately started playing. Sprite was slower now and had a lot of pain. Luke seemed to know that, but still, they were two dogs playing in a small room.

"Come on out here," Nate said, gesturing me to follow. We stepped into the combination kitchen-dining room. "Jess, this here's Sheriff Colt McCormick," Nate said, recapturing my attention. "Sheriff, Jess Cooper. The best we got."

I felt my face grow hot.

"Colt," the sheriff said, shaking my hand. "Good to meet you. Where do you want to start?"

The kitchen, like the living room, was too small and full of knickknacks. Still, there was a good oak table we could work on. "I'll need topo maps," I said.

"We got 'em."

"I'll want to see where you searched, Nate, but first ... Laura, has your mom wandered off before?" Dementia patients, I knew, were prone to wandering. They'd often get lost even in familiar places. Part of that was because their visual field narrowed. They'd focus straight ahead instead of glancing off to the sides for familiar markers. They often moved straight ahead too.

Laura took a deep breath. Worry lines etched her face. "My mom was born and raised in the woods. Whenever things got tense at home, she'd head for these here hills. Found solace in hiking them."

"So she knows these woods," I said, clarifying.

"Like the back of her hand. But she has been getting confused and, of course, if she's fallen, knowing these woods doesn't amount to a hill of beans."

"How has she been getting confused?"

"Sometimes she can't come up with names."

"Of people?"

"Or even some things. She's been putting things away in wrong places. When I come up here, I've been finding bills and bank statements under the couch cushions and canned food in with the mixing bowls. When I ask her about it, she laughs."

"But she still recognizes you."

"Yes."

"And you can still converse with her."

"Yes."

I was asking these questions to try to discern the level of Miss Etta's dementia. Severely affected people may wander randomly and won't go far. Those with milder dementia, like it sounded as if Miss Etta was experiencing, would be more goal-directed. They'd walk straight toward something until they got stuck. Usually. According to Koester.

Nate broke in. "Laura and me, we want her to come live with us, but so far, she's resisted."

"She says she don't want to be no bother," Laura explained, using air quotes. "I know if anybody can convince her, it's Nate. She loves Nate. But so far, even he has struck out."

I smiled. "Let me see the topo maps." The sheriff pulled out a set and spread them over the table. He and Nate and I bent over them, each of us pointing out features as we saw them. Then I straightened up. "Okay, let's do this. I'll need a walker. Sheriff, could that be you? Then we'll start by searching the easiest path from the house, unless Luke picks up a scent first."

"I'll be your walker," Nate said. "The sheriff, he's got other things to do." I opened my mouth to protest, thinking of Nate's artificial leg, but he continued. "Miss Etta, she'll come to me if I call her. I cain't say that'd be true with someone else."

"Okay." I looked around. "We'll start by presuming she went out the back door. Laura, really quick, see what's missing in the house."

Laura moved quickly. A few minutes later, she reported, "Her parka's missing. Plus a thick sweater and her quilt off the bed."

I nodded. "Luke, come on, buddy." He came and I put on his vest and the flashing light I used on him at night. Then I shouldered my pack and leashed him up. I put on a headlamp and a hat and picked up the big flashlight I'd taken out of my pack. I started to walk through the small L-shaped kitchen and out the back door.

Nate stopped short. He'd noticed something. He pointed to a corner. "Right there she kept a shotgun." He looked at me. "Must've took it with her."

"Does she hunt? Could she think it's deer season?"

"She don't hunt. Not no more. Maybe she was scared of somethin'?"

That put a whole new twist on things.

We walked outside, and I peered into the dark forest. There was no moon and no ambient light—not a gas station or shopping center for miles around. A shiver ran through me. I was glad Nate was with me.

I checked the wind, pointed in the general direction I wanted to go, and sent Luke. "Seek, Luke. Seek!" He took off, his little red light flashing through the trees as he zigzagged back and forth trying to catch a scent.

We had gone about twenty yards into the woods, maintaining approximately the same altitude, when Luke retraced his steps to take a second sniff at something. "You mark it?" I quietly asked Nate.

"Yep."

I urged Luke forward, but he quickly circled back and took off up a rock-strewn hill. Within a few minutes, I was puffing. "Could she do this?" I asked Nate over my shoulder.

"She might."

Sure enough, I heard a scrambling sound as Luke returned. He plowed into me and grabbed the tug on my belt. Nate had to put a hand on my back to keep me from falling. Then Luke took off again. I quickened my pace. Suddenly, I heard a shotgun blast.

Had she shot him? Shot my dog? My heart jumped. "Luke, come!" I screamed, panic raising the pitch of my voice.

"Let me go first!" Nate said, pushing past me. "Etta! Miss Etta. It's me, Nate!"

Luke came rushing back. I ran my hands all over him. Not a scratch. Relief.

We found her huddled up against the hill in the shelter of a fallen oak. She was wrapped in her parka and a quilt and a wool hat, and her shotgun was in her right hand, propped at her side. Of course, she couldn't see us, not with our flashlights shining in her face. So she aimed the shotgun. "Who is it?" she said. "I will shoot."

"Miss Etta it's me, Nathan. Laura's man."

"Nathan?" She put the gun down. "Come help me up, son."

He was so gentle with her. I was still shaking with anxiety and adrenaline, but Nate kept it together. He moved toward her, took the shotgun, and handed it back to me. I instantly unloaded it, pocketing the shells.

"Come on, Miss Etta. Let's go home," Nate said, helping her to her feet.

WALKING BACK to the house was no mean feat. Nate with his leg, Etta being old, and me, well, between two searches in one day and the anxiety they both brought to me, I was beat to shreds. Still, Miss Etta let me take hold of her and help her down that hill. As soon as I had a cell signal, I called Laura, and she and the sheriff met us coming out of the woods.

As we walked in the door, Miss Etta turned to Nate. "You put that shotgun right in that corner, Nathan."

"Momma, let's have a cup of tea," Laura said, guiding her to the kitchen table. She glanced at Nate, and I suspected she was hoping he'd take that gun out to their car.

But Miss Etta watched Nate like a hawk to make sure he put

that gun where she wanted. Then she sat down and looked at me, squinting. "Who's this?"

Her sudden attention took me aback, but Nate quickly chimed in. "This here's Jess, a good friend of ours. She does search and rescue."

Miss Etta nodded. "That's a big dog you got there. I mighta thought him a wolf 'cept for him wagging his tail so hard."

"That's Luke," I said. He had plopped down inside the back door and thumped his tail at his name. "Did he scare you? Did you shoot at him?" Even I heard the edge in my voice.

"Heavens no! I'd seen that jacket he had on. Like Nathan's dogs. I shot in the air to tell y'all where I was."

I took a little solace in that, but tension still gripped me.

Laura put a cup of steaming liquid in front of her mother. It was light, like green tea or lemon and ginger tea. "You want some, Jess?"

"No, thanks."

"Have a seat." She nodded toward the other chair. I glanced at Nate, who shook his head, indicating he'd stand. So I sat down. Laura turned toward Etta. "Momma, why'd you go in the woods?"

Miss Etta sipped her tea before she answered. She was a small woman, probably five foot two, and wiry. Her long, gray hair was caught up in a bun, but thin wisps framed her temples. Wrinkles etched her face. She still wore her wedding ring. "I seen a man I don't know three days now, near the road out front. Just back of it, in the woods. No broken-down car, no lost dog, no reason why he should be there. Every now and then he'd take a look at my house.

"Today, or maybe yesterday, I seen him again, only this time, another man's with him. The first guy, he's starin' at my house. Pacing. Then he started up my lane, at first walkin', then joggin'. I cain't see his friend. So I grab my jacket and my quilt, my purse and my gun, and I head out back. Them boys gonna have to work to find me, I said to the Lord. I knew where that oak tree had dropped. I figured they wouldn't climb that hill. Wouldn't think I could. So I went up there. Figured I'd start back when it got light, 'til I heard you, son."

"What did these men look like?" the sheriff asked.

Miss Etta gave the most generic of all possible descriptions. "One's 'bout your height, one taller. Dark hair. Jeans, boots. One had a blue jacket, the other camo. Scared me, they did."

The sheriff said he'd send someone around in the morning to check out the woods and take a statement from Miss Etta. Then he left, shaking his head. It was clear to me he thought she was seeing things.

After talking some more, Laura said, "Momma, let's go to bed."

"You all stayin'?"

"Yes ma'am," Nate said. "We'll be right here."

While Laura tucked her mom into bed. I texted Scott and told him I was too tired to drive, and I'd crash in Clear Springs.

Laura emerged from the bedroom. "I need another cup of tea. Jess?"

This time I accepted. "Yes, please."

She came back a few minutes later with two steaming cups, and we all sat down together. "I think Momma panicked," Laura said. "Those men could have been surveyors, or property hunters, or who knows what."

"Or a couple of kids. Does the school bus let off here?" I asked.

"I never noticed it," Laura said. "But it could have been kids. Or parents! That could be it."

"I've dealt with a lot of dementia patients through SAR," I said. "It's not at all unusual for them to wander off or see things. Or get a little paranoid." We batted theories back and forth for quite a while, both of us convinced there was no real threat, except the threat of Etta hurting herself in the woods.

Nate sat silently that whole time, holding his empty pipe in his mouth, his hand stroking Sprite lying in his lap. I kept glancing at him, but I couldn't read his expression.

Finally, he spoke. "Miss Etta seemed lucid to me when we found her."

"The dementia comes and goes," Laura said.

"I get that. But I don't think you should write off what she says. Somethin' scared her enough to head for the hills. I think she really saw somebody." He stared straight at Laura as he said it. The look in his eyes sent a shiver through me.

4

Driving home the next morning I did my best to push Nate's concerns out of my mind. After all, he hadn't been around Miss Etta very much lately. Laura usually went to see her mom on her own. I'd seen plenty of dementia patients with hallucinations or paranoid delusions, people who thought their longtime caregiver was stealing from them or trying to kill them. When the brain is affected by disease, anything can happen. So I forced myself to think forward to positive things—to my home and my husband and our life together.

Scott was already at work, according to the text I'd received at 7:00 a.m. He'd gone in early so he could come home early.

Still with the Behavioral Analysis Unit at Quantico, Scott had gone through four months of training to become certified as a profiler. He'd had classes in death investigations, pathology, linguistics, interview techniques, psychopathy, and other topics. He'd worked cases with more experienced profilers. Now, he spent most of his time working mass-shooting incidents and domestic terrorism. Which meant he deployed a lot. The bureau had pushed him to get his PhD, and he'd accomplished the degree work during COVID. He only had his dissertation to finish.

Did I mention Scott is supersmart?

Still, it's hard on a person to be so immersed professionally in criminal behavior—to process fact after fact about the most heinous acts without becoming hardened or a little sick yourself. I'd seen the toll it took on him. I knew when he went straight to the barn after work that he needed time, time to relax, time to let the horses he loved recalibrate his soul, time to reconnect with all that was good and natural and beautiful in life. Scott needed those horses like I needed Luke. And I was fine with that.

As for me, I was pretty happy doing search and rescue, continuing my consulting work, and building my PI business. I could not imagine going into an office every day. I'm too restless. Plus I wouldn't want to leave Luke at home alone. We are partners.

When Scott traveled too much I'd get lonely, and my feet would get itchy. I'd start thinking about hiking in the mountains or rock climbing again, anything outdoors. During COVID I'd started a garden, but I don't care what they say, you can talk to plants all you want and they will not even nod their little heads in response. And have you ever seen a tomato hornworm?

Eventually, I found a group that did trail running in the mountains. Perfect! Great exercise and I liked the people. Plus, they let me bring Luke. So I started running with them a couple times a week. I think Scott was just glad I wasn't out there by myself.

All those thoughts occupied me as I drove home from Clear Springs. My life was good. Not perfect. But good. And I thanked God for it.

The bright sun flared in my eyes as I turned into our lane at the Dark Horse Farm sign. Such a beautiful day. I'd forgotten Ember would be at our house, so her barking surprised me when I got out of my Jeep. Luke knew who it was though. His tail banged against his crate, and he jumped down eagerly when I opened it. I grabbed my go bag, thermos, and cooler and opened the front door, sending the swirl of two German shepherds eager to play outside. I texted Scott that I was home, hoping he'd text back *Almost done here.* But no, that was too much to ask for.

So I washed out my thermos and the cooler, tossed my dirty clothes in the laundry, and took a shower. I threw on jeans and a burgundy turtleneck and sat down in front of my laptop. I had inquiries from three lawyers about what I called "cheating heart cases"—suspected infidelities. One was too far away, but the others were pretty close, so I asked a few questions, cited my fees, and replied. I also had emails from two groups looking to book a talk on SAR. I usually did those for free. And I checked the Battlefield SAR website for the location of the next practice.

Nate called around eleven to see if I could keep Ember the rest of the day. Of course, I could. He had driven straight from Clear Springs to work. Laura had decided to stay with her mom for a few days.

"She shouldn't be living alone," I suggested. They had room again now that the dad and daughter they'd been helping, Charles and Harper Lee, were out on their own again.

Laura had met little Harper Lee through a friend who was fostering her. Motherless, she'd been removed from her home because she'd stopped speaking, and social workers were concerned about her care. Laura thought maybe relating to horses would help Harper. Eventually, her theory proved right.

Scott met Charles Lee when his house blew up. Scott had been chasing a serial bomber, who turned out to be Charles's neighbor. Charles recovered from his injuries, and Nate and Laura took him and his daughter in until they could get back on their feet. The Tanner House of Healing gained another couple of graduates.

"We want Miss Etta to move in," Nate said, "but she don't want to leave her hills."

"Did the sheriff investigate those men further?"

"He sent a deputy, a kid who sized Miss Etta up as elderly and therefore unreliable. Fit Laura's theory fine."

I could tell he still didn't agree. Nate can be pretty stubborn. "Well," I said, "since she's staying up there, at least Laura can see for herself what's going on."

"Right. I'll come get Ember after work. Be here around three-thirty."

I did the math. He would have had to leave Clear Springs before five in the morning to be able to work a full day and get home that early. "Nate, you've had a lot of driving already today. How about if I bring her to you?"

After an initial protest, he agreed, and so at two o'clock Luke, Ember, and I climbed in my Jeep and headed south, past fields full of dried cornstalks and pumpkin patches, and green, rolling hills dotted with black Angus cattle. We got to Nate's early enough for me to feed and water the horses. I was surprised to find their stalls in good shape since Nate and Laura had been gone.

"Who'd you get to take care of the horses?" I asked Nate when he arrived.

His eyes were rimmed with fatigue. "Amanda done it."

"Amanda? Scott's Amanda?" Scott's daughter had been MIA at our house for weeks and weeks.

"Yep. She comes up to ride now and then."

I blinked my confusion.

"Scott knows. I told him. Amanda's more like her daddy than she wants to admit."

Okay then.

I kept my time short at Nate's so I'd be home when Scott got there, but I couldn't resist stopping at a farm stand to buy burgundy and gold mums for the front porch and a gallon of cider. It was fall after all. As my Jeep nosed around the trees lining our lane, I saw Scott had beaten me home. He stood out near the barn, in his shirtsleeves, dress pants tucked into barn boots, his arms draped across Ace's withers, his head down. Something was bothering him.

He heard my car, looked up and waved, patted Ace goodbye, and started walking toward me. I parked and let Luke out. He went running for Scott, who bent down and ruffled the coat around Luke's neck. I smiled, thinking about the first time I met Scott. We'd found a body on federal land, and Scott, Mr. FBI, had come to investigate. He seemed so stiff, so formal, so OCD. It took a while—years—for the real Scott to break out of that shell.

I moved toward him and smiled. Tall, dark, and handsome, he took me in his arms and kissed me.

"I'm glad you're home," he said.

I ran my hand up his neck to the back of his head, feeling his skin, his hair, and absorbing the scent of him. "Me too."

He nodded toward the open back of the Jeep. "Need some help?"

"Can you grab those mums?"

He took one in each hand. I picked up the cider, and together we walked toward our home. Leaves fallen from the woods had blown into our front yard. They crackled under our feet.

"How was work?"

Scott shrugged.

"Something going on?"

"Not really." I suspect he knew I wasn't going to let him get away with that evasion because he continued. "Politics."

Jack. He'd been talking to Jack Conway.

Years ago, Scott had gotten into trouble for almost assaulting a prisoner he was interviewing. He was totally justified, trust me. Although Scott barely knew him, Jack had advocated for him. He helped Scott dodge a bullet, and over time, their relationship had grown to the point Scott now considered him a friend. A former street agent, Jack worked in DC and sometimes he'd unload his frustrations with the politicized top brass on Scott.

I slipped my hand into Scott's arm, and together we mounted the three concrete steps that led to our front porch. "These go here?" Scott asked, gesturing with the mums.

"Yes. One on each side, next to the porch posts."

I whistled for Luke, who'd run down to see his buddy Ace. Scott took off his boots, and together we went inside. "You want a fire?" Scott asked.

"No," I said. "Why don't you go relax? Dinner'll be ready at six."

"I'm going up to change. Then I want to hear about your searches."

OVER GRILLED SALMON, Caesar salad, and garlic knots, we talked, first about the search for little Brody. I could still see the image of his little moon face in that pond, the only part of his body above the surface. I told Scott about the woods, the little depression under the fence, and the farm pond surrounded by cows. "Who knows what was in that water! On the way home I called Luke's vet to see if I should put him on an antibiotic just in case." I stuffed the last piece of garlic knot in my mouth.

My husband stopped chewing. He cocked his head. He raised his eyebrows. "And then you called your own doctor and asked about yourself?"

I felt my face grow hot. My lips pressed into a line. "Well no, not really."

"How is there any *really* about that? You either did or you didn't."

I rolled my eyes. "Okay, I didn't. I didn't even think about it."

Scott reached over and took my hand. We'd found this old oak farm table at an estate sale, and together we had cleaned and polished it, wondering what stories its nicks and scratches told. Now our hands rested on it, two people with their own nicks and scratches and a good bit of trauma too. "You need to take care of yourself, Jess," Scott said softly. "I don't want anything to happen to you."

I nodded. "I'll call her." Then I squeezed his hand and let go. While we finished eating, I told him about Etta. "I really think it was her imagination," I said, "which is really sad."

As we were cleaning up, my phone rang. It was Brody's dad, Sheriff Ward. His call brought tears to my eyes.

"What?" Scott asked when I hung up. He'd seen my reaction.

"The little boy's going to be fine. He was treated for hypothermia and given antibiotics. They kept him overnight and released him. His dad says he's running around like nothing ever happened."

"That's awesome! Good for you." Scott gave me a hug.

"It was Luke. I just followed him."

"You followed him right into a dangerous situation."

I leaned my head against Scott's chest, his heart thumping in my ear, my arms holding onto him like the anchor he was. "I could not let that little boy drown."

"No. Of course not. Good job, Jess."

THE NEXT COUPLE of weeks went smoothly. The leaves deepened to golds and russets and bright yellows, contrasting beautifully with the black tree trunks when it rained. God truly is the Master Artist.

Scott was able to work from home some, which gave him more time to complete his projects around the house. We were about to tear out the kitchen, a scary prospect for me, but Scott promised me we'd figure it out.

While Scott worked, I trained with Luke, rode Beau, and prepared for my next teaching engagement. I worked the two cheating heart cases, quickly confirming the wives' worst fears. My SAR group had a couple of callouts. In one, the kid was found before we even arrived on the scene. In the other, police found the missing man dead in his car, which was off the road and in a ditch just out of sight. I was glad I didn't have to see that. Years ago, that could have been me.

Early in the afternoon on a bright, sunny day in mid-October, I drove down to Nate's. He'd taken half the day off and asked me to come help him work with his five-year-old quarter horse, Chief. I still didn't have a vision for how he planned to do SAR on horseback, and I was anxious to learn.

When I drove up, Chief stood saddled and waiting outside the small barn, his copper-colored coat gleaming in the sun. I let Luke out of the back of my Jeep. Nate heard us and emerged from the barn, Ember following him. She raced toward Luke.

"Thanks for coming," Nate said, giving me a quick hug.

"Glad to. What are we doing?"

"The goal is to get Chief used to unusual things. We're gonna start in the pasture. I've put Abby up and been puttin' things out —a tarp, a trash bag full of cans, a small jump. I need you to move stuff around. Then we'll try workin' in the woods."

"Sounds great." I hesitated. "Should I put the dogs in the house?"

"Yep."

I did that, then followed Nate over to the barn. I introduced myself to Chief again. I hadn't been around him much, and I wanted him to see and smell me.

"Laura's been teachin' me about hosses," Nate said. "About their body language and all. She's the expert."

"And what does she think of your plan?" I scratched Chief's neck.

"If it has to do with hosses, she's in." He checked the western saddle, making sure it was on well. "She's been ridin' him some when Harper comes over. Lettin' Harper take Abby on the trails."

"Really?"

"Yep. 'Bout twice a week. Laura's more sure of Abby, so she

gives her to Harper, and she takes Chief. So far, she said he's been good. She likes him."

I moved away as Nate slipped the reins over Chief's head, took off the halter, and handed it to me. I hung the empty halter on the fence post and watched as Nate slipped the bit in the horse's mouth, pulled on the bridle, and buckled it.

"Ready?" Nate said.

"Yes."

He moved to the "off" side, the horse's right, as his artificial leg wouldn't let him mount on the left. I went to open the gate. "Wait," Nate said. "I'm trying to teach him to let me do that. You go through the barn."

I got through quick enough to see what he was doing, getting Chief to move sideways next to the gate. "Easy now, easy boy," Nate said in a low tone. Chief's ears flickered. He moved into position, and Nate leaned down and unlatched the gate. It swung open, and Chief moved through. I could tell he wanted to keep on going, but Nate made him sidle up to the gate again so he could close it. "Good hoss, good boy," Nate said, after he succeeded on the third try.

He turned Chief toward the obstacles he'd arranged in the paddock, then nodded to me. "When we get past the barrel, put the slicker down."

"Got it."

Chief easily walked over the crossed arms jump, but he shied and snorted at the black plastic tarp Nate had laid on the ground, tossing his head and backing up. Nate circled him around, patiently talking to him, and tried again. Finally, he called me and asked me to walk across it. That did the trick. Chief followed my example, and the second time around didn't even hesitate. Nate told me later that to the horse, the black tarp looked like it could be a bottomless pond. No wonder he was shy about walking on it.

All in all, we spent about half an hour working in the pasture.

Nate was his usual, calm, patient self, and I could tell he would end up being a good horse trainer just as he was brilliant with dogs.

He let Chief relax by walking him around the yard while I went out on the trail and planted different obstacles—a white rag hung from a tree, a slicker on the ground, a barrel on its side, a small jump which I created from a downed tree, and things like that. When I was finished, Nate rode Chief through the course. He did well, except that, oddly, the white rag threw him. He tossed his head and stamped his foot. Nate remained patient, speaking softly to Chief, patting his neck, allowing him to approach it again and again. Finally, something clicked, and the little gelding screwed up his courage and walked past it.

Nate had Chief walk that trail a few more times, with me changing things up a bit every time. Then he indicated he was done. I disassembled the jump, gathered up the portable distractions, and walked back to the barn.

5

NATE ALREADY HAD Chief's saddle off and was brushing him down by the time I got back there. Chief leaned into the brush, turning his head to nuzzle Nate.

"So you've charmed him too," I said.

Nate grinned, but he didn't stop brushing. "It's what I do."

It's a gift, I thought as I put the white rag and the slicker in the barn. "Hey, I'm going to go let the dogs out."

"Okay. I'll be along soon enough."

"Want some tea?"

"Sure."

I walked to the house and let Ember, Luke, and Sprite out. Ember took off, looking for Nate, but the other two did what they needed to do and came back inside with me. I busied myself boiling water and setting out mugs and teabags. I looked out when I heard the crunch of gravel on the driveway. Laura, home from work. I took out another mug.

After our search for Miss Etta, Laura stayed in Clear Springs for a few days, but then she had to get back to work. Miss Etta refused to leave with her. "I got things to do," she protested. Finally, Laura had no choice but to let her mother stay...alone.

"Hey, Laura," I said, as Nate's wife opened the back door.

"Jess, how are you?" she put down her tote and gave me a quick hug.

"I'm good! I was helping Nate work with Chief. Want some tea?"

Nate walked in, Ember sliding in with him like a black shadow. "There's my girl," he said. He hugged his wife but looked at me over her shoulder. "I smell like hoss, but that's the way she likes me."

I laughed and poured boiling water over the teabags in three mugs, then turned and set them on the table. "Have time to talk?"

"Sure. Let's do it," Laura said.

So we sat and talked about our lives. I told them about my searches and the big renovation Scott and I were about to do. "I want to get the house done, then we can relax," I said. I asked about Harper.

"I don't know if I'm more of an aunt or a grandmother." Laura laughed. "I try not to spoil her, but I love her!"

"And she's talking?" I asked.

"Too much," Nate said, his eyes crinkling in amusement. "She's like a squirrel in a tree, chattering away about nothin'."

"Her dad's working?"

"Yep. Got hisself a job with the county, workin' at the dumpster site. Takes it serious, he does." Nate made a clicking sound with his mouth. "Ain't nothin' like almost dying to set a man straight."

"Are you still discipling him?"

Nate nodded. "Sunday nights. I'm learnin' mor'n he is."

I doubted that. "What about Miss Etta? How's she doing?" I saw a look pass between my friends.

Laura took a deep breath. "She won't come down here. We have room. Nate's happy to have her. But she won't leave those hills."

"Has she seen those men again?"

Laura's mouth straightened into a line. "I don't think she ever saw anyone." Her eyes stayed fixed on her husband.

Nate's jaw twitched, but he kept silent.

"She says her friends from church are checking on her, Martha and someone named Catherine Grace. I met Martha once when I was up there. She's in her late seventies but still driving and helps Momma a lot. This Catherine Grace—she's new. Her name's just started coming up."

A red flag popped up in my mind. I was well aware of scams perpetrated on older people. "Is she from your mom's church?" I kept my tone casual.

"I think so. Momma says she comes over and they 'have a chat' as she puts it."

"That's nice," I said, glancing at Nate. He remained impassive.

"I'm thankful she's not sitting there by herself."

My phone vibrated. A text. I glanced at it. "Scott's leaving work," I said, pushing back my chair. "I'd better run."

They both stood, and Laura hugged me goodbye. "I'll walk you out," Nate said.

I called Luke and we left the house, out of the kitchen door, and down the ramp we'd built for Nate when he lost his leg. I opened the back of my Jeep, and Luke jumped in his crate. Then I closed it.

"Thank you for your help today," Nate said.

I hugged him. "I was glad to do it."

I got in the driver's seat but before I could close the door, Nate leaned in. "Let Laura deal with her mom, okay?"

"What?"

"I saw you react when she mentioned those women stopping by."

"Not both women. Just the younger one, the one Laura doesn't know."

Nate shook his head. "Leave it alone. Laura's private. She don't like snooping."

I felt a little sting. I had "snooped" before, checking out Harper Lee and her family online. It's what I do. I'm a curious person. I don't want my friends taken advantage of. Back then my snooping turned out all right, but I had offended Laura ... and by extension, Nate.

So I nodded. "I'll turn off my Inner PI and let you guys handle it."

"Good." Nate shut my door.

But all the way home the thought of this "Catherine Grace" visiting Miss Etta bothered me. I mean, she could be anybody. I wondered if Laura monitored Miss Etta's bank accounts. I started to call her to ask, but Nate's words stopped me.

I had to let them handle it.

I flipped on the radio to distract myself. I shouldn't have. Another school shooting, this one in Montana. *Why?* Four dead, including a teacher. The increasing frequency of these violent events made my skin crawl. It felt like evil was spreading, like there was a deadly, dark shadow seeping over the country, settling in different places like a fog, poisoning the land.

Maybe I should be thankful we didn't have children. What kind of world would they grow up in?

Then another thought struck me. Scott. Would he have to leave? Go to Montana? He was one of the resident experts on mass shootings at BAU. Would they send him to Bozeman?

He called soon after. "Hey, what do you say we take a sunset ride?"

I swallowed hard. "Sure. I'm almost home. I was going to start dinner—"

"Forget dinner," he said. "Ride with me."

He was definitely going.

I girded my loins. Prepared for battle. Me and Scott vs. Evil, the evil that would perpetrate horrible shootings. The evil that would try to interfere with our marriage. The evil that would keep me perpetually scared about the future. "Okay. I'll saddle the horses," I said, keeping my voice light. "See you soon."

I WAS HEFTING Scott's big western saddle onto Ace's tall back when I heard his SUV on the gravel driveway. I had to use a step-stool to saddle Ace, and even then it was a struggle. I glanced toward the house in time to see Scott dash inside. He'd change into jeans and boots, I knew, before coming to meet me. I finished tacking the horses and, grabbing both sets of reins, I led them up to the house.

That's when an idea popped into my head. For Christmas, I'd have someone install a hitching post in front. I smiled. Colorado-born Scott would love that. *Bringing the West east,* he'd call it.

Scott emerged from the back of the house, but I'd stood in a place where he could see me. "Well, aren't you something?" he said, grinning. He kissed me hello, even before he patted Ace! "You want a leg up?"

"No, I got it," I said, arranging Beau's reins and inserting my left foot in the stirrup. *Maybe a hitching post and a mounting block.* I hopped twice and boosted myself into the saddle. I saw Scott check Ace's girth. The gelding had a habit of holding his breath as he was being saddled. Then he mounted. "We have just enough time," he said.

In mid-October it was still light until sevenish and my watch read 6:04. We rode side by side down the hill behind our house toward the creek. Luke trotted along with us. These rides had become one of my dog's favorite things. He stayed in our general vicinity but tended to follow fence lines, nose to the ground.

"He's checking the perimeter," Scott said. I found out later he was exactly right. That's something herding dogs did instinctively, guarding the flock. "Maybe we should get a big ol' Great Pyrenees to keep him company."

I laughed. "We don't have enough dog hair in the house?" My

voice sounded light, but my body was tight. I was waiting for the shoe to drop, for him to say he had to leave.

The sun dropped behind the mountains to the west. A golden glow spread over the land, our land, igniting the tops of the trees with brilliant red, orange, and yellow fire. I felt a rush of gratitude and breathed a silent prayer of thanks.

The horses heads bobbed in unison as they walked. The creak of saddle leather combined with the smell of horses mixed with fresh air did its best to relax me. Scott rode tall in his saddle in his jeans; his red, white, and blue western shirt; and his black hat. He told me once when he rode a horse without a hat he felt undressed. He glanced over at me. "Let's pick it up once we cross the creek."

Scott led us down a slight incline and over the three-foot-wide creek. When we were both on the other side, he urged Ace into a lope. Beau and I followed. Then Scott took off, his horse galloping across the cut pasture, flinging mud behind him. Beau took his lead, and soon we were racing across the field, my hair streaming behind me, my horse working hard. By the time we pulled up, I was breathless. Scott turned toward me, grinning.

"That was fun!" I said.

"Ready to go back?"

I nodded. We turned and walked the horses side by side back toward the barn. Scott looked at me. "How'd I get so lucky?"

The sun dipped behind the hills as late afternoon yielded to the deep blue of evening. In the east a star popped out.

"You're going, aren't you?" I said, looking straight ahead.

Scott hesitated. "Yes."

"When?"

"Tomorrow morning."

My throat closed. We were supposed to start tearing out the kitchen tomorrow. I hadn't told him about Catherine Grace and my suspicions. My mother's birthday was coming up, and now I'd probably have to head up there alone. A laundry list of reasons I would miss him marched through my mind.

"I'm sorry," he said.

What could I say? "I know." I shoved my list into a back corner of my mind and let go of his hand. "It's your job. I get it." I smiled. "I'll be fine. I've got plenty to do." I was determined not to be *that* law-enforcement wife, the one who complained all the time. I knew what Scott did when I married him. For crying out loud, I'd been an officer myself for eight years.

"Ethan said he'd come help with the horses." He glanced at me. "Don't start on the kitchen. Wait 'til I get back."

"Okay."

We got to the barn and dismounted. We untacked, brushed out, and fed the horses silently, each of us lost in our own thoughts. When I finished with Beau, I turned him out and said, "I'll go start dinner."

"I'll be up in a minute." He paused. "Hey, do we have any more ibuprofen somewhere? I'm out."

"Sure, in the kitchen."

"Good. I want to take some with me."

SCOTT'S FLIGHT departed from Dulles at six in the morning, which meant he had to leave our house at two. I woke up when he kissed me goodbye and lay in bed listening as he went downstairs and out the door. I heard the crunch of his tires on the driveway and prayed for him, for safe travels and a quick return. Then I snuggled deeper into the covers and pretended not to notice when Luke climbed up on Scott's side of the bed. My dog had seen the suitcase. He knew what that meant.

I slept in until about six-thirty. Outside, the world remained dark. Glancing at my phone I saw I had an *I love you* text from Scott, sent when he was about to board at 5:40 a.m. I sent a heart in return, then checked my weather app. Partly cloudy. High of 67. Sunrise 7:21. Perfect.

I threw on running clothes and proceeded downstairs. Opening the back door, I let Luke out and saw dawn stretching out from the east. Then I went in the kitchen and started coffee brewing. I put some plain yogurt in a dish and topped it with granola and blueberries and the tiniest bit of turbinado sugar.

Luke scratched at the back door. I let him in, then I grabbed my Bible and sat down at the table to eat and read 1 Corinthians. I turned to the page marked by my ribbon. Chapter 13. The love chapter.

Love is patient and kind; love does not envy or boast; it is not arrogant or rude. It does not insist on its own way; it is not irritable or resentful, it does not rejoice at wrongdoing, but rejoices with the truth. Love bears all things, believes all things, hopes all things, endures all things.

THOSE WORDS WOULD GIVE me something to think about all day.

After praying for Scott and Nate and Laura and yes, my family, I felt ready to start my day. My running group planned to meet up at eleven, which gave me a couple of hours to get some work done.

I fed Luke and sat down at my desk in the corner of the living room. Opening my laptop, I couldn't resist reading about Scott's Montana school shooting. Four dead. The suspected shooter was a now-deceased, sixteen-year-old boy, stopped in his rampage by the gym teacher who tackled him from behind. The boy's gun discharged as he fell on it. How very sad. Once again I found myself praying, for Scott and the other investigators, for the survivors, and the community as a whole. I tried to imagine what it would be like to be in school these days, to have to think about a shooter, to have to practice "run-hide-fight." It would be like living in the wilderness with wild beasts. How awful.

I turned to my PI cases. Most of them were the usual. Divorce cases and background checks remained my bread and butter. I did have one interesting one though. A forty-year-old man trying to track down the origins of a painting he'd bought at an antiques store. "I'm not an art dealer," I protested, when I called the man's lawyer. "I know nothing about art."

"They told me it came from an estate sale in Madison County, Virginia," Harrison Langford responded. "If you'll find who owned the house where it came from, I'll take it from there."

I insisted on him sending a large digital picture of the painting. Once I received it, I took the case. It was a beautiful oil of a little blonde-headed girl having a picnic in a meadow with her collie. A red-and-white gingham tablecloth lay on the ground, covered with plates of cheese and cookies, some of which were bone-shaped, and a teapot with matching teacups.

The sable-and-white collie sat regally across from the girl, his white ruff fluffed out, his dainty white front feet placed carefully on the edge of the cloth. The girl wore a light blue dress with a white collar. She appeared to be offering the dog a cookie. Incongruously, a tear rolled down one cheek.

Why was she crying? The scene was idyllic. Why had the artist included that tear? And who was the artist? He or she had signed the painting, but the signature was a scrawl.

I am a curious person. So I took the case. First I looked up estate sales in Madison County. That involved some investigative work, since most of them are advertised on Facebook these days, and they disappear after a time. Just in case, though, I checked the local newspaper archives. I called numbers for every private sale I could find over the last sixty days and got no leads.

Then I called the professional sellers. Finally, I hit pay dirt. A lady at Smith Bros. Estate Sales remembered a painting being part of a collection. She looked up the records and emailed me two days later. The painting came from an estate in Highland County. She gave me the name and number of the person who'd arranged for Smith Bros. to clean out a house and sell everything in it.

I called that number. The man who answered sounded annoyed. "I have no idea what my mother had in that house. I haven't been there in ten years."

Sad, I thought. "Where do you live now?"

"California. She died and I told Smith to get what he could out of the junk that was in there so I could sell the place."

"So you've sold it?"

"What did I want with a house in Virginia?"

"Do you remember a painting?" I described it.

"Nope."

I verified the address with him. After we hung up, I scheduled a trip to Highland County to look up property records. But today I planned to work cases on my computer before leaving for my 11:00 a.m. run.

Easy peasy. Or not.

6

IF YOU ASK ME, partly cloudy and in the high sixties is perfect running weather. I'd put on a light sweatshirt but anticipated leaving it in the car. I expected to get sweaty running in the mountains.

I pulled up to the trailhead to wait for the three other people who said they were running that day. *Four is a good number*, I thought. This trail was an old fire road, wide enough in most places for two people to run abreast.

I let Luke out. He watered the bushes and began sniffing around. I took off my sweatshirt and put my fanny pack around my waist. *Oops.* I'd forgotten the Garmin InReach.

Regrouping, I put my cellphone in the pack, along with my small pocket wallet. Then I retrieved Luke's light leash out of the back and closed up the car. I peered in the windows to make sure nothing looked inviting enough to break into my Jeep, and I locked it.

Still waiting for my friends, I jogged in place a little, anxious to get my muscles warmed up. I saw a bicyclist pass by on the road and then two cars, but by 11:15 when my friends hadn't shown up I began texting them.

Their replies? One excuse after another. *I don't feel good. Something came up. No can do, sorry.*

People!

When I glanced up from my phone, Luke was looking at me like, *What are we doing?* "We're gonna run, buddy, you and me," I said.

People? Who needs people.

So we set off, running downhill on a wide trail under a breathtaking forest canopy. Reds, oranges, browns, and yellows rained down on us in a multicolored shower. A squirrel chattered at us from his post on a tree trunk, and overhead, a blue jay squawked. The trail formed an eleven-mile loop, but I'd decided already to do a shorter run, three down and three back. The three back would be mostly uphill, giving me a challenge at the end.

Since mine was the only car at the trailhead, I was pretty sure we were alone, so I let Luke off leash. I still had to force myself to free him after he got lost a few years ago. I eventually recognized my paranoia was inhibiting his joy and carving a deep rut in my behavior that did not serve me well. Nate graciously kept his *I told you so's* to himself.

Luke crashed joyously through the underbrush a few yards off the trail, paralleling me as I ran. I had to watch for rocks, loose gravel, and tree roots, but soon that became automatic, and my mind turned, as it often did, to the world and the evil I saw spreading everywhere. It wasn't only the school shootings, there were violent mass events in all kinds of places, kidnappings and rapes, child abuse, domestic violence, trafficking, and porn. Weird stuff. Politics was uglier than I'd ever seen it, and the Internet had become a cyber Tower of Babel.

How long, O Lord?

Partly, it's the curse of the law-enforcement mindset. You see the dark side all the time. It's easy to get overwhelmed. Nate, recognizing this tendency in me, had taught me to practice focusing on beauty—the colors of the trees, the songs of the birds, the glint of sun off my dog's glossy coat, the look in Luke's brown eyes.

"These are gifts from the Lord," he told me, "to help us get through."

But all too often, I felt like the disciples on the boat in the stormy sea of Galilee, hands gripping the gunwales, eyes wide with fear, glaring at the Savior sleeping aft. *How long, O Lord, will you let this go on?*

I stumbled, just thinking about it.

The Savior is not sleeping, oh me of little faith.

I'd reached the bottom of the decline. The trail leveled off here and ran along the creek for a time. Luke took advantage of that, splashing in the water, then he took off again, chasing some random scent, maybe a fox or a rabbit, hopefully not a bear.

Ahead I could see a place where a rocky outcropping forced the trail to take a bend to the right. I had just shifted my weight to make that turn when a man stepped out of the woods, right into my path.

My heart jumped. I caught my breath. I automatically noted his description—height, weight, appearance, clothing. My hand went to my fanny pack. No gun. Adrenaline flashed through me. The man moved forward. Was that a smirk on his face?

I did the smartest thing I could do. I yelled for my dog.

Luke came racing through the woods and planted himself between me and that man, growling. My heart drumming, I put my hand on Luke's collar like I was holding him back. "Move, please," I said, "so we can get by."

The man's eyes, small and dark, flitted between me and Luke. Then he held his hands up in a gesture of innocence. "No problem," he said and moved just enough to let me by.

"If I let go, he'll go straight for your throat," I said. Of course, that was not true, but the guy didn't know that.

My body tense, I led Luke past the man, staying as far away as I could. I braced for an attack, contingencies forming quickly in my mind. My ears stayed alert for sounds he was following. When I glanced back, he was sauntering up the trail we'd just come down.

Had I imagined his evil intent? I didn't know, but I took some safety measures anyway. I leashed up my dog to keep him close. I moved us off the trail. We'd go back through the woods, so our path was less predictable. Steep inclines, rock scrambles, and some deep, dry, creek beds made our going slow. Keeping an eye out for that man made it even slower.

After a hard slog, we made it back to my Jeep. I breathed a prayer of thanks when we reached the trailhead parking lot.

DRIVING HOME, I kept going over the incident in my head. Was I paranoid? Imagining things? Was I a younger Miss Etta? Why did everything seem so threatening right now?

Embarrassed that I'd forgotten the Garmin InReach, I avoided telling Scott about it when he called that night. He had enough on his mind anyway. The sixteen-year-old shooter was from a "good" family. He had no history of being bullied. No history of depression. He hadn't left a note or a social media post explaining his actions. So Scott had a mystery on his hands.

It turns out, so did I. A few days after my encounter with that man, a woman reported being assaulted on another trail nearby.

I admit my hands shook as I called the sheriff's office in that county. I identified myself and told the officer what had happened to me. He asked me to come in. The next day, I did.

After years as a police officer, it felt awkward being on the "wrong" side of the interview table. Deputy Charles Browning took my statement. I stuck to the facts, avoiding the emotions that surged in me. When he asked me if I'd be willing to work with the sketch artist, I readily agreed. That man's face had stuck to the walls of my mind. I'd rather have it plastered all over the news.

Afterward, the thought of going home to my empty house

chilled me. I needed to talk, so I called Nate. He was on his way home. I headed that direction and arrived just as he was maneuvering his old pickup loaded with hay bales up next to the barn.

"Hey," I called out, "want some help?"

"Sure! You want to work up or down?"

"I'll take up." I let Luke out of the Jeep, went into the barn, and climbed up the ladder to the loft. Nate had rigged a simple winch and pulley system to lift hay bales up four at a time using an "iron claw," a wicked looking piece of equipment he bought from some farmer up in the mountains. I think he loved using simple, old farm equipment. He could get twenty-six bales on his truck, and while I know he'd loaded hay into the loft by himself before, it would go a lot quicker with two of us.

I hooked the iron claw to the rope and carefully guided it out of the window and down to Nate, who stood on the top bales. He grabbed the claw and stabbed it into the bales on both sides, then waved his hand. I started the electric winch, and the bales lifted toward the loft. I brought them in, released the claw, and sent it down again. It was like playing with the claw machine at the arcade, I'd told Nate once.

We repeated our actions over and over until all twenty-six bales were stacked in the loft. Then he came up and joined me so we could arrange them neatly.

While we worked side by side, I told him my story. He listened carefully and asked me questions, drawing my emotions out as deftly as a surgeon lancing a boil. A couple of times I felt my throat tighten. I pushed through.

"Something about him had me on high alert," I said. "Every bone in my body was ready to fight."

"He scared you."

"Yes."

"And when you told the deputy that, did he take you serious?"

"Yes! Of course. Why wouldn't he?" Then it hit me. Miss Etta. I pursed my lips. "I don't know if it's the same..."

A little shake of his head told me Nate didn't agree. He hefted the last bale into place. "You got good instincts. So does Miss Etta, even if she is old." Nate detached the iron claw and put it off in a corner of the loft. We climbed down and brushed off the wisps of hay and dust collected on our clothing. Then he moved his truck next to the woodpile where it belonged.

I walked toward him. "I guess I'd better go."

Nate nodded. "You tell Scott what happened?"

"He's got enough to worry about."

"You need to tell him." He hugged me. "Thanks for your help."

I started to get into my Jeep, then I turned back to Nate. "Why is all this happening?"

"All what?"

"The school shootings, mass murder at a Christmas parade, the weird domestics, road rage, random anger ... I feel like we've all gone a little crazy since the pandemic. Is it just me? Have there been other times like this?"

Nate's jaw shifted. "That's a good question. Let's you and me take a look at Second Timothy sometime soon. Let's see what the Word says."

I nodded. I missed those teaching times with him. Then I had another thought. "Hey, I've got to go up to Clear Springs. Want me to check in on Miss Etta?"

Nate frowned and scratched his head. "Let me ask Laura. I'll get back to you on that." He paused. "She's not as concerned about that woman what showed up."

"Why's that?"

"Turns out she's a local teacher."

"Okay, then."

I left it at that, but on the way home I thought, it should be easy to find out if there's a school teacher named Catherine Grace in that small county.

I let go of that thought. No snooping, I told myself. When I got home, I took care of the horses, fed Luke, and heated up some leftovers for myself.

THE NEXT MORNING I left Luke at home and drove up to Highland County. That meant crossing over the mountains on winding back roads full of hairpin turns and switchbacks, but it also meant driving through hardwood forests fully decked out in the beauty of fall. I would have lost myself in the color if I hadn't had to pay close attention to the narrow roads. I wished Scott could share it with me.

My mission in Clear Springs was to check the history of the house where the painting was found in the attic. I decided to drive by it first, and I chose to take the road into town Miss Etta lived on. I slowed down as I approached her house, peering into the woods and inspecting her property. Everything seemed quiet. Her old car, which she hadn't driven in years, sat on the side, weeds growing around it. A gray cat sat on a planter out front, licking its paw.

So I continued on. My target house, located on a side street off the main road, was a cute little dressed-up Cape Cod cottage. Every double-hung window had an arched window above it. Two dormers popped out of the second floor. Twin pillars on the small entry porch held up the roof topped by a false balcony complete with balustrade. The siding on the house was a very light gray with white trim, the landscaping around it neat.

Looking at the side of the house, I could see a small attic window. My heart did a double-beat, thinking I was seeing the attic that held that mysterious painting. I turned around, drove past the house again, then parked a few doors down so I could discreetly take some pictures. I had a story ready in case anyone asked me what I was doing—I was studying the design. Because it was really cute.

I went on to the courthouse, where a kindly, fiftyish clerk named Hazel walked me through the records search process. The physical records had been scanned in and some were hard to read, she admitted. "Just what place is it you're interested in?" she asked. I gave her the address. "Oh, land! I know that house. Cute little thing. Just sold too. Let's see if we can find it."

She came out from behind the counter and walked me over to a computer station. Leaning over the machine, she typed in some codes, then the address. She stood up straight. "Right there you have it," she said.

"Thanks so much!" I sat down at the computer station and scrolled back page after page until I reached the year the house was built—1952. It sold for $7,900, a pretty good sum for that town in that day, Hazel told me later. Part of a plot of land called Mead's Addition, the house stayed in the hands of the original owners for six years, then they sold it.

I tracked the house's history through the years, taking notes the old-fashioned way, in a spiral notebook, because my cell phone wasn't allowed in the courthouse. Finally, I arrived at the listing showing Esther Mayfield, the mother of the man who'd consigned the painting, as the owner. But that wasn't the current owner. I knew that.

Puzzled, I pushed back from the computer where I'd been searching and walked back up to the counter where Hazel worked. "Did you get what you needed?" she asked.

"Everything but the current owner. You said it sold recently?"

"Well, yes, I remember it. But that sale probably isn't in our system yet. Let me check on that for you."

I waited while she walked into a back office. I could see her standing at a desk, talking on a phone, then writing something down. She returned a few minutes later. "Here you go," she said, handing me a piece of paper. "The deed's been registered. It just hasn't sifted down."

I looked down at the name, then my head jerked up. "This is the new owner?"

"Yes ma'am."

I blinked as I looked at the paper again. A warm rush went through me. The name was "Kathryn Grace McCaskill."

7

NOT CATHERINE. Kathryn. *Kathryn Grace*? The one who'd been visiting Miss Etta?

I sat out in my car for a few minutes, stunned. I mean, it seemed likely it was the same person, even though I'd had "Catherine-with-a-C" not "Kathryn-with-a-K" in my head all this time.

Overwhelmed with curiosity, I pulled out my phone to check the public school website. No signal. So I drove to the library, figuring they'd have Wi-Fi, and they did. I accessed it, and in short order I'd pulled up the site. And there she was, Kathryn Grace McCaskill, English teacher. She used her whole name.

She looked young. Long brunette hair fell down around her shoulders. She had pretty green eyes, and there was something about her smile that seemed familiar. Friendly. If she was the one visiting Miss Etta, maybe I felt better about it.

But then, how much can you tell from a headshot?

I DROVE ON HOME, passing by Kathryn Grace McCaskill's house again as well as Miss Etta's. Was it possible there was another

Kathryn Grace in this tiny town? If the house owner was the one visiting Miss Etta, how'd she find out about her (or vice versa)? How'd they connect? I rolled ideas around in my head about how I could find out.

Then I remembered what Nate said about snooping.

I didn't want to offend Laura. I don't make friends easily. I sure didn't want to lose the only two I had.

I flipped on an audiobook to distract myself, a mystery. It didn't hold my interest, and soon I was thinking about Kathryn Grace and Miss Etta again. Nate said Kathryn was a "friend of a friend." Who was that friend? Someone from church? A woman with a child in Kathryn's class? A neighbor?

Should I tell Nate and Laura about the fact that Kathryn was the owner of the house I was investigating? Wait, had I even told Nate about that job? Or the painting?

Did I have a justifiable reason to talk to Kathryn Grace? Would the subject of Miss Etta come up? Could I bring her up?

I almost turned my car around, then my conscience rose up and played killjoy. Nate said leave it alone. I gripped the wheel and kept driving east, away from Clear Springs.

I ARRIVED home feeling slightly depressed, empty, as if my trip had been a failure even though it hadn't. I'd gotten the information about the house that my client asked me for. All I had to do was type it up and email it to him along with my bill.

So what was bothering me?

I unlocked the house and went in. Luke greeted me, wagging his tail, ears back, ducking his head. I set down my bag and ruffled his collar, telling him what a good boy he'd been, I hoped. I glanced around and saw he'd pulled the pillows off the couch and left them on the floor, a mild protest about being left behind.

"Go on out," I told him, gesturing outside. "I've got to change. Go on. Go poop." I closed the front door after him, put the pillows back on the couch, and went upstairs. I switched into barn clothes, put on a sweatshirt, and went back down, trying to remember where I'd left my muck boots, front or back porch.

Back, I decided. I went out that way, found them, and headed for the barn, whistling for Luke. "Come on," I said, when he bounded up. "We've got to muck the stalls." I had just gotten started on the barn when I heard gravel crunching in the drive-way. Luke took off, barking. I looked out and saw a black Toyota Tacoma pickup. Ethan! I waved.

He came into the barn a few minutes later, his jeans tucked into muck boots.

"You're just in time," I said.

"In time for what? Dinner?" He grinned at me, his white teeth flashing against his tanned face. His strong jaw and short hair screamed *law enforcement*.

"I could arrange that."

Ethan grabbed a second stall fork and started working on Ace's bedding, pulling out the manure. Having him working nearby energized me, and it wasn't long before the stalls were clean and swept. "You want to re-bed them?" he asked me.

"Yes." Scott liked his horses to be outside 24/7 if the weather was good, but he also liked the stalls to be ready if we needed to bring them in.

"Straw?" Ethan called out.

"Yep, that's right. There's some in the loft. I just need half of one for Beau. He's pretty clean." I heard two thumps as Ethan threw down the bales. I was just about to move the wheelbarrow to the manure pile when he came down the ladder.

"I'll do that," he said.

"Are you sure?"

"Yes, ma'am." He looked around. "I can finish up here."

"I'll go start dinner."

That grin. I didn't know how Amanda could resist it.

· · ·

OVER LEFTOVER CHICKEN CASSEROLE, salad, and bread I gleaned what I could from Ethan about his life. Amanda wouldn't answer his calls or texts. Scott had told him to back off, leave her alone, and he had, but he still loved her. "I don't know what to do," he said. "Right now, I'm just praying. That's what Mr. Scott said to do."

Mr. Scott? My Scott?

Pausing with fork in midair, he continued. "I feel like she's searching for something. Maybe it's because she's on the East Coast. Maybe California would suit her better. Or maybe she misses her mom." He looked at me. "Do you think she misses her mom?"

I hesitated, trying to decide how much to say. Scott's ex-wife was a manipulative mess. You'd miss her like you'd miss having a root canal. "Amanda may miss what she wishes her mom was like." And her dad, to be honest. Scott was MIA during much of Amanda's childhood.

Ethan cocked his head. I could see he was trying to absorb that thought. It was probably too deep for a young man, so I changed the subject and asked about his schooling.

He said school was going well. He should graduate with a bachelor's degree in criminal justice in May. "Then I'll start applying to police departments. Mr. Scott said he'd give me a reference."

"What departments are you going for?" I asked.

"Charlottesville and the counties around it. Albemarle. Nelson. Madison."

To stay near Amanda, of course.

I reached over and touched his arm. "Amanda may be processing the trauma of what she went through a couple of years ago or maybe things from her childhood. I'm not exactly sure what's going on, because she's not hanging out here, either. She may come out of it and you two will get back together. In the meantime, you build your own life. And keep praying." I squeezed his arm. "Scott thinks the world of you." I grinned. "Maybe that's Amanda's problem."

AFTER ETHAN LEFT, I put on my lighted visor, grabbed a flashlight, and walked Luke down our long driveway to the road and back. The night sky looked like an inverted black bowl. Stars by the thousands twinkled overhead, and I saw a shooting star streak across the sky.

Luke had been cooped up much of the day. I knew he needed a little exercise. That's why we were out here. Hearing him joyously crash through the woods made me smile. But I did attach a little blinking red light to his collar before we went out.

Back inside, Luke slumped contentedly to the floor, and I sat down at the computer, but before I could start typing up my findings on the house in Clear Springs, I got a text from Scott. *Coming home. Next flight.*

They must have had a breakthrough! And now I had a great excuse for not telling him about running alone and the man in the mountains and giving a statement to the police. It could wait. Right? He'd be home soon.

I went back to my report, but I did stray a little. I did a little research on the house's owner in case my client asked. *Kathryn Grace McCaskill has a B.A. in history from George Mason University and an M.Ed. from the same school. She grew up in Northern Virginia. Her hobbies are horseback riding and genealogy.*

That wasn't snooping exactly. It was right there in her short bio on the school division's website.

I sent my report and my invoice, took a shower, and changed the sheets. Scott might surprise me in the middle of the night or early in the morning. One way or the other, he'd be home tomorrow.

I went to bed about ten. Two hours later a callout woke me up: a female hiker missing up on a trail near where I'd seen that man. *Abducted?* The thought instantly flashed through my mind because that was definitely the vibe I'd gotten from that guy. I notified the incident commander, Bill, that Luke and I would respond. Then I texted Nate and asked him if he was going.

Yes. See you up there.

I called him. "You know where this is, right? Up near where that man accosted me on the trail."

"I thought maybe that was the case." He paused. "Bringing your gun?"

"Yes." Searching armed was not the norm. In fact, it was frowned on. But no way I was going in those woods again without protection. "You bringing Ember?"

"Yep."

That was cool. After Ember's original owner realized it would be a long time before he'd recovered enough from cancer to take care of her, he'd offered her to Nate, who agreed to adopt the black German shepherd. He'd used the COVID years to get her certified as a Wilderness SAR K-9. She was pretty good.

"See you soon."

Luke, already pacing because of the late-night phone call, went crazy, turning in circles and barking when I pulled out my SAR clothes and pack. I quickly got dressed, checked to make sure I had the Garmin, and left. I heard one of the horses nicker as I loaded Luke in the Jeep. Thirty-five minutes later, I arrived at the scene. Passing by the law-enforcement cars lining the road, I parked. I joined Bill, a colleague from Battlefield Search and Rescue, and two other teams, including Nate and Ember at the SUV serving as command center.

"So what we've got," said Bill, "is a twenty-eight-year-old female, an experienced outdoorswoman, who we believe was solo hiking on this trail." He pointed to a marked trail on the topographic map. "Her name is Alice Ragnorelli. Her boyfriend came looking for her when she was three hours overdue and found her car at the trailhead. He couldn't catch a cell signal, so he drove uphill until he found one and called 911."

"Where is he now?" I asked.

Bill nodded toward the cluster of people standing next to the road. "Over there."

In the middle of a group of law-enforcement officers stood a young man, head bent, his hand over his eyes, obviously upset. I felt for him.

"The park rangers and state police did a hasty search of the trail and a couple of side tracks but came up with nothing. The boyfriend is concerned. He says it isn't like Alice to be late." Bill looked up. We were all paying attention. "Here's what I think we should do. Nate, you take the main trail. There's one scramble here," he said, pointing to a spot on the map where rocks had slid over the trail, "but otherwise you should be okay. Emily, you take this offshoot, running down from here. And Jess, you head west. It'll make you climb, but you can do it."

"Sounds good," I said.

"Who are the walkers?" Nate asked.

"I have two deputies and a new SAR recruit."

"I'll take the recruit. Give them the deputies." Nate nodded toward me and Emily.

My deputy turned out to be a guy named Butch, who'd lived in these hills all his life and sounded like it. He'd hunted deer around here since he was in grade school, and while he was a little fumble-fingered with the GPS, he liked dogs and seemed happy to help however he could.

We searched for two hours over mountainous, rocky terrain. We saw half a dozen deer, three possums, and several raccoons. The air turned crisp as an apple, keeping me wide awake.

We reached the end of our assigned search zone and returned to base by a slightly different route. Toward the end, I asked Butch to hide, and I let Luke find him to get his reward.

Both Emily and Nate returned before us. Alice Ragnorelli was still MIA. I could see the discouragement on everyone's faces. Nate huddled with Bill to strategize a secondary search plan. I took Luke to my Jeep and fed him some beef jerky along with some kibble while I snacked on trail mix and a protein bar. A big drink of water for each of us, and we were ready to go again.

I'd rather do almost anything than wait. Give me a swamp to push through, a tick-infested field to hike, a slick rocky outcropping to cross over—any outdoor challenge, except maybe a farm pond—but don't make me sit around and wait. Luke felt the same way. Already he had bumped my leg with his nose twice, dog-language for *Let's go!*

Finally Nate called me over. "We're going to call it for the night. You can go home," he said to me.

"What?" I said, my heart rate quickening. "We can't go home. We haven't found her." The face of the man I'd seen in the woods flashed in my mind. My gut tightened.

"We've done all we can in the dark. The sheriff agrees. It ain't safe."

"But what if she's hurt? We can't just leave her out here." *Or what if that man has her trapped?*

"We'll start again in the morning. We got another group comin'."

"Wait, can I see the maps? Let me see the maps." Why I thought I was smarter than Nate I don't know.

Patiently, he showed me the maps, starting with the trailhead where she'd parked and expanding the search area to include the part Luke and I covered. "To the north is the road. If she'd gotten off the trail but stumbled on the road ..."

"... she would have walked down the road to where she'd left her car," I said, finishing his sentence.

"Right. To the south is a sheer cliff face. No way can we search that at night. You took the western route, Emily went here, and Ember and I, we checked this part."

"Ember's new at this. What if she missed her in the dark? I

mean, she could be lying out there hurt, unconscious, and Ember just missed her."

I could almost hear Nate counting to ten. He took a deep breath and blew it out. "If you want to go over that area again with Luke, okay. But I don't think Ember missed anything."

"Yes, I want to!"

Nate shook his head, his lips pressed into a line. "Bill?" The search commander came over. "Jess here wants to try this area again with Luke."

Bill looked at me like I was crazy. "Knock yourself out. I'm sending the others home."

"I aim to walk it with her," Nate said.

"What? No!" I said. He was already limping. I couldn't put that pressure on him. "Butch'll go." I looked around for my deputy.

"The sheriff pulled his deputies back," Nate said.

"Then Emily can walk it with me. Em?"

Nowhere in sight.

"Let's go, Jess," Nate said.

What could I do? With Nate following as my walker for the next hour and a half, Luke and I went back over the route he and Ember had covered. Luke ran all around, sniffing, working hard, but in the end, I'd inflicted pain on my friend and insulted his dog for nothing. I felt sick. Silently, I reported back to search headquarters and documented my failure in the log. Then I walked Luke back over to my Jeep. "You tried, buddy," I said, rubbing him behind the ears. "It's not your fault. I'm sorry."

He read my defeated tone, slurped me across the face, and jumped up into his crate. He lay down with a huff, then thumped his tail as I locked him in. He'd had almost four hours of running in the woods at night. He was happy.

I closed the back of the Jeep and heard Nate say, "Hey, girl."

I turned around. "I'm sorry, Nate."

He hugged me. "We mighta got lucky. Who knows?"

"I couldn't leave without trying everything to see if she was out there."

"I know." He shifted his weight. "Text me when you get home."

"I'll be okay."

"No. You do this one my way. Text me. I don't want Scott comin' after me 'cause I *figured* you'd be okay and then you weren't."

He wasn't kidding. So I agreed to text him and then I watched as he limped back to his car. I got in my Jeep and steered out of the trailhead parking lot, past the deputy assigned to stay in case the hiker returned to her car. I drove home down empty dark roads beneath a black velvet sky, images of Alice Ragnorelli, the lost hiker, flashing through my mind. Were we abandoning her? Was she hurt? Did that man have her? Was she going to end up another body in the woods?

8

Leaving the search for Alice Ragnorelli twisted my gut. I hated every mile I traveled away. I thought of Geraldine Largay, the Appalachian Trail thru-hiker who'd simply left the trail to use the bathroom and gotten lost. What if Alice was in the same boat? Yes, she was an experienced hiker, but so was Geraldine Largay.

"God," I began to pray, "where is she? Why couldn't we find her? Her boyfriend seemed devastated. Please help them find her tomorrow. Please let her be safe. Please." I adjusted my grip on the steering wheel. "Hurt is okay," I bargained. "Just please let her be alive."

I went on, talking to God about lost hikers, school shooters, men who have affairs, and the sadness I felt because I couldn't find Alice. I asked him to help Scott with the school shooter case and bring him home safely. I told him about Miss Etta and her dementia, and why did that seem so common? And how sad was that to end your life that way? Then I brought up Nate and his leg, and I asked God to heal it quickly.

"And please help me not snoop even though I'm concerned about Miss Etta and her visitors. Don't let her fall for any scams, Lord. Keep her safe, please."

Why even pray? God's gonna do what he wants to anyway.

Sometimes the devil gets into my mind. I had to reject that right away. "Thank you, God, that you hear my prayers and answer them in due time."

The sky grew light in the east as I guided my Jeep into our driveway. Emerging from the woods at the beginning of our lane I saw the horses were in the field, already cropping grass. Beyond them a fox trotted toward the creek. A curl of smoke rose from our nearest neighbor's chimney. Woodstove season had arrived.

God has given us a peaceful refuge in a world of hurt, I thought. I thanked him, but Alice Ragnorelli remained lodged in my mind.

I SLEPT for four hours before the sound of my cellphone woke me up. Checking the caller ID, I expected it to be Scott, but it wasn't, it was Nate. "Hey, what's up?"

"They found the girl."

I sat straight up in bed. "Alice? Where? Is she okay?"

"She's dead."

I swung my legs over the side. "Where? Where'd they find her?" *Please don't let it be where Luke and I searched.*

"In the trunk of the boyfriend's car."

"What?" Shock propelled me to my feet. "Are you kidding?"

"Something made the sheriff suspicious. He sent his deputies home, 'cept the one sittin' on Alice's car, but he hung back, watchin' the boyfriend. The kid said he'd left his car up the road, where he'd found the cell signal. The sheriff offered him a lift. The kid said he'd walk. That was a red flag.

"So the sheriff pretended to leave, but then followed him on foot. When the kid got to his car a mile or so up the road, he backed into the woods—"

"To dump the body." I finished his thought as I paced.

"Right. To dump the body. And the sheriff caught him."

"Oh, Nate. He seemed so ... devastated. Heartbroken."

"People ain't always like they seem."

PEOPLE AIN'T ALWAYS *like they seem.* Nate's words bounced around in my mind like billiard balls smacked by a sharp cue as I went through my morning routine. Get dressed. Make up the bed. Brush teeth. Try to figure out what would make a "nice" young man kill his girlfriend.

The young man—what was his name? Reed something?—seemed authentically upset when I saw him. Crushed. Frightened. In fact, I saw him shaking as he stood waiting for us to get started searching. Of course, he could have been shaking from the cold, or from fear he'd be found out.

What tipped the sheriff off that he killed her? It was him refusing a ride. Choosing to walk up the mountain in the middle of the night by himself.

Come to think of it, when I arrived, I'd noticed all the parked cars I passed on the way to the trailhead were law enforcement or familiar SAR team members' cars. Of course, Reed couldn't park his car there. Someone, most certainly the dogs, would smell the body. Why hadn't I noticed that suspicious behavior?

Before I got a good grip on my familiar self-flagellation whip, I reminded myself that the sheriff had interviewed him, and I had seen him only briefly and at a distance. Plus, I was focused on my job and my dog.

Still, this development stunned me. I pride myself on being sharply observant.

I heard a noise downstairs. Luke jumped up with a big "Woof!" and headed that direction.

"Dad? Jess?" a voice called.

"Amanda?" Wow, why was she home? "I'm coming."

She stood just inside the front door, her long flaxen hair

streaming down her back like a waterfall. Tall and lean, dressed in jeans, a flannel shirt, a sky blue parka, and short boots, she could have been a model for REI or L.L. Bean. She looked up at me, her eyes blue like Scott's, as I descended the stairs. "What a surprise," I said. "So good to see you." I gave her a hug.

"Dad's not home?"

"He had to go to Montana."

"What happened this time?"

"Another school shooting."

She tossed her head. "I don't know how you stand it."

I let that one drop. "What brings you out here?"

"Do you have any coffee?"

"Sure! Come on."

I led the way out to the kitchen, pulled out the large coffee pot, and began making the dark brew. She took off her parka and draped it on the back of a chair, then sat down. "We've missed you!" I said. "How's everything going?"

She didn't answer right away so I pressed the start button on the brewer and turned to look at her. Her chin was slightly raised, her eyes intense. "I think I may be pregnant. If I am, I'm getting an abortion and I want to know if Dad's insurance will cover it."

Her words ignited a bomb inside me. *Oh, no! Abortion? How could you? Why can't I get pregnant?* Followed by *Help me, Jesus! Help me.*

Amanda's eyes dared me to judge her. I took a deep breath. I sat down next to her. Behind me, the coffee pot gurgled. An image flashed in my mind. When it came into focus, I realized I was imagining Jesus talking to the woman caught in adultery. Grace, grace.

I reached over and put my hand over Amanda's. "I'm sorry. This must be very scary for you."

She jerked her hand away and burst into tears. "Dad's going to kill me."

I rose, moved toward her, and hugged her. My eyes were full

of tears, too, tears of fear and anger and rage and sorrow. Grief for the child I'd never conceived. Fear for Amanda's future. Concern for Scott. Tension locked up my joints and froze my jaw.

I let go of Amanda and retrieved a box of tissues while I tried to manage my emotions. I poured two mugs of coffee and placed them on the table. "Cream?"

She nodded.

I grabbed the half-and-half from the fridge and a spoon from the drawer for her. The sugar lived on the table in a kitschy little bowl shaped like a fat puppy. I moved it toward her as I sat down. My hand shook. I prayed urgent little arrow prayers, half-sentences, desperate pleas, and syllables begging for wisdom. Nate and I had talked a lot about grace, and now here was Amanda, needing it, and I was so scared I wouldn't have the words for it. Or the heart. That I'd be so wrapped up in my own frustration and anger at my infertility that I couldn't feel for her.

"Amanda." I cleared my throat. "First of all, your dad isn't going to kill you. He loves you. More than you know." She looked across the room, trying to dodge that thought. "Have you taken a pregnancy test?"

Amanda shook her head. "I'm just late. And I'm never late."

"Well, wouldn't that be a good first step? Before you ..." I started to say 'panic' but changed my mind. "... before you get too concerned?"

"I couldn't face it."

"Maybe you could do it here. Then we could face it together." I must have been channeling Nate to say something like that! I couldn't believe my own words.

She tossed her head. "When's dad going to be home?"

"He was supposed to fly in last night or early this morning. I haven't heard from him."

She started to get up. "I don't want to see him. This was a mistake."

I reached out and touched her hand. She sat back down. "Who's the guy?" I asked.

She dropped her head, resting her forehead in her hand, hiding. "It was the stupidest thing."

"Tell me about it."

"A bunch of us were out, celebrating after a game. We were going from bar to bar downtown. I got separated from my friends and kind of lost. A guy ... this guy came up to me and said he'd help me get home. We were walking through this park." Tears began running down Amanda's face. "I was drunk, Jess. Too drunk. And he was all over me and ..."

"And he raped you." My head felt like it had a steel band around it.

Amanda's eyes filled with tears. "It was my fault," she whispered.

Her shame spilled out like ink on fresh white paper. I could feel it, feel it as if it were my own. "No." I shook my head. "Amanda, that was rape. It wasn't your fault." I rose and hugged her, and she sobbed. *How many women had this same story?* "Being drunk," I said gently, "is not an invitation for sex." My voice remained calm but anger made my pulse pound. I felt hot. Scared for her. Angry at the guy.

What I knew of Amanda's life unfolded in my mind. She'd been abused by at least one of her mother's boyfriends. After coming to live with her father, she'd been abducted, trafficked by a boy who was a friend of a friend, and nearly raped. And now this. Were men picking up on her vulnerability? She'd had counseling, but had it been good trauma counseling? Did she need more?

"Amanda, I hate that this happened to you. I have some ideas on how we could get you some help processing it. To give you some hope."

"I need to get rid of it," she said. Then she fixed her eyes on me. "You don't believe in that, do you? You'd call me a baby killer. But I can't do this! I'm not ready for a baby! Especially that guy's." She grimaced. "I don't even know his name. I was so stupid!"

I bit my cheek, hard, to keep from responding. I'd been longing for a baby for over two years. Every month I struggled with disappointment and grief. And she would just ... just throw this life away? The irony scoured my gut. *God,* I thought, *this is crazy. Help me!*

I forced my voice to be calm. *Let him who is without sin be the first to cast a stone.* "Amanda, your dad and I both believe that unborn babies are gifts from God. But we wouldn't call you a baby killer. We'd call you a precious daughter who we both love. You are a beautiful, courageous young woman in a difficult situation. Don't prejudge us." *Like I so often used to do.*

Amanda looked at me like she was trying to believe me. I imagined for a moment the woman caught in adultery searching Jesus' eyes to see if his compassion was real. It was real. I knew what those eyes looked like. I'd seen them myself.

I swallowed hard and opened my mouth to share that with her. Just then, I heard a knock at the door. It opened. And I heard Ethan say, "Miss Jessica? Did you know Beau is out?"

Amanda panicked. She half rose, her eyes wild. "He's here?" she whispered.

I called out to him. "Thanks, Ethan. I'll be right there." I kept my eyes on Amanda. I lowered my voice. "You stay here. Or go upstairs if you want. I've got to get the horse. I'll make sure Ethan doesn't come in."

She nodded. I hugged her, grabbed my jacket, called Luke, and raced out of the house.

THE COLD AIR hit me like a slap. I shoved Amanda's problems— and mine—into the back of my mind. Beau was down by the creek. How had he gotten out of the pasture? Ethan was trotting toward my horse, a bucket in his hand. Grain.

Grabbing a lead rope off the fence near the barn, I began running. Luke dashed ahead of me. I almost called him back, but then I saw he had figured out both the problem and his role in solving it. He made a wide arc to the left. He was going to herd Beau back toward Ethan and me.

German shepherds were bred to both move livestock and protect them. Luke didn't get to use the herding part much, but watching him now, I was glad he had that drive.

Beau dodged Ethan as he got close, but he couldn't avoid Luke. Two big "woofs" and Beau began moving back toward the barn. "Hey, buddy. Hey, Beau," I called as he came in my direction. I'd done a lot of what Scott calls groundwork with him. That day it paid off. Beau responded to my invitation to follow, I looped the rope around his neck, and soon he was back in the pasture.

"We need to figure out how he got out," I said to Ethan when he joined me.

"I'll walk the fence," he responded. "I came over to clean the tack, but I'll do that instead." He looked down at the ground. "Amanda's here?" He'd seen her car.

I hesitated. "She's having a moment." I watched to see if he understood what I was saying.

He nodded. "I won't come up to the house."

Good. "Text me if you need help with something." I turned. "Let me know if you find a hole!"

"Will do."

I walked back to the house, Amanda's problems—and mine— emerging from the back of my mind like a bear coming out of a cave. I focused on the ground, thinking as I walked. Frost edged each fallen leaf in silver and sparkled in the sun. Beauty.

Beauty from ashes, Lord. Bring the beauty.

. . .

AMANDA WAS NOT in the kitchen, so I went upstairs, Luke following behind. By the time I found her in her bedroom, I'd found the picture I wanted on my iPhone.

She was sitting on the edge of her bed, the bed she'd slept in maybe half a dozen times in the two years we'd owned this house. Scott blamed himself. He said he'd left her alone all her growing up years, and that's what felt normal to her. I tried to comfort him, but the truth is, like my own dad, he might not have wanted to be an absentee father, but he was one. And Amanda did have a hard time feeling his love.

I sat down next to Amanda and showed her the picture on my phone. It was a shot of Scott in ICU after he'd nearly lost his life saving her from traffickers. He was unconscious, tubes everywhere, monitors recording his every heartbeat. We'd thought we'd lose him that night, he'd lost so much blood.

Amanda looked at the picture, then looked away. Then she took my phone in her hand and studied it. She scrolled forward through some other shots taken at that time. And she began crying, tears streaming down her face.

"He saved your life, and then you saved his. Remember?" After he'd plucked her from the traffickers and been shot, she'd driven like crazy toward the hospital, then recognized my Jeep on the road and flagged me down.

I retrieved another box of tissues. "He loves you," I said softly, putting them down next to her. "I understand it may be hard for you to feel it. But I think you also need each other. He is one hurting man right now, missing you." I put my hand on her back, and as I did, I had a flash of insight. By staying away from him she was protecting herself from the pain of him leaving her, or worse, dying. "I think if you bring your problem to him he'll be that warrior dad, who will fight for you, the one who almost died protecting you. Trust me, Amanda. He loves you. And he needs you."

She shrugged.

"I think there's a reason you came to this house today, and it doesn't have to do with insurance."

She looked at me, and I saw in her eyes I was right. And she leaned her head on my shoulder, and I hugged her.

9

By the time Amanda left an hour later, I was exhausted emotionally and physically. The stress of the search, the despair over Alice Ragnorelli's murder, and then Amanda's problems had washed everything out of me. All my feelings were dead. All my energy was gone.

I stripped off my dirty jeans and climbed into bed, and that's where I was when I got the text from Scott two hours later saying he was on the way home. Sound asleep. In bed.

There'd better be some steaks in the freezer, I thought, rousing myself.

Luke, who was sleeping on the floor nearby, yawned and stretched. He came over to me, wagging his tail. I rubbed him behind his ears and told him I loved him. Then I slid into some fresh socks and jeans and a prettier T-shirt; brushed my teeth again and headed downstairs.

Yes, there were steaks. Fresh broccoli. Some good rolls. We had propane for the grill. And when Scott walked in an hour later, we had fresh flowers for the table, a beautiful bouquet of pale pink roses and baby's breath.

I'd been fussing around trying to remember what I had told

him, and what I needed to tell him, and if Amanda was on that second list, or if I should wait for her to tell him. But when Scott walked in my fussing stopped. I melted into his arms, the strength of his body and his sheer presence calming my heart. I silently thanked God for this man. I breathed in his scent and kissed him.

"I missed you," he said.

I wondered if he could hear my heart pounding. "I missed you too."

He kissed me again. "Let's go see the horses."

Well, at least he came in the house first.

I called Luke and we went outside and walked toward the barn. Scott took my hand. "So tell me about your trip," I said.

He stared straight forward. The muscle in his jaw flexed. "I will in a while. How have you been?" He squeezed my hand.

"Good." Okay, that was partly a lie. But I was alive, in one piece, up on my feet. That qualified as "good," didn't it?

I told him about the curious case I had—the origins of the painting of the little girl and the collie.

He grinned and asked, "If it had been an old truck, or a landscape, or a classic house, would you have taken that job? The answer is *no*. It had to be a girl and a dog."

I laughed. "Yes, I took that job because it was a girl and a dog, even though they were having a tea party, which is kind of ridiculous in my opinion."

He put his arm around me and drew me close, kissing the side of my head. "No frills for my girl."

"And that's just the way you like it," I retorted.

"You bet. So did you figure it out? Where the painting came from?"

"Yes! But here's the weird thing—it was in an estate auction in Madison County, but it came from the attic of a house in Clear Springs. I checked that out, identified the owners back to 1954, and found the current owner is the younger woman who's been visiting Miss Etta." I looked at Scott, anticipating his surprise.

Nothing. "Clear Springs is a small town."

I guess next to figuring out a clean-cut school shooter, a coincidence like that wasn't much. I kept going. "She's a school teacher."

"So did you tell Laura?"

"Not yet." As soon as those words came out of my mouth I realized how crazy they sounded. Why wouldn't I tell her? Immediately?

Because I was afraid she'd think I was snooping.

We stepped up to the paddock fence. Scott whistled and Ace came running. "Hey buddy! Hey boy."

Scott let go of my hand, reached up, and petted his horse. He touched his horse's cheek and his neck, then he climbed up on the board fence and jumped into the paddock next to him. The affection between the two of them was clear. I smiled as I watched them.

Luke had slipped through the boards of the fence and was dancing around Ace. I wasn't sure whether he was trying to get Ace's attention or Scott's. Beau remained in the far end of the paddock. I guess I hadn't bonded with him enough yet to bring him running. I climbed up on the fence and sat on the top board.

Scott stood next to Ace, pulling weed fragments and hay out of Ace's mane. He had the same magic touch with horses that Nate did with dogs. I loved watching them together.

I debated with myself about which issue to bring up next— the man on the trail when I was running alone, the search for Alice Ragnorelli and the fact she was murdered, or Amanda and the possibility she was pregnant.

Scott a grandfather? I couldn't see it. He wasn't old enough.

Ace curled his head around Scott's body, a sign of affection. "He looks good," Scott said. "Thank you for taking care of him."

"Of course! Ethan came by and helped." I hesitated. "We had a search while you were gone."

"Just one?" He flashed a grin at me.

"A tough one." I went on to tell him about the lost hiker and the boyfriend and the sheriff finding her body in the kid's trunk. "I can't believe I didn't suspect him! He seemed so sincere."

Scott frowned. "An argument that escalated do you think?"

"I don't know. I guess we'll find out more eventually."

Scott ran his hand over Ace's chest, his girth, his haunches. He picked up each of the horse's feet in turn. He must have been happy with what he saw, because he patted Ace's neck and said, "Good boy."

I only had two subjects left in my quiver, Scott's daughter and the man I saw while running alone. "Amanda stopped by."

Scott raised his eyebrows.

"She didn't know you were out of town. You didn't text her?"

"No. Didn't think to."

"You ought to invite her out to ride. Before winter really sets in."

He walked over to the gate, opened it, and left the paddock. I climbed down from the fence. "That's a good idea. What's for dinner?"

An escape! Call me chicken, but I really didn't want to get further into a difficult topic just then. He'd just gotten home! "Steak, salad, bread. The usual."

"Sounds perfect to me. Let me give them some grain and then I'll be up. I'll do the steaks on the grill."

"C'mon, Luke." On the way to the house, I texted Amanda: *Your dad's home.* Maybe she'd call.

TWENTY MINUTES later we sat down at our farm table. Scott said grace. The smell of the grilled steak and the fresh bread competed for my attention. We dug in. Then Scott began to talk.

"You know, if bad guys all looked grizzled and nasty and smelled like cigarettes and beer it'd be easy. But when the bad guy is a fresh-faced, clean-cut kid from a good family, smart, healthy, just sixteen with his whole life ahead of him, I don't know, it's tough." He clenched and unclenched his left fist. "It seemed wrong."

My eyebrows raised. "Wrong?"

"Unnatural. Like something had gotten ahold of him." Scott glanced quickly at me. "I know, if you'd suggested something like that to me three years ago, I would have said you were crazy. But I've been face-to-face with evil. And this felt evil even though, rationally, there was no evidence of it." He paused. "Look, global warming or climate change, whatever you want to call it, is a problem. You might even call it an emergency. But one that requires violent action? That's over the line. And to have a good kid like this go off the rails in such a dramatic way, it just felt weird to me."

"Did you get to talk to his parents?"

"Yeah. Solid people. The kind you'd want to be friends with."

"People ain't always like they seem."

Scott laughed. "Quoting Nate?"

"Yes."

"But in this case, I think they are just what they appear to be. I mean, I grilled 'em. I talked to the parents, their daughter, a bunch of kids from his school, his teachers, their pastor, some youth group members. Nobody saw this coming. Said he was a good kid, a serious kid. Wanted to become an environmental lawyer."

"How'd the shooting go down? All I've read are the media reports."

Scott continued to eat as he talked. "The kid, Everett, walks into school late and goes to his locker. The hall's empty—just Everett and his buddy. He puts his backpack down on the floor and unzips it. Then he takes out the gun to show it to his friend.

"Another kid comes around the corner, sees the gun, and starts yelling. Just then the bell rings. Kids pour into the hallway. Everett panics, they wrestle for the gun, it fires, and kids get shot. Finally, the gym teacher tackles Everett. Everett falls on the gun, shoots himself in the gut, and bleeds out."

Right at that moment, Scott's phone rang. He looked at the caller ID. "I'm sorry. I have to take this." He got up and walked out the back door and shut it behind him.

My head spun. Everett's plan, if he had one, didn't sound very well thought out. I mean, why would he pull the gun out in the hallway where anyone could see it? Was the kid who tried to grab it one of the ones killed? Was the gym teacher hurt?

I heard the door open and looked up. Scott walked in with a look on his face that I can only describe as "intense." He bent down to kiss me. "Jess, I'm sorry. I've got to go back to work."

I blinked. I cocked my head, silently questioning him. Fatigue edged his eyes. He'd been on the go for how long? And now he was going in again?

"Come upstairs. I'll tell you while I get dressed."

I stared at our half-eaten dinners. "Okay, then." Because that's what you do when you love somebody. You leave the steak and follow him.

By the time we reached our bedroom he was half-undressed. "Quick shower," he said.

I gathered up his discarded clothes, retrieving his wallet and phone and a small packet of ibuprofen from his pockets, and laid them on the bed, then threw the clothes in the hamper. He emerged from the shower and redressed in fresh clothes, a suit this time, a good one.

While he dressed, he spoke. "What I'm going to tell you can't go anywhere else, not even to Nate."

I nodded. "Okay."

"The evidence response team went over the family's house, including the kid's room. They're usually pretty thorough.

Found nothing that would indicate why Everett did this. No manifesto. No more weapons. No plans." Scott's face was animated. "For some reason I decided to take a look myself. When I walked in that kid's room it was neat as a pin. Organized. Everything in its place. But I could feel something. Maybe it was too neat.

"So I started going over it again. I looked in the dresser, behind the dresser, under the bed. I checked the desk. I took out the drawers and even checked behind them. The evidence people had taken his laptop, but I looked everywhere else.

"Then," he paused, "you know that floorboard upstairs that drives me crazy? The one that gives a little when you step on it?"

"Yes."

"I was standing next to his bed trying to think like a sixteen-year-old kid, and I felt something like that. A little give in the floor. I got down on my knees and started looking. I saw a barely imperceptible line in the carpet, so I tugged on it. It came up. So did a piece of the hardwood flooring below it." Scott turned toward me, his eyes bright. "That kid had created a secret compartment under the floor beneath his bed, and inside was a second laptop. His parents had never seen it before, and neither had his sister."

"Scott that's brilliant! Good for you."

"That's why I came back early. I wanted to bring it personally to the tech guys. There's a reason why it was hidden."

"It could hold the motive."

"It did hold the motive. That was the phone call."

Navy blue suit, white shirt, and a gray, white, and blue striped tie. Mr. FBI. He looked sharp.

"Remember I told you Everett wanted to be an environmental lawyer? He found an underground environmental group on the Internet. They radicalized him. Got him panicking about global warming. The group is organizing coordinated 'climate action now' terror attacks in every state on an unknown date to get everyone's attention. Demanding an end to fossil fuel and other changes. Everett was the Montana connection."

"So was that the attack?"

"No. I think he was showing off, trying to get his buddies involved. He's only sixteen, for crying out loud."

"So he was practicing sneaking a gun into school? He wasn't very good at it, was he?"

"No."

"But there are more attacks coming?"

"Unless we stop them. I'm going in with my boss to brief the head of CIRG. If he buys it, we'll go see the deputy assistant director. Then," he leaned over and kissed me, "I'll be back."

"When?" It was a fair question. He was in the process of throwing fresh clothes in a backpack.

"Soon as I can."

I followed Scott downstairs, my heart sinking with every step. He turned at the door. "If you see Amanda, tell her I love her and would like to have her out for a ride soon." Then he hugged me and kissed me. "I'm so sorry to leave you again. I love you."

And he was gone.

10

I TEXTED SCOTT'S DAUGHTER. *Sorry, Amanda. He had to go back to work. Please don't do anything before we talk. Please.*

I slumped down in my favorite living room chair—a green, old-fashioned wingback I'd found at a yard sale. I leaned my cheek against the "wing." I loved Scott. But sometimes I hated his job.

But I would not complain. It was a package deal.

Luke came to me and nudged my arm. That's when I realized I hadn't fed him. So I lurched to my feet and walked out to the kitchen. I scooped two cups of kibble out of the bin and put them in his bowl. Within seconds he was crunching away.

I turned and saw our half-finished meal on the table. I'd lost my appetite for it, so I cut the meat off the steak bones and tossed it in Luke's dish. "Here you go, buddy. Enjoy." Then I scraped the bones and the salad into the trash, wrapped the rolls in foil, and loaded the dishwasher. By the time I was done, Luke was too. "You want to go out?" I asked him.

Of course he did. I grabbed my coat, slid into my boots, and flashlight in hand, we went outside. My original thought was to walk the driveway as usual, but for some reason I turned toward the creek, and we walked through the field instead.

Loneliness held me in its grip, and sorrow dogged at my heels. I was alone except for Luke. Thank God for Luke. And thank God for God. "I'm not alone and I will never be alone," I said out loud. I was affirming a truth I'd first heard lying in the mud with a knife in my side.

The sun had long since dropped behind the hills. The sky had turned from deep blue to purple. Here and there a star had popped out. Normally, I would have relished the beauty, but on this night sadness overwhelmed me. I stared into the sky feeling all alone in the vast universe, my mind searching for a Scripture verse, a promise to claim. My mind went blank.

Lost in thought, I walked across the creek and all the way to our property line. Then I whistled for my dog. "Hey, buddy, let's go back," I called out. Luke came to me, and I ruffled the coat on his neck. "Let's go home."

On the way back to the house in the dark, a sudden fear came over me. *What if Scott doesn't come home? Like my father.*

What? Where did that come from?

A cold chill iced my veins. I literally stumbled and cried out. Luke came close and stuck his nose in my hand. "I'm all right," I said.

But I wasn't. *What if he doesn't come back?*

My father had left for work as usual on 9/11, kissing me goodbye just as I was waking up for school. It was a Tuesday. What can be more normal than a Tuesday? But less than three hours later, he was dead, along with twenty-five hundred other people in the World Trade Center.

What if Scott dies like that?

I fought back with logic. Scott's not a street agent anymore; he studies mass shootings. He didn't have to do car chases or fugitive warrants or undercover work. *He's a careful driver. He rarely drinks. All he's doing is driving to DC. He said he'd be back. He will.*

You have no control over that.
What if ... what if ... what if ... ?

BY THIS TIME my heart was beating erratically, and a cold sweat dampened my neck. I began jogging, then running through the darkness. When I reached the house I took the back steps two at a time, entered the brightly lit kitchen, and turned to let Luke in.

He wasn't there. He wasn't anywhere. "Luke!" I yelled, my voice high with fear. "Luke!" I looked wildly around, peering into the night, fumbling with my flashlight. *Where was he?* "Luke, come!"

Then I heard him. He came charging back from the horses' paddock, tail wagging.

"Inside," I said, and I shut the door behind him and locked it.

My heart raced. My old nemesis, fear, had grabbed control.

God, help me, I prayed. *Help.*

My mouth felt like a desert. My breath came in shallow gasps. I was on the brink of an anxiety attack, my first in a long time. *Help me.*

Breathe. *In for four, hold for seven, out for eight.* I heard Nate's voice in my head. *It'll go by. Just wait it out,* he used to tell me. *Ground yourself in something physical. Plant your feet. Grab a post.* I leaned against the wall.

Luke came over and nudged my leg with his nose. I slid down and sat on the floor. He sat in my lap, or tried to, and I rested my cheek on his shoulders, inhaling his scent, so grateful for him.

I spent the next fifteen minutes petting my dog and praying to my God. I rose to my feet calmer but discouraged. I thought I'd gotten past those attacks.

I had to shift my focus. "Come on, buddy," I said to Luke, and I went upstairs to the room we used as an office. I sat down at my computer and looked up crisis pregnancy centers. I found several near UVA. I made a document containing their names, addresses, phone numbers, and websites. I wrote a note to Amanda, saying I loved her and would go with her to support her if she wanted to go to one of these crisis pregnancy centers.

My hand hovered over the keyboard, debating whether I should send the email. My phone rang. *Nate.* "Hey," I said, answering it.

"You okay?"

"Sure. Why?"

"I felt a nudge to call you is all. Is Scott home?"

Clear as day I saw I was at a crossroads. I could hide and deny anything was wrong or I could open up. I took a deep breath and made a choice. I told him about Scott. I told him about my near-anxiety attack after Scott's leaving triggered the trauma of losing my dad. And then I swore him to secrecy and told him about Amanda, about my concern for her, and my worries about her relationship with Scott and maybe getting an abortion.

My words spilled out like a flood. Nate listened in silence, letting me take the bit in my teeth and run, as Scott would say. Then he spoke. "Jess, you got a lot going on. It ain't no shame to get overwhelmed by life sometimes." He paused, letting that thought sink in. "How'd you deal with it?"

So I told him about controlling my breathing, grounding myself, petting Luke, and praying. "Then I just waited it out," I said.

"You did perfect. I'm proud of you."

"Thank you," I whispered.

He asked me some more questions, about when I thought Scott might be back and did I need help with the horses or anything around the house. I told him I had no idea when he'd be back and no, I didn't need help. Then he said, "Let me check with Laura, but how about you come for dinner tomorrow night if Scott is still gone? Let's catch up."

That sounded great. "Yes, I'd like that."

11

THE HEAD of the Critical Incident Response Group listened carefully as Scott outlined his concern that the incident in Montana was just the beginning of a campaign of violence promoted by the group Contra2+ and designed to force action on climate change. But expanding the probe into that group's plans beyond Montana required a step up the chain of command.

"Knowing the deputy assistant director," CIRG Chief Marcus Walker said, "I think it would be best to go to his office."

"Now?" Scott's boss, Jeff Bennett, asked.

"Yes, now."

"It's late."

"I know."

Scott chose to drive to DC separately from the other two men. His home would be a different direction from theirs when they were done.

By the time he rolled into Washington, the city was draped in darkness. He accessed the secure parking at the J. Edgar Hoover Building, grabbed his attaché case, checked his watch, and took the elevator up to Jack Conway's office. He had time to see his friend, now a deputy assistant director himself.

Jack had been a street agent, initially in Detroit, then worked his way up the ladder in New York, LA, and then Washington. Scott could relate to him. He wasn't sure about the other guy.

Fortunately, Jack was in and had a few minutes. "Give me the *Reader's Digest* version," Jack said. He gestured toward a leather chair. "Sit down."

"Thanks, but I don't have time to sit. They'll be here any second." He summarized his concerns, then asked, "So tell me about this guy, Kai Oliver. What am I facing?"

Jack made a clicking noise with his mouth. "He's a holdover from the last administration. A lawyer...came over from Justice. Originally from California. I don't know, Scott. A lot of those guys were too political for my taste. But hey, it sounds like you have a good case. So run it up the flagpole."

"Right."

THREE MINUTES later Scott met his boss, Jeff Bennett, and Marcus Walker outside Kai Oliver's office. "The Deputy AD wants to bring in someone from the General Counsel's office," Marcus said.

Scott raised his eyebrows.

Marcus shrugged. "Sensitive issues."

The secretary ushered them toward the inner office door, and the three men walked in.

Kai Oliver was on the phone. Another man sat in one of the chairs in front of his desk. He was small and lean and dressed in a black suit, white shirt, and red tie. He looked at the three men entering as if he were measuring them, but he never made eye contact.

Oliver waved toward the empty chairs, and the men sat down. Behind him, the windows looked out toward the Capitol building, a glistening white dome against a black sky.

Scott felt like he always did in situations like this—on edge.

The plush blue carpet, fancy walnut desk, and creaky leather chairs spoke of power and privilege. They were a far cry from the low-ceilinged offices, government-issued desks, and short-napped, neutral carpets he was used to. He was still three organizational levels down from the director, maybe more, and a long, long way up from the street.

Oliver got off the phone. His cropped blond hair and tanned good looks announced the fact that he was born and raised in California. As tan as he was, at this time of year and living in DC, Scott figured he had to be using a tanning salon. Behind Oliver on the credenza was a framed photo of a beautiful blonde woman, his wife apparently. No kids. The rest of the photos were grip-and-grins with the president, the attorney general, and members of Congress.

He was a political appointee, and so, probably, was the guy from the general counsel's office. Scott felt the muscles in his back stiffen.

"Talk to me," Oliver said, without introducing the fifth person in the room. "Why are we here? A school shooting? Why do I care?"

Marcus Walker spoke up. "Cooper here is with the Behavioral Analysis Unit. He's got concerns about it. Scott, why don't you take over."

Scott's jaw flexed. He didn't like speaking out with an unknown person in the room. It didn't set right with him. So he took control. He stood and extended his hand. "Supervisory Special Agent Scott Cooper, Behavioral Analysis Unit. I don't believe we've met."

The man's eyes widened. Scott towered over him. "Elroy Frank," the man said. "Office of the General Counsel."

Scott nodded and sat down. The two men with him, his boss and the head of CIRG, followed his lead and introduced themselves. Then he looked at Oliver. "To answer your question, sir, the Montana case started out as a school shooting. But I think it's beyond that." Scott recapped the incident, from the morning shooting at the school to the laptop he'd discovered hidden in the kid's room to the radical environmentalists. "The boy was Everett Voight, age sixteen, from Bozeman. He developed an interest in climate change about a year ago. Started talking about becoming an environmental lawyer. Not coincidentally, his dad works for the Montana Petroleum Association. Apparently, there were some interesting discussions around the house, but his dad didn't think a lot of it. His kid was smart. And what kid doesn't try to push back against his father?"

"Montana's too gun friendly," Oliver said, tapping his pen on his pad.

"The gun was purchased legally and secured in a locked box. But Everett was smart and old enough to know how to get into it."

"So the parents are liable. I really don't see the point—"

Scott interrupted him. "The point is, sir, that Everett does not fit the profile of a typical, alienated school shooter." He could tell from Oliver's face he'd made him mad by interrupting him, but Scott continued. "Everett was smart, well-adjusted. He did a lot of research on the Internet, and sometime in the last six months he connected with a radical environmental group called Contra2+." He glanced at Elroy Frank to see if he was tracking.

"Contra2+ has been in existence for five years. Last year, they had a big shakeup. People got frustrated by what they saw as the inaction of the previous leader and kicked him out.

"Now it appears they're reaching out to young people concerned about climate change, like Everett, and radicalizing them. They've issued a call to action, attacks to take place in all fifty states and DC between now and Earth Day, April 22, to force legislative and other changes."

"More school shootings? Is that all?"

Scott forced himself to be patient. "No sir. From what we can tell from Everett Voight's computer—"

"He's the boy—"

"Yes, sir. From what we can tell, Everett was trying to get a couple of other kids to join him in whatever action was supposed to take place in Montana. He told them he had access to a gun. They didn't believe him, so he brought the gun to school to show them. He wasn't planning the shooting. He's not a 'normal' school shooter. I don't even think he'd planned to kill himself."

Oliver frowned. "You're saying he brings a gun to school and shoots, but he's not a school shooter."

"Not in the normal sense, no. Nearly 90 percent of school shooters have a plan that they leak to friends or on social media ahead of time. They study other school shooters. They have notebooks or computer files full of data. They have grievances, they've been bullied, or feel on the edge of the school culture. This kid had none of that. He was a good student. Fairly popular. Smart. And pretty OCD. I saw his room—spotless. I think he got enamored with the teaching of this group online and went overboard. Became obsessed with it. When we interview the friends he was trying to recruit, I bet we'll find out they were shocked he had access to a gun, much less planned to use it."

"We've got to do something about the guns in this country."

"Sir, you know as well as I do, that if we banned guns today, we'd still have enough firearms to last until Eternity." Scott's face felt hot.

"But you want to blame this on environmentalism."

"No, sir. Concern about the environment and climate change is valid. But the radical ideology that it can lead to is not. I'm concerned about this one organization, Contra2+."

"The president receives strong support from the green community," Elroy Frank said.

"I understand that. But I'm sure the president doesn't want fifty domestic terror attacks going down in the next five months."

"Climate change is a big problem! We should be supporting groups spreading that word."

Scott felt his pulse pounding in his head. "Concern about

climate change is one thing. Domestic terrorism to force social change is another thing altogether. The FBI's priority is criminal activity, and that's what I'm talking about. Criminal activity."

"So what's your recommendation?" Oliver played with his pen.

"I think we need to tell the Joint Terrorism Task Forces in every field office to investigate the activity of this group, Contra2+, particularly regarding contacts with K-12 students, and I think we need to get eyes on its leadership. Immediately. I think we need analysts following them."

Oliver grimaced.

"I think we need to track their Internet activity and possibly plant agents in the group. Because I think they're planning a campaign, and we need to short-circuit it."

Oliver blew out a breath, stood up, and stared out the window. The lights of Washington glittered outside like precious stones. He turned back around and looked at Walker. "Marcus?"

"Cooper knows his stuff," the head of CIRG responded. "I support him."

Oliver sat back down and fiddled with his pen, tapping the point, then the top, on the desk pad. Scott's muscles ached with tension. Finally, Oliver raised his head and focused on Elroy Frank. "What's your take?"

Scott felt his heartrate quicken.

"I'll inform the general counsel. He'll probably want to consult with the attorney general."

Scott knew immediately what that meant. A streak of anger shot up his spine. This would be a political decision. Nothing to do with law enforcement. Just politics. His heart started pounding.

He moved forward in his chair, ready to argue his case further, but Oliver short-circuited him. He stood and said, "Gentlemen, we'll be in touch."

Scott opened his mouth to protest but caught the look his boss shot him that said, *Don't*.

"Thank you, sir," Marcus said, rising to lead the way to the door.

At the threshold, Scott turned and said to Oliver, "And this group? This Contra2+?"

Oliver dismissed him with a wave of his hand.

Scott thought his head was about to explode. He started to blindly follow the others back to the elevator but then realized he was too angry to ride down with them. He might say something he'd regret.

So he mumbled something about seeing a friend and turned right, down the hall toward Jack Conway's office.

"All done?" Jack said when Scott appeared at his door.

"They're gonna kill it. They just couldn't tell me to my face."

"They?"

"He wanted the OGC there. Some guy named Elroy Frank."

Jack shook his head. Then he looked at Scott and said, "I need a drink. Come with me. I know a great bar right down the street."

Man could he use a drink! That sounded so good. A nice smooth... but then an image of Jess appeared in his mind. He fought the temptation. His fists clenched. *Get behind me, Satan.* "Sorry, Jack, I can't. I've got a two-hour drive and a wife who's waiting for me."

"Lucky you." Jack put his hand on Scott's shoulder. "I'm sorry about how that went down."

"Me, too."

Scott turned away from his friend and stepped onto the elevator. *Lord, just get me out of this building.* It was all he could do to keep from slamming his fist into the wall. *What a snake pit!* Anger burned in his gut. Politics! Now politics trumped law enforcement?

He entered the garage, jerked his car door open, and got in. Then he exited the building and drove down Pennsylvania

Avenue toward I-66. The beauty of the White House, the Washington Monument, and the other federal buildings was lost on him, blocked by his anger. He found the entrance to I-66 and headed west out of town, out to where life made sense.

He had barely made it into Virginia when his boss called him.

"Scott, the Deputy AD says treat the Montana case as a school shooting."

"What?"

"It's one more screwed-up kid and an all-too-readily available gun. That's the way he wants to play it."

"And this group? This Contra2+?"

"Leave them alone, he said. According to the OGC, they're exercising their First Amendment rights."

Scott cursed.

"I know this didn't turn out the way you wanted, the way any of us wanted. But this is not a battle you want to fight," Jeff said.

Oh yes he did! He wanted to fight it with every bone in his body.

Scott barely managed to cool down enough to get out a "yes sir" before he hung up. Then he hit the accelerator, racing through the traffic like a teenager, blowing off steam.

Common sense prevailed. He settled down and blended into the traffic. But he kept going over in his mind what Oliver had said and what he, Scott, should have said. What recourse did he have now?

That was easy—none. No options. If the deputy assistant director said drop it, they had to drop it. And if there was a plan to carry out attacks, well, they'd have to deal with them when they happened.

But it was so stupid. And the more he thought about what Oliver and Frank had done, the angrier he got until he whipped across three lanes and took the next exit. He drove to a gas station, pulled in and parked, and got out of his car. In the dark, he walked off to the side into a small stand of trees.

He pulled out his FBI phone and his personal phone. Copying a contact from his bureau phone, he called someone he thought he could trust in Montana on his personal phone. "Joe," he said, glancing around to be sure he was alone, "I got two people I need you to interview and report back to me. Just me. Verbally. No official report. No 302. Got it?" Then he continued, giving the names of the two kids Everett Voight was trying to recruit. "I want to know everything they know," he said. "Yeah, use this number. Call me. Thanks, buddy."

Drop it? Not quite yet. Scott jerked open his car door, got in, and started the car. His head pounded. He rubbed his temples, then fumbled in the center console and pulled out a bottle of ibuprofen he kept there. He swallowed four of them with a big gulp of water.

Reentering the flood of seventy-mile-an-hour traffic on I-66, he moved to the middle lane and continued driving west toward home. He tried to think about Jess, about the horses, about anything but the foo-foo at work.

Suddenly, he felt a sharp pain in his chest, pain like a linebacker had just hit him, pain like a strong hand squeezing his heart. He pressed his fist to his sternum. *What? What's going on?* He gripped the steering wheel. His vision grew dark on the edges. *I'm having a heart attack.* Instinctively, he began moving his car across lanes to the right. *God help!* Finally, he reached the shoulder. He threw the car into PARK, put on the flashers, and fumbled for the emergency button on his watch, his vision growing darker as he did. He pressed it hard and tried to breathe.

12

EVENINGS in the late fall and winter seem endless to me. It's so dark I think it must be time for bed, then I look at my watch and its only 8:30. That feeling is amplified when Scott is gone, and it was even worse tonight. The battle with anxiety had worn me out.

Luke had plopped down in the office next to the wall, so I decided to do a little PI work to distract myself until bedtime. My inbox contained two inquiries about possible investigations: a missing adult child and a business looking for a background check. I quoted my prices and sent emails back to both of them.

Then I got an email from the lawyer for my girl-with-collie painting purchaser, Andrew Gerhardt. The lawyer said Mr. Gerhardt wondered if I'd be willing to contact the new owner of the house and see if there were any other paintings left there. Also, could I possibly get photos of the attic? And could I try again to identify the artist?

Wow, he's really interested in this, I thought. My curiosity piqued, I asked the lawyer a couple more questions. First, *What's Mr. Gerhardt's interest in this?* And, *May I do a brief background check on him?* I certainly didn't want to aid a stalker or predator or even complicate Kathryn Grace McCaskill's life with a weirdo.

To my surprise, the lawyer must have been working late because he emailed me back right away. He wrote, *Mr. Gerhardt was adopted as a young child. He has vague memories of his early life, which is why he bought that painting. He's hoping that house or the name of the artist, will trigger more memories. Both of his adoptive parents are dead. Feel free to do a background check. You'll find he's a successful businessman, married with children, and has no criminal record. By the way, he's also doing DNA research into his background. Here's his date of birth.*

Interesting! I emailed back my thanks and said I'd get right on it. I plugged the information in and did a quick check. Indeed, Mr. Gerhardt was exactly as his lawyer said. That made me feel better about contacting Kathryn Grace. I put it on my calendar for the next day.

Scott liked to do a night check on the horses right before bed. I dreaded going out there, afraid the darkness would trigger my anxiety again. I also knew the longer I put it off the more anxious I was likely to become, so I woke up my dog and we went downstairs. I put on my jacket and grabbed the big-beam flashlight from the kitchen cabinet. "C'mon, Luke."

I'd have to pray my way through it. I know Jesus says "Be anxious for nothing," but he was going to have to help me if I was going to achieve that standard at this point in my life. Right now, I was anxious about everything—women being killed, school shootings, men in the woods. And Scott. I thought he was pushing it, going back to DC tonight. I knew it had to be important, but I also knew he had to be exhausted. So I prayed he'd get back home safely. Tonight.

Just as we were about to go out, my watch signaled a text. I looked at it and frowned, confused. I grabbed my phone out of my back pocket and turned it on so I could see the text better. What? It was an automatic message saying Scott's phone had called emergency services.

My heart began pounding for the second time that night.

The text gave his location on a tiny map. It looked like I-66. Had he had an accident? I tried calling him. No answer. I fumbled with my phone. Googled Fairfax County PD's non-emergency number. Called them. Got no information.

What should I do?

Luke whined. I looked at him. His tail wagged slowly. He cocked his head, as if to say, *What are we waiting for?*

I swallowed the lump in my throat. I had to find Scott. Now. And something told me to leave Luke at home.

I let Luke out to pee, then called him back in. "I can't take you, buddy. Not this time." I patted him goodbye, shut the door, and locked it. Then I jumped in my Jeep and took off.

Although it was hard to tell from the little map exactly where Scott was, I knew I was at least a good hour and a half away. I felt panic rising in me. Had emergency services responded? Was someone helping him? Police? An ambulance?

I began praying out loud, babbling really. "God you know, you know what's going on. Help him, Lord. If he's hurt, save him. Get help to him. If it's just the car, that's no problem. We can fix cars."

I thought about calling Nate, but honestly if I did, I thought I'd just start crying. Thankfully, traffic was light. I kept the speedometer at ten to fifteen over, fast enough to make some time but not so fast to be a danger.

About forty minutes into my drive my phone rang. I looked at the screen, hoping it was Scott. No. It was Scott's good friend Mike Perez, another FBI agent. He'd worked with Scott on the bombing case.

"Mike, what's going on?" I blurted out as I answered it.

"Where are you?" he asked.

I had no idea where I was. "On 29 somewhere." Then I saw a sign. "I'm just crossing the Rappahannock at Remington."

"Okay, good. On the other side of Warrenton, on 15, there's a commuter lot on the left. Near a tennis club. I'll meet you there."

"Mike, where's Scott?"

"Stay calm. It's probably nothing. He had some chest pains driving home and called 911."

Stay calm? Chest pains? He's too young for that!

"He's at a hospital in Fair Oaks. They're checking him out. He knew you'd be upset and asked me to drive you in, so I'll meet you in the commuter lot, okay?"

"Okay. Right."

"I'm in a bureau SUV. Are you driving your Jeep?"

"Yes."

"Okay. Be safe. See you soon."

Be safe? Be safe? Scott? A heart attack? My own heart thumped like a scared rabbit. My most eloquent prayer sounded like *OhGodOhGodOhGod.* I had resisted calling Nate three times already. I didn't want to wake him. Bother him. Be dependent on him.

I gave that up in a heartbeat, grabbed my phone, and voice-texted a message. *Scott's at a hospital in Fair Oaks. Chest pains? Headed there now. Please pray.*

He called thirty seconds later. "What's going on?"

I told him.

"Where are you?"

I told him that too.

"What can I do?"

"Pray! I'll update you when I know more." I paused. "I left Luke at home."

"Okay. I'll get him if I need to. Let's pray right now."

The sound of his voice as he prayed brought me to the throne of God, as it always did. My heart rate dropped to the level of "very concerned rabbit." For the millionth time I thanked God for Nate.

I promised to call him and hung up, focusing on my driving. Mike was already in the commuter lot when I arrived, and I admit I was relieved to settle into the passenger seat and let him take over. Plus he got to the hospital much faster than I could have.

As I walked into that hospital I had flashbacks from when Scott was shot before. Mike used his creds to get us past the front desk. My gut was tense as we walked back to Room 7, my fingers tingling with fear.

I stepped in. Scott was in bed, bare-chested, covered in monitor lead stickers, his head elevated, his eyes closed. But his color was good. And the numbers on the monitor—heart rate, blood pressure, respiration—were all close to normal.

He must have heard us. He opened his eyes, and I rushed forward, hugging him awkwardly, my cheek next to his, hot tears on my lashes.

"Hey," he said, whispering in my ear, "you're ruining my makeup."

I grinned and pulled back. "What's going on? Why are you here? You scared me!"

"I scared myself!" Then he told me what happened—the drive, the chest pain, the fear. "I don't know what caused it and neither do the docs. My bloodwork looks good. The EKG was normal. They're going to do an echocardiogram and a nuclear stress test as soon as they can get me scheduled."

"Are you still in pain?"

"Some. But not like it was."

I sagged down into the chair next to his bed. He took my hand and squeezed it. His grip was strong. Then he looked at Mike. "Thanks."

Mike had recently been detailed to Scott's unit, BAU, and they'd grown even closer lately. I was glad of that.

"I'll go find your bucar," Mike said.

"I appreciate it. I asked the cops who responded to secure it. Who knows where it is."

"At least it's not on the side of the road."

"Right."

I was still in investigator/EMT mode. "Scott, what was going on before the chest pain? Were you dizzy?" He shook his head. "Was your stomach upset?"

"No." He looked off to the side, frowning. "I don't know what triggered it."

"Does your family have a history of early heart disease?"

"My uncle died pretty early, in his fifties. Otherwise, no, not that I know of."

"Did you have other symptoms, like pain in your arm, or shortness of breath?"

He grimaced. "Not really."

I took another stab at an explanation. "What went on earlier this evening? You were meeting with someone?"

"I got pretty mad." He turned sharply toward me. "I mean, really mad."

"At?"

He shook his head. "I can't tell you. Not here. But yeah, I was angry."

Could anger bring on a heart attack? Or angina? Or could it be something else?

Before I could ask any more questions, two patient transport workers came in and wheeled Scott out for an echocardiogram. "I'm going to grab some coffee," I told him as he left. He acknowledged me with a wave. I found the coffee machine and a quiet corner where I could call Nate.

And that's the way the rest of the night went. Scott was in and out for tests. Nurses came and went. I sat in the chair sipping really bad machine coffee, black. Each of us dozed off once in a while. When the sun came up, Scott was still alive, both of us were exhausted, and the tests showed nothing. So the hospital released him with instructions to follow through with his family doctor, a cardiologist, and possibly a gastroenterologist. Mike, who was working, arranged for an agent from the Northern Virginia office to pick us up and drive us to Warrenton, where we retrieved my Jeep.

Scott dozed all the way home. By the time we drove past the DARK HORSE FARM sign and into our lane, I felt limp as a wet noodle. Exhausted. But there was an energetic German shepherd waiting for me and two horses who needed care.

Imagine my relief when we rounded the bend, emerged from the woods, and saw Nate's Tahoe parked in front.

13

WE SLEPT. Nate had taken care of everything—the horses, the dog. He'd even brought in more wood in case we wanted a fire. So we dragged ourselves up to bed and held each other closely while we slept. Three hours later I slipped out of bed, grabbed some clean clothes, and left the bedroom, softly closing the door behind me.

Luke was waiting in the hallway, his brown eyes curious, his tail wagging slowly. "Let's go," I whispered, and together we went downstairs. He raced me down and turned at the bottom of the stairs, asking *What's next?* with his look. "I need coffee," I told him, and led the way to the kitchen.

What is next? I thought as I put coffee grounds in my pour over and water in the kettle. Scott was supposed to follow up with his family doctor who, we were told, would probably recommend he see a cardiologist. I wondered about that. After some good sleep, would Scott put that off? Decide he was really okay? Would the FBI call him in? Would he put his job before everything else? As usual?

As my coffee brewed, I decided to be proactive. I picked up my phone and called our family doctor and made Scott an appointment for Friday, two days later. Then I called the hospital and asked that they send the results of the tests they'd done over to our doctor. I couldn't make Scott do anything, but I could make it harder for him to resist.

I let Luke out for a brief moment, then grabbed a Kind bar and a cheese stick to go with my coffee, and we went back upstairs to the small bedroom I used as an office. It felt chilly, and I wished I'd grabbed a sweatshirt. But I wanted to get some work done while Scott slept. I gave Luke a chewy to keep him occupied while I worked.

First, Kathryn Grace McCaskill. I'd found her phone number and though I figured she'd already be at school, I decided to call. I left a message in my most friendly and reassuring voice, asking her if I could meet her at her house.

After that, I worked on my talk: "Out of the Gate: Smart Searching Before SAR Arrives." Cops were always first on the scene when a person was missing. Actions that they take can make or break a search. As a former law-enforcement officer and a current SAR volunteer, I had credibility in this area. I'd been asked to do an in-service training class—on Friday—in Staunton. When I looked at the invitation more closely, I realized Augusta County was hosting it, but Bath and Highland County deputies as well as Staunton police would be there too.

Highland County included Clear Springs. Maybe I could combine the trip with a visit to Kathryn Grace McCaskill.

But what about Scott's appointment? *Scott's a big boy,* I told myself. *He can get himself to the doctor.*

But what about that chest pain? Should he be driving?

I picked up my phone again and called Amanda. I told her about Scott's appointment and asked her if she could take him. She said she could. Was I meddling? Maybe. But Scott was her dad.

I turned my attention to work. I pulled up the document for my standard presentation and read it through. Then I did a deep dive into the demographics and geology of the counties. Virtually all of their searches would be wilderness searches. There was no "urban" in that part of Virginia, although Staunton was a good-sized city.

Still, I decided to focus on wilderness searches. I looked up available trails, including many in the George Washington and Jefferson National Forests, and quickly confirmed one of the biggest problems would be lack of cell service once you got into the mountains. Hikers from more populated areas might not be prepared for that.

I described how to establish a PLS, point last seen, and the difference between a PLS and an LKP, last known position, which could be the person's car in a parking lot at a trailhead. I outlined the importance of doing a hasty search—a quick reconnaissance on foot of the most likely places the lost person could be. I always recommended deputies be paired up, not side by side, but at least within sight of each other, and that they cover the ground at a jog if possible. Hasty searches eliminate the most likely scenarios, leaving the more complicated options for the SAR teams.

I pulled out Koester's book, *Lost Person Behavior*, and refreshed my memory on some of his points that would be particularly applicable to mountainous western Virginia. I expanded the section of my talk on errors in following trails—the likelihood that poor signage, missing trail markers, or taking shortcuts caused the hiker to become lost.

I heard Scott stirring in the next room. Quickly, I finished polishing my presentation, then I changed out pictures in the PowerPoint to make them local to western Virginia. I saved everything just as the bedroom door opened.

At that sound, Luke jumped up, left his chewy, and ran to my husband, wagging his tail and turning circles around Scott's legs. Scott thumped Luke's side.

"Good morning," I said, smiling. Scott had pulled on jeans and a plaid shirt. "How are you feeling?"

"All right."

"Pain?"

He shook his head.

"You're taking the day off?"

"Comp time. You working?"

"Just finished. Come on. You want some breakfast?"

Once again Luke raced us downstairs, turning again at the bottom in hopes of some fun adventure. I opened the front door and told him to go "check the horses." He knew what that meant and took off toward the barn.

Scott didn't want a big breakfast, just granola and yogurt. Not even coffee. I asked him questions about his trip and his meeting last night in DC. His terse, short answers told me he didn't want to talk about it. Not yet, anyway. Maybe later.

"What's on your schedule for today?" he asked me.

"I have a presentation on Friday in Staunton. Eight o'clock. So I either need to leave here at six that morning or go up the night before and stay in the motel." I told him I was hoping to connect with Kathryn Grace McCaskill today, reminding him who that was. "Except for taking that phone call, I'm free."

Then I took a deep breath and told him about making the appointment with the doctor. "It's for Friday, when I'll be in Staunton. I'll cancel if you want me to."

"No, don't do that."

"I figured you'd say that, so I called Amanda to see if she can take you."

Scott frowned. "I'm a big boy. I can drive myself to the doctor." Just like I said.

"I wasn't sure how you'd be feeling."

"I'm fine. I think it was just something ... weird."

"Well, it would be good to follow through just to be sure." I put my hand on his.

He sighed. "I know. I hate this." He rose to his feet, walked to the sink, rinsed his bowl, and put it in the dishwasher. I followed with my coffee mug. "I'm going to go down to the barn," he said.

I wrapped my arms around Scott. "I love you."

"I love you too." He kissed me. "I'm sorry if I scared you."

"Hey," I said, pulling back and grinning at him, "it's what we do."

He started to leave, then turned back to me. "Jess, can we have a real family Thanksgiving this year?"

My eyes widened. "Like what?"

"Like have people over—Amanda, Nate and Laura, your family maybe. Make a turkey ..."

I'd never cooked a turkey.

"... and you know, pumpkin pie. The whole deal." He ran his hand through his hair. "It's been a long time."

Probably since his mother died. That's what I guessed. "Sure," I said. "We can do that." My phone rang before I could go further. "Hold on," I said, staring at the caller ID. "This is my call."

"We can talk later." Scott waved and walked toward the door.

"Miss McCaskill! Thanks for calling me back." I pressed the phone to my ear. I explained about Andrew Gerhardt, about his curiosity regarding the painting, and the house it was found in. I kept talking, although honestly I felt like I was pushing a boulder uphill. She seemed reluctant—understandably!—to let me in her house. I told her I'd be glad to send her references. I told her I'd done a cursory background check on Andrew Gerhardt, and what I'd found. Then I went one step further and told her Gerhardt had been adopted and was trying to trace his biological family.

Suddenly, the boulder tipped over the ridge and raced downhill. "I'll tell you what," she said, "let me make a phone call and I'll get right back to you."

Not ten minutes later she called back. "Okay!" she said. "You can come. When can we do this?"

I told her about my in-service in Staunton on Friday. I

expected her to suggest meeting her on Saturday but no. Friday was a teacher workday. She'd get off at three and could meet me at her house then.

"Perfect," I said. Elated, I clicked off my phone, grabbed my jacket, and raced to catch up with Scott.

I OPTED to leave home at 5:30 in the morning on Friday rather than spending Thursday night in the hotel where the in-service would be held. I wanted to be with Scott every minute that I could. I left Luke with him, knowing my dog would have more fun with Scott at the farm than he would with me.

"Look," I told Luke, holding out my empty hands. "No pack. You stay here. Take care of Scott."

My dog sighed and started back upstairs, glancing at me twice to make sure I was serious.

The cold air hit me with a jolt as I left the house. The black sky seemed hard as glass, and the wind cut across my face. Thankfully, my Jeep started right up. I eased out of our lane and began my ninety-minute journey to Staunton. I'd have a long day, what with the side trip to Clear Springs, but at least I wouldn't have to spend the night somewhere. *I'll be home tonight,* I said to myself, *with Scott.*

I spent the first twenty minutes of the trip talking to God. I try to use the acrostic ACTS when I pray on the run, so I don't regress to simply reciting my laundry list of wants and needs. Adoration helps me focus on God's attributes. Nate calls it "entering into God's beauty." I'm not sure what he means by that. Confession keeps me humble. Thanksgiving stimulates my gratitude. And supplication—well, I always have a ton of prayer requests, topped that day by my concern for my husband's health.

· · ·

I ARRIVED in Staunton with plenty of time to get a decent cup of coffee before meeting my contact at the Holiday Inn. Soon, I was standing at the head of a long narrow room filled with cops, clicking through my PowerPoint and explaining the smartest ways to start searching for a lost person.

I love cops. Yes, some are knuckleheads and others are knuckle-draggers, and back in the day some hurt me a lot. But most are great people who just want to help keep the world in order. I love their energy, their focus, and their comradery. I even love their jokes and jibes.

My new gig, giving these lectures about SAR, was healing something in me. I'd been driven from my job as a Fairfax County detective by some bad players. Now, I had the opportunity to overcome that, diffusing its power by layering in new, positive memories. I wondered if Nate knew that would happen when he suggested these talks to me.

I spoke for an hour and fifteen minutes, gave them a fifteen-minute break, then resumed. I left half an hour at the end for questions.

The thirty-five officers in the room were attentive. Involved. They asked good questions and listened carefully to the answers. They kept me on my toes. The time flew by. I just wasn't prepared for how the morning would end.

At 10:50, my contact, Sheriff Josh Brown of Augusta County, walked up and took the mic. He thanked me for sharing my expertise and invited everyone to give me a round of applause. That's when I expected a little envelope to come out, filled with gift cards for Starbucks or Dunkin' Donuts or whatever.

Instead, the side door opened and Sheriff Skip Ward from Rockingham County walked in. Brody's dad.

To say I was shocked was an understatement. He walked up, gave me a hug, and I stood there speechless as he took the mic and told the story of how I saved his son, Brody.

"She never hesitated," he said. "She went right in that farm pond and held my boy up until I could get there."

Then the side door opened again and in walked the boy himself, Brody. Actually, he ran in. I bent down and gave him a big hug, inhaling the scent of his hair and feeling the life in his body. Tears formed in my eyes.

I stood up as Sheriff Ward continued to speak. "So, Jessica Cooper, I'd like to present you with the Sheriff's Valor Award for saving my son." He held out a beautiful, printed certificate. "And this is a gift card for a weekend at the Eagle Mountain Resort for you and your husband and, of course, Luke. Good anytime."

Everyone in the room stood up and applauded as I accepted the certificate and envelope and shook Sheriff Ward's hand. The applause thundered in the room, which was a good thing, my throat so tight I couldn't say a word.

If that had been the only surprise, it would have been a good day.

14

AFTER MY TALK, the Augusta County sheriff took me to lunch, along with one of his K-9 handlers. We talked dogs and law enforcement and families, and when they found out my husband was an FBI agent, they jokingly started guessing how long we'd last together.

Law enforcement is tough on marriages, I know. Look at my parents. Of course, I'd always blamed my mother for their problems, but now that I'd been a police officer myself and had married an agent, I had more sympathy. I could see how the focus that law enforcement requires and the stress it creates could make a spouse feel neglected.

Armed with a fresh cup of coffee, I left Staunton at about 1:30. Even with most of the leaves off the trees, the drive through the mountains still seemed beautiful to me. I guess I like anything that isn't civilization. I called Scott to tell him about the recognition I'd received from Sheriff Ward but apparently he was not finished at the doctor's office. My call went to voicemail.

So I tried Nate. I caught him at work, between projects, in his office. He was pleased Sheriff Ward had recognized me, he said, but "the main thing is, you saved that boy. Where you headed now?" he asked.

"Clear Springs. So if Laura wants me to check in on her mom, text me. I'll be leaving by five o'clock though. I want to get home tonight."

That's when the cell service began breaking up, so I quickly said goodbye and concentrated on driving.

Clear Springs is just a wisp of a town nestled among the hills and mountains of western Virginia. It's a step back in time, a return to simpler days, but I knew it was not necessarily easy living there. Driving those mountain roads in winter would be dicey. While there was a family practice doctor in town, the nearest specialist had to be an hour and a half or two hours away. People were neighborly and helped each other, but like in any small town, I'm sure everyone knew your business. Not for me, but I was happy visiting.

I arrived at Kathryn Grace McCaskill's house at 2:45 and parked on the street out front. I sat looking at her house, impressed once again with its beauty. The arches above the double-hung windows, the shutters, the neat little dormers on the second floor, and the false balcony testified that somebody cared about design, even in a small house.

She had a little driveway, but no garage. I could see the back-yard was fenced, and I wondered if she had a dog. As old as that house was, anyone could have installed that fence.

At 3:10, a new blue Subaru Forester pulled into the small driveway and Kathryn Grace McCaskill emerged. She waved. I grabbed my tote and my phone and got out of the Jeep, locking it as I walked toward her. I didn't bother grabbing my jacket. That was a mistake. It was colder up here in the mountains, and the wind cut right through my blazer and trousers.

"Miss McCaskill? I'm Jessica Cooper," I said, extending my hand.

"Come inside," she replied after giving me a firm handshake. "It's freezing out here."

I followed her. Like many houses of that era, there was no foyer or entry hall. You stepped right into the living room onto a ten-by-ten tiled area. Kathryn hung her coat on a peg on the left-hand wall and took off her boots. I started to remove mine. "You don't need to do that," she told me. "I'm just in the habit. How about some tea?"

Tea sounded great. Kathryn led me back to the kitchen where she put a kettle on what looked like an ancient gas stove. "Earl Grey? Lemon Lift? Irish Breakfast Tea?"

"Lemon Lift," I said. "Thank you." I looked around at the small kitchen. It probably hadn't been updated in years, but instead of appearing shabby and old, it looked classic. Flat-front cabinets painted white, a gray-and-white speckled laminate countertop, and a light-gray tile floor all appeared perfectly preserved. The window above the sink looked into the deep back-yard. Above the window hung a wooden sign that read, "In the morning when I rise, give me Jesus."

"Let's sit at the table," Kathryn said, gesturing toward the four-seat maple table in the small adjoining dining room. She placed the steaming mugs of tea down on blue-and-white place-mats and turned to grab sugar and teaspoons.

"This house is great," I said. "How long have you lived here?" I knew the answer to that question from the property records. I was just making conversation.

"I've been in Clear Springs about a year and a half. But I bought this house just a little over a month ago."

"It's so pretty. What brought you to Clear Springs?"

"Work. They had an opening for a middle-school English teacher in the middle of last year. I took the job on a lark and loved the area so much I decided to stay." She switched the subject. "What kind of PI work do you do?"

I explained about my job and a couple of the more interesting cases I'd worked on. "But my real passion is K-9 search and rescue," I said.

I felt instantly comfortable with her. She seemed steady, down to earth, likeable. She'd pulled her wavy brown hair back into a low ponytail. Silver miniature apple earrings bobbed from her ears. Her eyes were a friendly brown, and she wore little, if any, makeup. There was nothing pretentious about Kathryn Grace McCaskill.

So I told her about Luke, and a little about Scott, and mentioned I'd been a Fairfax County detective before deciding to work as a PI.

"What brought you to Fairfax?"

"I'm from Long Island originally, but my dad died on 9/11. My mom remarried and we moved to Fairfax. I spent my teen years in Burke."

"Burke! Seriously? I grew up in Clifton. We were practically neighbors."

We shared which high schools we'd attended and stories about the area. Kathryn was a few years younger than me, so we had no mutual friends, but we had shopped at the same places and had a mutual hatred for Northern Virginia traffic. Hers had a more personal basis.

"My parents," she told me, her eyes growing sad, "were both killed by a wrong-way drunk driver crash on the Beltway."

"Oh, no," I said, shaking my head. "That's terrible! When did this happen?"

"I was nineteen, a freshman at George Mason. I had just begun my second semester. I was in my dorm room, studying, when I got the call." She looked at me, tears glistening on her lashes. "I'm adopted. An only child. I had no one to call. A nice police officer came and picked me up. I had to identify them, and the rest … the rest is a blur." She took a deep breath.

"Thankfully, a couple from our church who loved my parents came along beside me. They helped me figure out who to notify and how to plan the funeral. I had to find burial plots and pick out caskets, decide what clothes they'd be buried in." She stood up suddenly, retrieved a box of tissues from the kitchen, and sat back down.

"Kathryn," I said, invoking familiarity with her first name, "I'm so sorry. How traumatic!"

"It was so bizarre. They were only in their fifties," she said after blowing her nose. "My parents' extended family all lived out of town. They came to the funeral. My mother's sister and her husband invited me to come live with them in Florida. But I was frozen, hardly capable of getting through the day, much less making a major move.

"In the end, I decided to stay at George Mason but move out of the dorm and back to our home while I sorted things out." She took a deep breath. "Well," she said, "I don't know how I got into all that. Let's turn to what you came for. Want to see the attic?"

"Sure!" I was full of questions still but decided to take her lead. "I'd like to take some pictures when we get up there if you don't mind."

"There's not much to see, but that's fine."

She led me up a small stairway to the second floor, which was divided into two bedrooms and a bathroom. An even smaller stairway with an angled turn in the middle took us up to the attic. Kathryn pulled the cord on a bare-bulb light, and the fully floored attic came into view. Except for the floor, it was unfinished, with bare beams overhead and three-foot high walls on the front and the back. There were windows at each end, allowing some light in. A single, four-drawer dresser sat at the far end.

"Is that yours?" I asked, gesturing toward it.

"No. My guess is they couldn't figure out how to get it out of here."

My camera whirred as I took pictures. Then, curious, I walked toward the dresser. "This is a nice piece."

"I know. It's heavy."

I opened the drawers, noted the tongue-and-groove construc-
tion, and solid frame. I hefted the dresser's weight. "You're right."
Then I spotted something. "Did you see this?" I pointed behind
the dresser, and moved away so Kathryn could get close enough
to see the small door hidden in the eaves.

"No! I didn't know that was there."

"Do you think we can move the dresser?"

"Let's try."

We both took hold of the heavy piece and moved it away from
the wall. "Do you mind if I look in there?" I asked her.

"Help yourself."

I put my camera on the dresser and knelt down. The door had
a single knob opener. It took a couple of tugs, but I got it open.
Then, using the flashlight on my cell phone, I peered inside.

Stunned, I quickly pulled back. "Oh my gosh, Kathryn.
There's more!"

"More?"

"Paintings! At least three that I can see. Hand me my camera,
would you please?" I snapped some pictures of the paintings in
their crawlspace.

"Can you pull them out?" Kathryn said.

"I'll have to crawl in. Here, take this." I handed back my
camera.

Thankfully, the storage area under the eaves was well-
floored, so I didn't have to worry about falling through to the
room below. I was a little concerned about mice, but my interest
in those painting pushed me forward. The three frames leaning
against the back wall hid a fourth smaller one. I passed them out,
one by one, to Kathryn, then I crawled back out and dusted off
my pants.

Kathryn had the paintings lined up against the wall and was
staring at them from a few feet away. She looked at me, eyes shining. "Whoever drew these loved that dog!"

The four pieces of art were all country scenes, landscapes and farms. But the collie was in each one somewhere, along with the little girl. "They're beautiful! Can you see the signature?"

"Not quite," Kathryn said. "We'll have to take them down-stairs. Is that all that's in there?"

"It's all I can see. But I'd come up with a better flashlight if I were you. Let me take shots of them in this space, and then we can carry them down."

On our way down, paintings in hand, my phone vibrated, signaling a text. As soon as I could, I checked it. Scott's message said, *More tests but I'm okay.* I breathed a sigh of relief.

After wiping the art down with rags, we lined them up in Kathryn's living room where we had good light. I took lots of pictures, including closeups of the signature area and even the backs. It looked like the artist's last name was Burns, although I couldn't honestly be sure. They made a beautiful collection.

"Are these mine, now, do you think?" Kathryn asked me.

"The former owner told the estate sale company to empty the house. I'll bet they never looked in the crawlspace. I think legally, now that you've closed on the house, they're abandoned property, so they're yours."

"Really?"

"Check with the lawyer who handled the sale. But that's what I think."

"I'm overwhelmed," she said. "This is really cool" She looked at me, eyes shining.

"Very nice." I checked my watch. "Well, I'd better get going." I started putting my boots back on.

Katherine still stared at the paintings. "I'm really curious about your client," she said suddenly.

"In what way?"

"He's adopted. I'm adopted. He's looking for his bio family. So am I."

"I can understand that."

"When I first moved here, I rented a room from an older

widow. I started going to church. A friend I made there told me about a widow who was alone. She visited her now and then to check on her. I went along one time, and I enjoyed that lady so much.

"So I decided to start visiting her too. Meanwhile, I kept working on getting my birth records. One day, I got a phone call from social services. And here's where it gets crazy. I found out my birth mother lived here in Clear Springs. So I started asking around. And Martha, the woman I was renting the room from, told me she thought she remembered something that happened thirty or so years ago. And that this woman I'd been visiting, Etta, might be my biological grandmother!"

I blinked, hard, unable to process what I'd just heard. *Etta? Etta could be her grandmother? Laura's mother?* My thoughts raced.

Kathryn continued. "I called social services back and told them about that. But I asked them to hold off contacting her. I needed time to process what I'd learned, and I didn't want to shock Etta."

Etta! Suddenly I could barely breathe.

"We have a good relationship as it is. Maybe that's enough. Maybe I shouldn't stir the pot. I have to think it out." Her face beaming, Kathryn said, "Such an answer to prayer!"

"That's amazing," I responded, forcing my voice to remain calm. "And she lives here?" Tension tightened my right hand into a ball.

"Less than three miles away."

My phone vibrated. I looked. A text from Scott. *Are you on your way home yet?* I looked at Kathryn. "I hope the rest of your search for your family goes well." I smiled to cover my inanity. "I need to get home. You've been more than helpful. Thank you! I'll get in touch with my client, and he'll pass the information on to Andrew Gerhardt."

"I'll ask around school, and if I learn who the artist is, I'll let you know."

"Thank you! I love your house! It's really sweet."

What a lame thing to say, I thought as I walked away. I felt stunned, off balance. How could Etta have a grandchild? Did Laura have a brother? A sister I didn't know about? Maybe a stepbrother or stepsister? Miss Etta had remarried after Laura's father left. Is that where Kathryn came from?

My thoughts spun like a merry-go-round on the drive home.

15

I'D ANTICIPATED BEING at Kathryn's house for an hour. Instead, with the tea and the conversation and the surprise discovery, it was nearly three hours. The sun had gone down long ago and clouds had moved in.

Between the dark, twisty, unfamiliar mountain roads and the erratic cell phone service, I felt alone. I missed Luke. It had been right to leave him at home, but still, I was so used to having him riding in his crate in the back, another beating heart in the car, that I felt empty without him.

Soon, focused ahead only as far as my headlights let me, I got lost in my thoughts— thoughts about Kathryn Grace and Etta, Amanda and Scott, people and relationships and how God saw it all, knew it all, and was exercising his sovereignty over it all.

I know that seems radical. Most people think we have "free will," that we make our own decisions. And that is true to an extent, but Nate always said that God is ultimately in control. I resisted that at first, proud of my independence. But the more I read the Bible and the closer I came to knowing God through good experiences and bad, the more I began to accept—actually *rely*—on his sovereignty. I was slowly learning to trust God, trust his love. Or as Nate put it, trust his heart even when I didn't understand what his hand was doing.

That doesn't mean I no longer got anxious. Ha! Are you kidding? Anxiety is my middle name. I am, as Nate frequently points out, a work in progress. "All of us are," he said. "I don't get it right all the time neither."

I love Nate. He is the brother I never had.

A clicking sound snapped my attention back to the road. I stared straight ahead. Ice pellets. Tiny ice pellets were hitting my Jeep and bouncing off. Was the road freezing? I gripped the steering wheel and dropped my speed.

Glancing at my cell phone I could see I had no signal. I wished I'd remembered to text Scott and tell him I was leaving. I wished I'd started a podcast or an audiobook, something to help me relax as I drove. There was no place to pull off and no side roads to turn down, not here anyway. I was going to have to white-knuckle it … and pray.

I ARRIVED home at 9:00 p.m., slowed by ice in the mountains and rain at lower elevations. Eighty pounds of German shepherd exuberance met me as I ran through the rain to the porch. Scott stood in the open door, the light behind him welcoming me.

"Looks like it was a nasty drive," Scott said. "Come on in!"

"I hit ice up in the mountains," I said, stepping into the warm foyer and petting Luke. "But by the time I drove down to Staunton it had turned to rain. Whew! I'm tired." Of course, I was about to bust with what I'd learned about Kathryn Grace and Etta, but I focused on him first. "What did your doctor say?"

"Come on, take your coat off. Let's sit down."

Scott had a nice little fire going in the fireplace, just enough to warm the room and add some flickering light. We sat down on the couch and snuggled, and I silently thanked God once again for this man. Luke plopped down and rested his head on my foot.

"I'm glad to be home," I said. Scott didn't respond, so I poked him gently in the ribs. "You there?"

"You had a visitor today."

I frowned and looked at him. "Who?"

"Deputy Browning from up west of here. He was in the area and had some mug shots he wanted you to look at. Said you had an incident up there, on a trail?"

Guilt burned my face. "Yes, I did."

"You didn't tell me."

I could hear the irritation in his voice. "I didn't want to worry you."

"I *want* you to worry me! I want to know what's going on in your life, especially if it's something that could threaten you or increase your anxiety."

"You were gone. I handled it." I made it sound like him being gone was the problem.

"I thought we agreed you'd be running with friends. He said you were running on the trail alone. Why?"

"I wasn't alone. Luke was with me."

"Jess, you know what I mean."

A stubborn resistance had swelled up in me, like a wave rising to a crest or an earthquake reaching its peak. I moved away from Scott. "I was supposed to meet my friends. They all copped out at the last minute. What can I say? I wanted to run so I did."

His jaw was tight. "Next time, how about change course. Run down here or at the gym. Running by yourself up there ... Jess, it's not safe. Clearly."

My heart pounded. I opened my mouth to ask him why he was being so controlling, but something made me shut up. Scott leaned over and kissed the side of my head. "Jess, it's a privilege to be your husband. Part of that is protecting you."

I inhaled, ready to retort.

"You're a hard woman to protect. You take risks. You got grit, as Nate says. But help me, please, by not taking foolish chances.

Jess, I love you. It would kill me if something happened to you."
His voice was gentle. He kissed me again.

Something made me lay down my arms. Beat my sword into a
plowshare. Maybe it was the Holy Spirit. "I'm sorry. I should have
told you. I was embarrassed because I'd said I wouldn't run alone.
Plus I'd forgotten the Garmin." I blew out a breath. "I took a
chance. So stupid. And yes, that man scared me." I moved toward
Scott again.

"I'm glad you had Luke with you. He looks tough anyway."

He put his arm around me. And you know what? It felt good.

We sat that way for a while, then it was my turn. "What'd your
doctor say?"

Scott took a deep breath. "He wants me to have an
endoscopy."

I raised my eyebrows.

"Tube down the throat to check for ulcers and other digestive
issues."

"Right. That's actually hopeful! Better than a heart
problem."

"Yes. But he also wants me to see a cardiologist. Recommended one in Culpeper."

"Great."

"They set up an appointment on Monday for me."

"Nice." He had his arm around me, and I snuggled deeper
into his shoulder. "Did you feel okay today?" I asked him.

"Yeah. Hung out with the horses. And Luke. Did a little work.
I felt fine."

"Did Amanda drive you?"

"No, I waved her off."

That disappointed me. I was hoping they would get to talk. I
had to tell Scott soon about her pregnancy. Somebody did
anyway.

"Mike's coming out tomorrow. I hope that's okay."

"Mike Perez? Sure."

He squeezed me. "So tell me about your day. How'd your talk go?"

"It went well." I started to get into details and his phone rang.

He pulled it out of his pocket. "I'm sorry. I have to take this."

He got up and walked out of the room, phone to his ear. I yawned. The warm fire was making me sleepy. Not to mention my long day. When Scott didn't come back right away I decided to lie down. Resting my head on the soft leather arm of the couch, I must have fallen asleep. Next thing I knew, Scott was jostling me awake.

"Come on, babe. Let's go upstairs," he said softly. And so we did.

THE NEXT MORNING, over the breakfast that he made for me, I was able to tell Scott about the trip, including the recognition from Sheriff Ward and my meeting with Kathryn Grace.

"She's very sweet. I liked her immediately," I said. "Down-to-earth, and from what she said it sounds like she has her priorities right. But I was shocked when she told me she might be Etta's granddaughter."

"I'll bet."

"Now I have dirty knowledge of that fact, and I'm trying to figure out what to do with it. I mean, does Laura have a brother or sister I don't know about? Did she have a sibling who had a child but then died young before I knew Laura? I'm scared she's going to think I was snooping, but I wasn't!" I took a big gulp of my black coffee. "On the other hand, it should comfort her to know the young woman visiting Etta might be a relative. Shouldn't it?"

Scott stayed focused on his breakfast. I wondered if he was working on his cases in his head while I chattered on. But then he put down his fork and wiped his mouth with his napkin and looked at me. "If this Kathryn Grace is Etta's granddaughter,

Laura might be pleased she's the one visiting Etta. On the other hand, she could be concerned Kathryn's after Etta's money."

"She doesn't have any money."

"Are you sure? Sometimes folks live poor but leave a big estate. Like your Miss Lottie."

"Right." Miss Lottie seemed to be barely scraping by when I first met her. She lived down near Williamsburg and hired me to find her long-lost daughter. She died, and with no surviving relatives, she left me a large amount of money out of gratitude for my work on her case. We used some of that to buy this house.

"What's more," Scott said, continuing, "Kathryn could be an imposter. She could have been trying out her story on you, to see if it flew. In any event, Laura needs to know what you know. And the longer you wait, the more it will seem like you're hiding information."

Scott was right. "What time's Mike coming?" I asked.

He looked at his watch. "He should be here about nine o'clock."

"All right. Are you okay if I go up to Nate's this morning if they're home?"

"Sure."

"I'll send my report on the paintings to my client, then I'll leave. I'll be gone a couple of hours. I'll take Luke. I'll bring something home for dinner, if Mike will stay."

"Great. That'll work."

TWENTY MINUTES LATER, I was on the road to Nate's with Luke in his crate in the back. The rain from the night before had ended, but my Jeep was dotted with droplets. I ran my wipers to clear the windshield.

My stomach felt knotted as I drove. Scott had raised some important concerns. But Kathryn certainly seemed sincere to me, thoughtful and kind. I didn't think she was trying to pull a fraud.

Still, *people ain't always as they seem,* as Nate would say. Regardless, I knew I had to get this information to Laura and, like Scott said, the sooner the better.

Luke stood up in his crate as I pulled up to the Tanners' house. He always seemed to know, either by smell or by the way the driveway felt under the tires, that we were at Nate's. I parked near Nate's Tahoe, got out, and let Luke out of the back. He went sniffing, looking for Nate or Sprite or Ember. His people.

I walked up the ramp and knocked on the back door. I used to simply walk in, but between the enforced separation of COVID and Scott and I having our own house, over time I'd become a little more formal.

"Come on in!" Nate yelled, so I opened the door.

"Okay to let the dogs out?" Sprite and Ember were both trying to get past me.

"Sure!"

I let them out to play with Luke, then I hung my jacket on the pegs and found Laura and Nate in the living room.

"Come on in. Sit down. Do you want some coffee?"

I swallowed, my throat thick. They looked like they'd been having a discussion. I could see tension lines in Laura's face and Nate's had that impassive, "I ain't gonna change my mind" look I was so familiar with.

"No, I'm fine. I had coffee in the car." I sat down on the hearth. Laura was on the couch, Nate in his chair to her left. "How are you two doing?"

"How's Scott? That's what we want to know," Nate said.

So I updated them on my husband's medical condition. "He's frustrated," I said. "Scott doesn't like down time. But his heart seems fine."

"Could it be stress?"

"Maybe. We'll know more after these other tests." Nate, I observed, was wearing his usual work-around-the-house clothes, but Laura was wearing nice slacks and a sweater twin-set, like she was going somewhere. "Did I interrupt something?" I asked, looking from one to the other.

Laura's mouth was a straight line. "I wanted to go see my mom," she said. "But they had an ice storm last night and Nate doesn't want me driving on those roads." She looked at him. "I've been driving up there my whole life!"

"And how many times have you ended up in a ditch?" he said, his voice gentle. "I just think you should wait. I don't want you gettin' hurt."

"He's being protective," I said, smiling, hoping to diffuse the tension. "Scott's like that too. Sometimes it drives me crazy. Nate's right though. The roads are bad up there. I ran into a little of it coming home last night."

"Were you in Clear Springs?" Laura said, surprised.

"Yes. Actually, that's what I wanted to talk to you about." I took a deep breath to stop the quivering in my gut. My pulse pounded in my ears. "Remember me telling you about the case I had up there? About the painting?"

"No," Laura said.

"I may not have told her," Nate said. "Start from the beginning."

So I did. I told them about the painting bought at an estate sale, about it being found among items from a house in Clear Springs, and about the house being owned by a woman named Kathryn Grace McCaskill.

Laura's head jerked up. "Kathryn Grace? The same as the young woman visiting my mother?"

Nate moved in his chair as if he were uncomfortable.

"Yes. I thought, could there be two people with that name in such a small town? So I looked her up ..."

"You went snooping," Laura said, stiffening her back.

"No. I was getting more information for my client. Nothing to do with Miss Etta. I found out Kathryn is a single woman, a school teacher, and new to the area."

Laura rolled her eyes. She got up and moved behind the couch.

"I thought that might make you feel better about her visiting your mom."

"Yes. That's reassuring, Laura, ain't it? She's got a legitimate job," Nate said.

Laura didn't respond.

"That's not all." I swallowed hard as both of them turned to me. "My client asked me to see if Ms. McCaskill would let me see the attic. The man who purchased the painting, Andrew Gerhardt, has been searching for his biological family, and the picture, and then the house, were clues for him."

I saw Nate glance quickly at Laura. I kept going.

"Through his lawyer, Gerhardt asked if I could visit the house and take pictures of the attic, which he thought he remembered. When I told her the situation, Ms. McCaskill was open to me coming by, so that's why I was there yesterday." I started pressing my thumbnail into my finger, something I do when I'm trying to ignore other pain. "It was a sweet little house that she bought a month ago. We went exploring and found a small closet under the eaves in the attic and four more paintings!"

"That's great," Nate said, as if he hoped that was the end of it.

"Ms. McCaskill is super nice. She told me why she'd let me visit the house. She, too, was adopted and is looking for her biological family."

"What?" Laura flung her crossed arms down. "Why don't these people leave well enough alone?"

Her vehemence surprised me, but I had no choice but to continue.

"In her case, I think it's because she has no other family. No brothers and sisters, and her adoptive parents were killed in a car crash on the Washington Beltway. So she started researching her own family history. She found out she'd been born in western

Virginia. She drove out there and loved the area, and so eventually she found a job there, teaching in Clear Springs."

Both Nate and Laura were frozen, staring at me, like people in Times Square waiting for the ball to drop. Or the Hindenburg to crash. Laura's face was red.

I gulped. "One day she went with a friend to visit an older woman. That's Etta. Kathryn said she loved her right away, loved her spunk and vitality. So she kept visiting." I rubbed the back of my neck, which was piano-wire tight. "Then the woman she was renting a room from told her Etta might be her grandmother."

Laura exploded. "Her grandmother? What made her say that?" Then she burst into tears.

Nate stood up. "Laura, honey, it's okay." He almost fell, trying to get to her. He wrapped his arms around her.

My heart beat hard. Tension ran up my spine and across my shoulders. My breath became shallow. "So I don't know if you had a sibling or ..."

Nate shot me a look that shut me up.

But there was one more thing I had to say. I held my hands up. "She hasn't told Etta. As far as Etta knows, she's just a young friend."

Laura pulled back from Nate and glared at me. "You! I asked you, as a friend, not to snoop. To leave my mother alone. Would you do that? No! You've got to poke your nose in other people's business. Stir up trouble."

Confused, I rose to my feet. I looked at Nate. I got no help.

"You're such a meddler! How could you do this to me? You need to leave. Do you hear me? Leave!"

"Laura, I ..."

"Would you get out! Get out!" she screamed, her face red.

Stunned, I moved toward the door. I halfway expected Nate to stop me, but no rescue came. As I closed the door behind me, I heard glass crashing.

16

I STUMBLED down the ramp and toward my car. I'd stepped on a land mine. Why? I called for Luke, my voice croaking with emotion. All three dogs came running. Hands shaking, I started to put Luke in his crate, then hesitated. I needed him close. So I had him jump in the front passenger seat, where he immediately curled up.

How about the other two dogs? Normally, I'd put them inside the house, but I didn't want to open that door again. Plus, was there broken glass in there? "C'mon, dogs," I said, and I started to lead them up the ramp. I'd make them lie down and stay. I saw Little Sprite limping, so I picked her up and impulsively kissed her head, tears stinging my eyes. I'd been banned from the house. Would I ever see Sprite again? Nate?

I made it a few miles down the road, before tears began flowing. What had I done? Why was Laura so angry? I grabbed a tissue and blew my nose. Luke looked at me, head cocked, like he was trying to figure out what was going on. I stroked his head, tears hot on my cheeks. Was Nate mad at me too? Was that fierce look on his face anger or protectiveness? Had I just lost my best friend?

The thought of that tore my heart. I cried like a baby.

Ten minutes later, I got a text from Nate. *She may be Laura's child. Sensitive subject.*

Laura's child? Laura's? I jerked my car over to the shoulder and texted back. *Did you know????*

Of course, he responded.

I quickly did the math in my head. If Kathryn was Laura's child, Laura had to have been a young teenager when she had that baby. There were only about fifteen years between them. So did Nate know then? And was it Nate's baby?

I had so many questions. Somehow, I had the sense not to ask them. Not right then. Maybe later. I put my phone down and drove on.

That contact from Nate moved me back from the ledge. Maybe I wouldn't lose him. I settled down enough to stop at the closest store to our home and buy steaks, salad, some fresh fruit, and frozen garlic knots. Dinner for three.

But by the time we got home I was teary again. Laura's voice, her anger, kept playing over and over in my head.

I expected Scott and Mike to be in the barn. They weren't. They were in the living room, talking. I hoped to avoid them, to drop the groceries in the kitchen, and scoot upstairs. That didn't happen. As soon as Scott heard me, he got up to see if he could help.

"Hey, what's wrong?" he asked, folding me into his arms when he saw I was upset. And it all spilled out. Right there. In front of Mike and everything. "It'll work out," Scott said gently. "You're not going to lose your friends."

"I'll tell you what. That would totally freak me out," Mike said, "having someone show up and say, 'Oh, by the way, I'm your kid.'"

I pulled away from Scott. "People are so hard to deal with!"

"Give Laura a few days," he said. "Let her have time to adjust to the idea."

"She was so angry."

"But that's not typical for her. She'll get over it."

"She's probably embarrassed," Mike suggested, picking up an apple from the bowl on the table and chomping into it.

Luke came up and shoved his nose into my leg. I sunk down on the floor and pulled him close. "I hate people," I said, and I buried my face in his ruff.

Mike laughed. "Present company excepted."

"Not always," Scott said. He stooped down to face me. Luke licked his face, which made me smile. He wiped dog slobber off with his sleeve. "Why don't you come down to the barn with Mike and me? Hang out with the horses. We'll try not to annoy you." He smiled softly. "Bring your dog. He's good company."

"I want to go curl up in a ball and make the world go away."

"I know," Scott said, touching my knee, "but why don't you hang out with me instead?"

Something made me do it. I went to the barn and the three of us played with the horses all afternoon. We groomed them and Scott filed their hooves. While I watched, he taught Mike some ground work, techniques used to establish the bond between horse and human before riding took place.

Mike was an eager learner. He was also funny. "Oh, I get it," he said to Scott after my husband taught him some nonverbal techniques to gain the horse's trust. "I've seen you do that with your wife." He grinned and looked my direction. Both Scott and I had to laugh. Soon he had Beau following him around the paddock.

"Why'd you name him Beau?" Mike asked me. "Did he come with that name?"

"No. Nate suggested it. I don't know why. But I liked the name so that's what I called him."

"You know," Mike said, "Beau's the name of Rooster Cogburn's horse in *True Grit*."

Scott and I looked at each other and started laughing.

"What?" Mike said.

"Nate's always saying, 'Girl, you got grit!'" Scott explained.

Mystery solved. Now I knew.

Although it was cold we went for a ride, Mike on Beau and me riding behind Scott on Ace. Luke happily trotted along with us. I almost fell off when Ace decided to bunny hop over the creek, but I hung on, and Scott loved it.

After being outside all day, the steaks and salad and bread tasted really good. After dinner Scott built a fire in the fireplace. I curled up on the couch, dozing while Scott and Mike talked.

They were talking about work, and I half-listened until Scott brought up Montana. Then my ears pricked up. I lay still, eyes closed, listening.

"So my guy out there, Joe, interviewed the two kids Everett Voight was supposedly trying to recruit. They said he'd gotten weird lately, that he was a really bright kid, but he'd become obsessed with climate change. His girlfriend broke up with him at the beginning of the school year over it. She said he was getting too radical. Climate change was all he wanted to talk about.

"Apparently, he was trying to get his friends to help him damage or destroy a power substation to bring attention to his cause. That would knock electricity out over a wide area, which in winter could be deadly. He saw himself as a warrior for ecology."

"Great."

"He was out there for sure. Living on the fringe."

"So why'd he shoot up the school?"

"That wasn't supposed to happen," Scott said. "There's a message on his computer. One of the eco-activists suggested he take the gun to school to prove to the others he had access to it, and he was serious about taking action against the power station. He was showing the gun to another kid. A third kid came around the corner, saw it, and started yelling. Everett apparently panicked. The gun went off, there was a scuffle, and that's how four people got killed."

"And he committed suicide."

"I'm not sure it was suicide. It was a self-inflicted gunshot wound in his gut. A teacher tackled him from behind. He was lucky the bullet didn't hit him. I think the shot could have been accidental," I heard Scott say. "Everett's dad taught him to shoot, but they didn't regularly practice handling guns."

"Hmm," Mike said. "So what all did the tech guys find?"

"In his computer they found lots of messages—texts and emails —between him and these radical activists. They were feeding him hardcore propaganda. Apparently, they want action against climate change in all fifty states between now and Earth Day."

"Do you think they're ecoterrorists?"

"That's what it sounds like. We'd have to investigate it further, but to me, it sounds like they're not simply expressing normal concern about global warming. It sounds like they think violent action is necessary and justified."

"The deputy assistant director said leave them alone."

"Right. And if this is ecoterrorism, I shouldn't be the point man. But I don't think we should drop it."

There was silence for a couple of minutes. "I don't know, man," Mike said. "Seems like the deputy AD called the play. If it's a bad call, step back and let him take the hit."

"Yeah, like that ever happens!"

"Still, he gave you an order. You can't ignore that."

I heard Scott take a deep breath. "He's tied my hands. Joe texted me and said the SAC in Salt Lake said to deep six the environmental aspect. Treat it as a school shooting."

"In other words, let the locals handle it."

"But I don't feel right about ignoring what's right in front of me."

I could hear the anger in Scott's voice.

"Watch your back, man. That's all I'm saying. Watch your back."

A WEEK WENT BY. I didn't hear from Nate, not even a text. We had three callouts, all of which I responded to. Nate was MIA on every single one. I called him, twice. He didn't answer. I texted him and got no response.

My heart ached.

In the meantime, Scott had more medical tests. While we waited for results, I pressed him, and he finally told me the chest pain came after a frustrating meeting with the deputy assistant director and a guy from the general counsel's office. "I haven't been that angry in a long time," he said.

"You've had lots of stress lately," I suggested.

"Yeah."

The diagnosis finally came—ulcers, lots of them, in his gut. The gastroenterologist prescribed medication and told him to stay away from caffeine, alcohol, and tobacco, as well as NSAIDS like aspirin or ibuprofen.

"I've been eating them like candy," Scott confessed to me. "I've had so many headaches."

At least it wasn't his heart. We felt grateful for that. We talked about some ways he could reduce his stress. Part of that was treating the Montana case as a school shooting, like the deputy AD ordered. It didn't sit well with him, but it wasn't a hill to die on, either.

Two weeks before Thanksgiving, I told Scott we'd better invoke Plan B for the "traditional Thanksgiving" he wanted to have. Plan B was to invite my mother, stepfather, and sister and Amanda. I didn't think Nate and Laura were coming.

Losing Nate's friendship had pierced a hole in my heart. It was like losing a brother. He was first my SAR mentor and then my spiritual guide. His faith was infectious. I felt lost without him.

And I felt so confused. I was the one who'd found Laura and reintroduced them when Nate was lying in the hospital after being injured on a search. Their long-lost love quickly reignited. They had so much in common. She shared his upbringing and his faith. He'd carried her picture in his wallet for twenty years. He clearly loved her.

They married quickly. I felt happy for them.

Now I wondered if I should have bothered getting involved. It had caused me a lot of trouble and grief. I'd never gotten close to her, although I have to admit that was typical of me. My friends tended to be men. And if she really was a Christian, how could she spew all that anger at me? And seriously, a child out of wedlock? Had she told Nate before they married? How much did he know about her before he committed to her?

I knew Nate well enough to know he'd stay with her regardless. So I wallowed in my judgment and pain, silently bitter, with no hope in sight.

A week before Thanksgiving, I got a call from Kathryn Grace McCaskill. "Didn't you tell me your husband works for the FBI?" she asked.

"Yes. He's an agent."

"I'm concerned about one of our students. Do you think I might run the situation past him and get his advice? I don't want to get this kid in trouble. He's struggling as it is. But still..."

I jumped at the chance to help her. "I think he'd be glad to talk to you," I said. Scott always said a lot of these mass shootings could be prevented if people would speak up when they observed a person going off the rails. "Let me check with him, and I'll call you right back."

Within fifteen minutes, the two of them connected and I got out of the middle. We had no idea at the time how that phone call would change all of our lives.

17

SCOTT CALLED me half an hour later. "Hey, didn't you say you met the Highland County sheriff?"

"Yes, when Miss Etta got lost."

"You want to take a drive?"

"With you? Sure!" I didn't ask where or why.

"I'll be home in an hour. Get packed up. Figure on two days."

"Are we taking Luke?"

"Yes. And your Jeep. There may be snow in the mountains."

EXACTLY NINETY MINUTES later we were on the road, headed for Clear Springs with me driving. Both of us had on khaki cargo pants and good boots. Scott wore a really nice light gray long-sleeved shirt and his favorite navy-blue down vest. I'd topped my outfit with a black turtleneck and a navy sweatshirt. "I guess this is how we dress up for a date," I joked.

"You look beautiful to me. Perfect," he responded.

My face grew warm.

Our heavy gear—parkas, thermal base layers, extra clothes, gloves, hats—was in the back. Scott had packed our guns in the locked metal safe he'd bolted behind the front seats, reachable from either one. Not that we were going to war. But an FBI agent is technically on duty 24/7. Scott needed to be prepared, so he'd installed that gun safe in my car not long after we were married.

My mother asked me one time how I felt about being surrounded by guns all the time. I said as long as they weren't pointed at me I was fine with it. What was she thinking? That they were going to rise up and kill me on their own? "The Revenge of the Glocks" or something like that? I was more worried about Alexa.

"So what's this date all about?" I asked once we were on the road.

"You know I talked to Kathryn McCaskill."

"Right."

"She found a notebook that belongs to a kid at her school, someone she's had her eye on for a while. She thinks he's troubled. The notebook is full of violent images—guns, angry-looking people, a school bus crashing, and then images about global warming—the earth on fire, trees falling, that sort of thing. She scanned some of the pictures and sent them to me."

Scott shifted in his seat. "This kid is also in her class, and the essays and stories he writes are full of pretty rough violence."

"And he's how old?"

"Fourteen."

"Has she talked to the school counselor about him? Do they even have school counselors?"

"Yes, she tried talking to the counselor, but he isn't concerned. He seems to think it's normal behavior. But I agree with her—I think it's over the top. What's more, I saw images and dates, including Earth Day, April 22, that look a lot like what I was seeing on Everett Voight's laptop."

"The kid in Montana."

"Right. So I want to go up to Clear Springs, talk to Kathryn, and maybe the sheriff and the school principal. I'm interested in preventing an incident and getting the kid help if he needs it."

"And what do you want me to do?"

"Oh, you're the eye candy," he said, grinning.

I reached over and punched his arm.

"I thought Kathryn might be more comfortable if you came along. Plus, I wanted to be with you for a change."

"I love it."

He rubbed my shoulder. "I know it's hard with me gone so much. But I think what we're doing is important. Both of us." He settled back in his seat. The day was gray, overcast, and the air smelled like snow. "By the way, I talked to Amanda."

I gripped the steering wheel. *Did she tell him?*

"She told me about the baby."

I noticed he said "baby," not "pregnancy." My stomach tightened. "How did you react?"

"To be honest," Scott said, "I wasn't surprised. She's been drinking too much, been putting herself in too many risky situations." He took a deep breath. "Been there, done that."

"It's not her fault. That guy forced himself on her."

"She could have been wiser." He shifted in his seat. "And maybe she would have been if I'd been more involved when she was growing up. I regret that. I just couldn't take living in California."

"So what did you tell her?"

"That I loved her. That I didn't believe in abortion. But I said that it was her decision and I'd continue to love her whatever she decided." He looked over at me. "It breaks my heart, but how could I condemn her? I've walked through that same swamp."

I nodded, speechless at his grace and wisdom.

"But I was furious at that guy," he said.

"Women always bear the consequences."

Scott sighed. "She doesn't know about God. To her, abortion is just a practical decision. It's just getting rid of a mistake."

I took his hand and squeezed it.

"So we'll see what she does." He shook his head. "I think my reaction surprised her."

"I'm sure it did." I kept my voice level, although an emptiness had opened in my gut, thinking about Amanda, and a baby, and the void in my own life. So many thoughts swirled in my head. If she had the baby, would she want us to raise it? And would I do that? Could I? *Maybe abortion would be better.*

I kicked that out of my head immediately. *Go away, Satan, you father of lies.*

But I honestly didn't know how we would work everything out. Or how I'd feel about it.

We kept driving through Bridgewater and onto the mountain road that snaked through the George Washington National Forest. Then my husband spoke again.

"I also called Nate," Scott said.

I stiffened. "Oh yeah?" I stared straight ahead.

"I wanted him to know we'd be in Clear Springs on bureau business."

I nodded, not trusting my voice.

"He said to tell you he's sorry."

"He's sorry?" I spit those words out.

"He said he had to help Laura through some stuff. And it wasn't a good time for him to call you right now."

"So that's it? She gets mad and I get ditched?"

I shut up after that, clenching my jaw to keep from saying more. My heart pounded like a war drum. Hurt, more than anger, drove it. *This is why I hate people,* I thought. *The minute you care about them, they disappear.* Dogs are so much easier.

Scott reached over and put his hand on my knee. He left it there, like he was trying to steady me. "Be patient, hon. It takes people time to work through these things. You know that."

Yes, I of all people should know that.

But I was still angry. Hurt. Hurt or angry. Maybe both.

"You haven't lost your friends. Not permanently."

"I was never close to her," I said, bending the truth. "I tried for his sake, but it didn't happen." I took a breath trying to calm down. I could smell Scott's body wash. I wanted to hold him and be held by him. I wanted the comfort of feeling his body next to mine, of being anchored skin-to-skin.

I reached down and wrapped my hand around his. He understood. He turned his hand to capture mine.

Then, to my utter shock, he prayed out loud, for me, for Nate and Laura, for the circumstances that had caused our conflict. He prayed for healing of our relationships and for courage and faith for me, faith that our mutual love for Jesus would restore us. Eventually.

My husband got me.

I POINTED out Miss Etta's house as we approached Clear Springs, and then Kathryn Grace McCaskill's cute little home. We arrived at the school after the buses had dispatched. I let Luke out of the back and took him to a grassy area where we could play. Throw the ball, watch him run for it, tell him to drop it, throw it again—over and over I repeated these actions. The process relaxed me. I loved watching Luke run. I loved the happy look on his face as he came back to me, ball wedged in his jaw, tongue lolling. I loved the way he crouched in anticipation of me tossing it again, eyeing me, trying to guess the direction of my throw.

Scott went inside to talk to Kathryn right before the snow began falling. At first it came in large flakes drifting lazily down from the gray clouds. Like a kid, I lifted my head and caught some on my tongue.

Then gradually the flakes became smaller, more intense, and started to collect on Luke's back and my shoulders. So we walked back to the Jeep. I gave Luke a drink, leashed him up, and we followed Scott through the unlocked front doors into the warmth of the rural school.

It was easy to tell where he and Kathryn were. Only one room had its door open, the light spilling out into the hall in a yellow rectangle. I tapped on the propped door and walked in to what was obviously an English classroom. Posters of some of the great writers hung above the old-fashioned blackboard: Shakespeare, Jane Austen, Walt Whitman, Longfellow, and Emily Dickenson. The assignment for the night was on the board. Near the window hung the American flag.

"Hey, come on in!" Kathryn Grace said. She rose from the desk where she'd been sitting, her dark hair falling around her shoulders, contrasting nicely with her cream-colored Fair Isle knit. "Is this Luke? Can I pet him?"

"Yes, this is Luke." My dog was already giving his permission, wagging his tail and grinning.

"He's beautiful," Kathryn said, smiling at me.

Scott stood up and stretched. Seeing him in this classroom reminded me again what a hunk my husband was.

"We were about to go down to see the principal," he said. "Do you want to come?"

"If it's okay."

"Sure," Kathryn said.

"Did you see it's snowing?" I said.

"No, I wasn't paying attention," Scott said, bending down to look out of the classroom window.

Kathryn looked too. "It's laying on the roads already. What are you all driving?"

"A Jeep," I said. "It's good in the snow."

"How much are we supposed to get?" Scott asked.

"Last thing I heard, six to eight inches," Kathryn replied.

"We're staying overnight. We have an appointment with the sheriff in the morning. But I think we'll be fine." Scott straightened up. "Do you have a good snow car?"

"Subaru," Kathryn replied. "So far, so good. But the roads can be treacherous."

We walked back down the hall I'd just come down. "Are your doors always unlocked?" I asked Kathryn.

She rolled her eyes. "Your husband has already gigged us on that." Then she smiled.

"The shootings are happening everywhere," Scott said.

"You're right."

We walked into the main office. A chest-high counter stood in front of us, chairs behind us lined up below the windows that looked into the hall. Three secretaries' desks were on the other side of the counter. I could see a thick black notebook labeled ATTENDANCE and another labeled FIELD TRIPS.

Field trips? Where in the world could kids go around here? To mountains, trails, waterfalls, historic markers, maybe an old house or two?

Still, I suspected the kids didn't think of themselves as deprived.

The principal, a short, bald-headed, robust-looking man named Clint Chambers, emerged from his office. Kathryn introduced us and he invited us all, including Luke, back into his office.

I could see there were only two guest chairs in his office. "Luke and I'll wait out here," I said, gesturing toward the outer office. I'd still be able to hear everything.

He nodded. "Suit yourself."

I sat and stroked my dog's head and neck, watching and listening as Scott explained to Chambers what his position was with the FBI and the studies they'd done on school shootings as well as other types of mass incidents. He spoke about the influence of the Internet and pointed out several school shootings in small towns, including the one he'd worked in Montana. "Sadly, being in a rural area is no longer a protection against violent incidents," Scott said.

"We're pretty close out here," Chambers replied. "I'd like to think we know what's going on in the kids' minds."

"Yes, sir," Scott said, "but all it takes is for one kid to go off the rails and you've got a problem. Every time we have an incident, people start talking about gun control, as if that's the only solution. You and I know, sir, Americans are not giving up their guns. So what we've found through our studies is this: In almost every incident, someone knew the shooter's plans before he carried them out. But they either didn't believe him or didn't want to get involved, and they just didn't say anything. We've found prevention—getting the shooter help before he takes action—is key. That's why I was glad Ms. McCaskill got in touch with me."

"Why'd you call the FBI?" Chambers said to Kathryn. He sounded a little aggressive to me. Maybe he was embarrassed.

"I'd talked to Mr. Donnelly several weeks ago." She looked at Scott. "He's the counselor." Then she continued, "He wasn't concerned, but Travis's drawings and stories still bothered me. I'd met Agent Cooper's wife, and I don't know—I felt like I wanted to run it by someone else." She paused. "Maybe I am being an alarmist, but I love my kids, and I want school to be safe."

"Miss McCaskill is new to teaching—" Chambers said.

Scott interrupted him. "Based on the studies we've done, I share her concern. The images in the notebook are disturbing and violent. What's more, they show some connection to images and texts in other cases we've had ... and at least one in which the kid acted out."

Scott's being careful not to name ecoterrorism, I thought. That was wise, considering the deputy AD's position. At this stage of the game, I knew he simply wanted someone to talk to the kid. Maybe help him process some of his thinking.

"The Internet links everybody, even kids in rural communities. That can be good, but it can also be bad if parents and teachers don't realize what's going on." Scott shifted in his seat. "There are radical groups online specifically targeting kids. If you have a kid who is troubled in some way, it can be easy for them to get hooked into some cause or mission bigger than themselves. It's a way to establish an identity that seems important."

"That seems far-fetched."

"I'm only suggesting that you take Ms. McCaskill's concerns seriously and have your counselor talk to this kid. See if he needs help."

My attention was riveted on this conversation. I watched Mr. Chambers through the door to see his response. I saw him frown, stare at his desk pad, then play with his pen. Then he looked up at Scott. "I guess that can't hurt." He rose to his feet. Scott and Kathryn did too.

"Thank you for hearing me out, sir," Scott said, shaking the man's hand. "You've got an idyllic place here. I hope it stays that way."

WE SAID goodbye to Kathryn and walked out of that school into a wintry wonderland. Half an inch of snow lay on the ground. I let Luke off leash, and he went racing around in it, chomping mouthfuls and being a general goofball.

"I like her," Scott said. He meant Kathryn Grace. "It took courage to confront the principal with that problem after being blown off by the counselor. Especially because she's new to teaching."

"Yes."

"She likes horses." Scott looked at me. "We were talking about it while you were outside, playing with Luke. She's never had one, but she took riding lessons as a kid. She says she's considering getting one now if she can find a nearby place to board it. I told her what we were doing with the horses, and I invited her down to ride."

"That could be interesting," I said.

"Is that okay?" He looked at me, eyebrows raised.

"Yes. I was thinking what would happen if Laura happened to be at our place." I shook my head. "I like her too, Scott. And I agree, she was brave to—"

"Jess! Scott!"

We turned. Kathryn was running after us, through the snow, no jacket. She stopped short, her face flushed and her breathing hard. "We have a school bus missing!"

18

"Parents are calling Mr. Chambers to say their kids still aren't home!" Kathryn's eyes were wide.

"An accident?" Scott asked.

"None reported."

"Do your buses have GPS trackers?"

Kathryn took a breath. "Not yet. The school board has talked about it, but it's expensive. Mr. Chambers is calling the sheriff to ask him to check the roads. He motioned for me to stop you."

Scott nodded. I could see the concern in the corners of his eyes. He looked at me. "Let's see this through."

"Go ahead," I said, nodding toward the school. "I'll be there after I get Luke."

Scott and Kathryn jogged back inside. Luke cocked his head, wondering why I was letting him out of his crate again. He hesitated, then jumped down and looked at me. "I don't know what we're doing," I said to my dog. "I think a school bus had an accident. Or something. We're hanging out to see if we can help. Come on." I leashed him up.

By the time we got inside, the three of them were bent over a map, tracing the route of Bus 16. "Let's get the names of the kids on that bus and start calling," Chambers said, racing back to his office. He emerged a minute later with a list of twenty-three kids.

"Some of these are my kids!" Kathryn said, her face distraught.

"Buses have a hard time in this kind of weather," Chambers said. "Hopefully, they've just slid off the road. Look, I'll take the first ten," he said. "Two of you split the others. We'll call and see if the kids are home." He looked at me. "Maybe you should call instead of your husband. Give 'em your first name and say you're a volunteer. If a man calls and says he's with the FBI all hell will break loose."

We agreed on staying low key. No point in starting a panic.

Luke was on a down-stay, watching us carefully, trying to figure out what was going on. I went behind the counter to a secretary's desk and began calling the six names on my list. As each of us got information, we gave it to Scott, and he marked it on the map. By the time we were done, we could see exactly where the last kid was successfully dropped off. In all, the driver and nine kids were missing.

Sheriff Colt McCormick arrived as we finished. Chambers introduced him to Scott, then me. "I know you," he said, frowning.

Thankfully, Chambers drew his attention before he could make the connection with the search we did for Etta. I hadn't explained to Kathryn that I knew her. "The last kid dropped off lives here," he said, pointing to the map. "These nine, plus the driver, are missing."

"We'll hone in on that area." The sheriff called his dispatcher and told her where to send the deputies searching for the bus.

The snow outside was falling heavier now, thin flakes outracing each other to the ground, clustering on tree limbs, and collecting in bright white clusters on the bushes. The sheriff's radio was tuned to both police and fire and ambulance. The fire and rescue services were all volunteer, and the dispatches were constant, accidents occurring all over the place.

WE STOOD WAITING FOR NEWS, waiting for our anxiety about the kids to be relieved. Then Kathryn got a phone call. "Oh, no," I heard her say. "I'll be there as soon as I can."

She clicked off her phone and looked at me. "Aren't you an EMT?"

"Yes." I'd recently been recertified.

"This elderly lady I've been helping fell outside her house. Her neighbor found her. She was able to get her inside, but she's bleeding. The neighbor called 911. They said it would be at least an hour before help would get there because of all the accidents."

"That's how I know you. Miss Etta!" the sheriff said.

Now it was Kathryn's turn to frown.

"No time to explain now. Let me grab my first-aid kit out of my Jeep."

"Is it okay if I go?" Kathryn asked her boss.

"Yes. Go. We'll let you know when we find the kids."

"Can you drive?" I asked. "I don't want Scott here without a car."

"Yes. And Luke can come with us."

I GRABBED MY GRIP, my first-aid kit, and Luke's bag and hopped into Kathryn's blue Forester. We headed for Miss Etta's. Kathryn's ability to keep cool and drive rationally despite the stress impressed me. The roads were slick and visibility low. Wipers brushed the dry snow off the windshield easily enough, but it was still hard to see.

"How do you know Miss Etta?" she asked me once we were on the main road.

How could I respond without revealing Laura's identity?

What could I say, ethically yet truthfully? I shot a silent prayer skyward. "She was lost in the woods, and Luke and I were on that search."

Very true. But not the whole truth.

"Oh, she told me about that! That was you? She said no one believed that she saw some men near her house."

Nate did, I thought. *Nate believed her.* A knot formed in my stomach. "She seemed ... disoriented."

"She is, sometimes." She braked carefully, shifting into a lower gear on a downhill stretch. "You must have met her daughter."

"Yes. Her daughter was there."

"My mother, I think. What's she like?"

"You look like her," I said, "and she is very ... kind. Compassionate." I had to change the subject. "Watch this guy," I said, pointing to a car headed toward a stop sign ahead and to our right.

Kathryn expertly navigated around the man who did not stop. "Good move," I said.

"My dad made sure I could drive in any weather. He'd take me out to big, empty parking lots and let me practice steering out of a skid." She grimaced. "It's ironic. He worked hard to make me safe on the road, and then he's the one who gets killed in an accident through no fault of his own."

"What a shock."

"Losing him and my mom in an instant like that broke me. I wasn't sure I'd ever get out of that black hole."

"I understand."

We were coming up on Etta's house. Kathryn eased her way down the hill, her left blinker on, and waited for a truck crawling up the other direction. She expertly turned into Etta's driveway.

"I'll leave Luke in the car until we see what's going on inside," I said. I grabbed my medical kit.

Kathryn had one more thing to say. "Jess."

I turned toward her.

"Remember, she doesn't know I think she's my grandmother."

"Got it."

Kathryn led the way to the house and walked right in. "Miss Etta, it's Kathryn!" The older woman was sitting in the living room in her recliner, her feet on the floor, an ice pack on her forehead held in place by her blue-veined hand. The neighbor, a fifty-something woman clothed in a housedress, sat on the couch. "What happened, Miss Etta?" Kathryn said.

Etta opened her eyes. She blinked at Kathryn. "Oh, honey, thank you for coming."

"Did you fall?"

She didn't respond. Instead, she looked beyond Kathryn to me. "I know you."

"Yes, ma'am," I said. "We met before. When you were lost in the woods."

"No 'lost' about it," she said. "I knew where I was."

"Yes, ma'am." I smiled. She hadn't lost her spunk. "Miss Etta, I'm a medic. Can I check you out? Make sure you're okay?"

"I'm fine, 'cept for my head. I knocked it good when I fell." She lowered the ice pack.

"You've got quite a bump," I said.

"Tell me about it."

I took out my little flashlight, clicked it on, and looked in her eyes. They were old eyes for sure, worn and tired, but they still held a spark of life. The pupils were the same size, a good sign. "Do you feel dizzy, Miss Etta?"

"Not no more."

"Did you walk up to the house after you fell?"

"Martha, here, she helped me."

I glanced over at the neighbor. "Did she walk okay?"

"A little shaky, but her legs worked and all. She said her shoulder hurt, the right one. When I first found her, she was lying on the snow. She seemed a little ... confused."

I continued, checking Etta's blood pressure, listening to her heart and lungs, checking her vision and her ability to move her arms and legs. I checked the relative strength in her hands, and I asked her to stand momentarily. "I think you're okay," I said, after checking her out.

"Well, I told you that!"

"What were you doing, Miss Etta? Why'd you go outside?"

She looked at Kathryn. "I seen them again. Them men. I said to myself, I got to see what they're up to. Sneak up on 'em. Watch 'em."

Kathryn stroked her hair. "So what did you see?"

Miss Etta stared at the ceiling across the room. Her mouth straightened into a line. "I seen them walk down the road and stand back in the woods a bit. After a time, I saw the bus. School bus. And ... and ..." she looked at Kathryn, "who's the boy drivin' it now? Herb? Herb Nowers?"

Kathryn nodded. "Yes."

"Herb musta stopped the bus and opened the door. I seen them men get on and then somethin' come flyin' out."

I swallowed hard. "Did you see a child or a teenager maybe get off the bus?"

"Ain't no houses down there. Bus don't stop there usually."

My law-enforcement brain went into gear. "So this thing you saw, flying off the bus. Was it something like a backpack? Or a jacket? What did you see, Miss Etta?"

Miss Etta looked straight at me. "It was somethin' like Herb."

"You stay here with her. I'll get Luke and go look," I said to Kathryn. "I called Scott but couldn't get through. I left a message."

"Try texting. That often works when the cell coverage doesn't."

"I will. But you try too. And call 911. Call anybody who you can get through to. And if you hear from Scott, tell him what she said."

I was glad I had brought my heavy SAR jacket with me from my car. It was beginning to get dark, the leaden sky deepening into a dark gray, cold as steel. Standing in the front door, Kathryn opened her hatch with the remote, and I got Luke out and leashed him up. We walked down Miss Etta's driveway, and I looked down the road, careful to note how far I could see.

Luke and I crossed over to the eastbound side. If I understood Miss Etta correctly, she saw the bus stop at a place where no houses lined the road. She saw two men get on the bus and something—the driver?—come flying off.

If that was accurate, I should find something in the snow—tracks, signs of a scuffle, or maybe even Herb.

The hill dropped off more steeply after the road passed Etta's house. I wished I had something—even a walking stick—to help me keep my balance. I slid a couple of times, despite my good boots. I kept Luke on my right, away from traffic, praying that the reflective stripes on the back of my jacket would keep us from getting hit. Visibility was getting bad.

The gravel shoulder of the road was only about two feet wide, then there was a ditch about fifteen inches deep, running alongside the road. The far side of the ditch formed a steep bank and beyond that a hill. Or a mountain. A good incline, whatever it was, and heavily wooded.

Luke began pulling. He smelled something, something more than asphalt and gravel and dirt and snow. "Easy, buddy," I said, fighting to keep my footing on the slippery slope. From the end of Miss Etta's driveway, I'd spotted a tree, a tall pine in amongst the oaks and poplars and maples. That was as far as I thought she could see because of the curve in the road, and that's where I headed. Short of that, about twenty feet, Luke got more animated. He dropped down into the ditch, pulling me with him. I hadn't

even told him to "seek," but I recognized the signs. He was on a
search with me along for the ride.

The bottom of the ditch was ragged with rocks and sticks and
limbs and leaves. I stumbled, and at that moment, Luke surged
ahead, jerking his leash out of my hand. I fell, hitting my face on
a rock. I looked up, used my sleeve to wipe the snow out of my
eyes, and saw Luke, lying on the ground, looking at me.

Lying on the ground is his indication. Worse, it's his "human
remains" indication. I braced myself for what I'd see, pushed
myself to my feet, and stumbled forward.

A man. Lying in the ditch. On his back. Hands splayed out to
the side. The school bus driver?

I felt for a pulse in his wrist. None. I checked his carotid
artery. Nothing. I touched his cheek. Cold.

Dead.

Where were the kids?

19

I JERKED my phone out of my pocket and tried Scott again. No signal. I texted him and Kathryn. I found out later, I'd accidentally copied Nate on it. I texted 911 on the off chance the sheriff's office had that capability set up.

I remembered Luke's reward. "Good boy, good boy, Luke!" I released him, found a stick, and threw it for him. He'd done his job and found a cadaver. Good boy. And how sad.

Luke was returning with the stick when I heard a sound. I turned and saw headlights coming straight for me. *What?* A truck, one of those big, massive pickups, was whipping back and forth, out of control on the slippery hill, its headlights swinging through a curtain of snow like a madman trying to beat his way onstage.

"Look out!" I screamed to Luke. I scrambled up the hill, grabbing trees and bushes to pull myself up. "Luke, Luke!" I slipped, fell, and scrambled again on my knees, desperate to get away from that truck. A horn blared. I half-stood, pushed off a rock, and pulled myself up past one more tree, and then I heard the truck slam into something solid below me.

It came to a stop not ten feet behind me. I heard the hiss of steam escaping. I could smell gas and oil and hot brakes. Then I heard a tree begin to creak. To my horror I saw a tree leaning, leaning straight away from that truck. I moved to the right, fell, and covered my head with my hands, screaming for Luke. Branches whipped me, flailing at my back, as the tree, groaning, hit the ground with a loud THUD!

"Luke!" I pushed through the branches covering me, rising to my knees. "Luke!"

He came to me, working his way through the fallen tree, jumping over the trunk, pushing through the branches. I grabbed him, tears coming to my eyes. "Oh, Luke! Are you okay?"

He was. God is good. So good. The trunk of that tree landed three feet to my left. My shoulders, bruised by a large branch, still worked. My back, my hips, my legs ... I was okay. Battered, but okay. And so was Luke.

I heard the "whoop-whoop" of a siren. A police car, lights flashing, pulled up behind the truck. I groped for Luke's leash and stumbled down the hill. The driver of the pickup was out of the car, talking to the officer. Both were shocked to see me emerge from the woods. Then I told them about the body.

THANKFULLY, the deputy's radio worked. Scott and the sheriff arrived within fifteen minutes. I could see Scott was shaken, feel it by the way he held me.

"I need to get her to a hospital to get checked out," he said, looking at the sheriff, lights flashing on both of their faces.

Sheriff McCormick shook his head. "Nearly sixty miles to the closest one. That's an hour and fifteen, without the snow complicatin' things."

I spoke up for myself. "Scott, I'm okay. Really. Everything works. I'm a little bruised, that's all."

"Tell me again how all this went down," the sheriff said to me.

So I did, starting with me checking out Miss Etta, her telling me about the men, something falling out of the bus, me walking down the road to check whether I could see anything, and Luke finding the body.

"The truck nearly killing us, that was a bonus, thrown in at no extra cost."

"So you're saying Herb's body is under that truck."

"There's a body of a man under the truck. You'll have to determine who it is. He was dead when I found him. I'm a certified EMT. I checked several ways." I began trembling, more from stress than cold, I think, although I was wet from being on the ground. Oh, and a tree falling on me.

Scott noticed me shaking. "Why don't you get in the car?"

"No." I didn't want to miss anything.

"You got a blanket in your vehicle?" he asked the sheriff.

"I'll get one," a deputy said. He returned seconds later with a rough but warm blanket. Scott wrapped it around me.

The sheriff looked at Scott. "So why would two men hijack a bus with kids on it? And where would they take them?"

Scott's jaw was tight. "I don't know, Sheriff. But if they've been kidnapped, the FBI will help, if you want us."

Things moved more slowly out in rural areas. I could see Sheriff McCormick's resistance on his face. He wasn't ready to call in the feds. But Scott is, well, Scott. "I know you'll want to stay ahead of this, Sheriff. You've already got the pickup driver over there on his phone." He nodded that direction.

I frowned. *How's his phone working? Must be a different carrier.* I felt a little jealous.

"At the very least," Scott said, continuing, "that guy is telling somebody about the dead body next to the road. And if he heard us talking about the school bus, well, it'll be all over the county soon."

Sheriff McCormick hitched up his pants. "We sure don't need folks panickin'."

"Why don't we go back to your office and strategize?"

"The strategy is to find 'em!"

"Yes, sir. But you're going to need organization and support to do that. If this is a kidnapping, it'll blow up quicker than you think."

I started to say something, but my teeth were chattering. Scott looked at me. "How about I get someone to take you to the B&B?"

"I don't want to be left out of this," I said.

"You need to get warmed up and take care of Luke. Then you can jump back in."

That made sense. "Okay. You're right. I need my car."

He raised his eyebrows.

"All my stuff is in it."

"All right. We will make that happen." He looked back at the sheriff. "Meet you at your office in half an hour?"

"Yep. The small white building next to the courthouse." He yelled for a deputy. "Jason, take these people and their dog back to the school so they can get their car. Then bring Agent Cooper to my office."

"Yes, sir."

As we walked to the deputy's car I heard the sheriff giving other orders. *You stay with the body. You call the medical examiner.* He was going to be unusually busy tonight.

About three inches of snow had fallen. The hill was super slippery. I wasn't sure we were going to get up it, but the deputy took it slow and we made it. I hadn't seen a truck spreading sand or salt the whole time we'd been there on the side of the road. I wondered how much snow mitigation they did up here. Did they plow? Use salt? I guessed I'd find out.

By the time we got back to the school I'd talked Scott into taking me back to Miss Etta's instead of the B&B. "I don't want to be isolated there," I said. "I can shower and eat at Etta's and stay in the loop." I had a feeling Kathryn Grace would spend the night there.

He agreed, reluctantly. I texted Kathryn, and she urged me to come. So we picked up my Jeep, and the deputy followed us to Miss Etta's to take Scott back to the sheriff's office. "Keep me posted!" I said, as Scott left.

As soon as I stepped into the warmth of Miss Etta's house I avalanched. Fatigue swept over me like warm syrup. I could see Miss Etta dozing in her chair. What I wouldn't give for a nap. I nodded her direction. "How is she?"

"Good," Kathryn whispered. "She was chatting away until a few minutes ago."

"I'll check her vitals again as soon as I get cleaned up."

"What happened down there?" Kathryn whispered.

"Let's go in the kitchen."

I took off my boots and we walked back there. "Does she have an old towel?" I asked.

Kathryn grinned. "Everything's old!" She went to the back and reemerged a few minutes later with a faded light-blue towel. I wiped down Luke. Thankfully, he was mostly wet, not muddy.

"Where's her laundry room?" I asked.

"In the basement. I worry about her navigating those stairs all the time. Here—I'll take the towel. What else do you need?"

"I need to feed Luke, and I need a shower."

"And food for yourself probably."

I really didn't feel like eating anything. "I'll feed Luke first."

While Kathryn ran the towel downstairs I fed Luke. I had a three-day supply of kibble in my SAR bag. If we stayed longer than that, I'd have to scramble to find more. While Luke crunched his dinner, I told Kathryn what we'd found down the hill. The shock on her face didn't surprise me.

"Was it Herb?" she asked.

"I don't know. It was the body of a fiftyish man dressed in dark-blue work pants and a parka. He was mostly bald and had a wedding ring on."

"That sounds like Herb. Poor man." Kathryn sank into a chair. "What could have happened to those kids?" Tears glistened in her eyes.

"How many are in your classes?"

"Of the nine, four are. Two thirteen-year-olds, Eric and Michael. Then a girl, Katie, also thirteen, and a boy, Jamie, who is fourteen. Why would anyone want to take them?"

I could think of several reasons, none of them good. "Scott's helping the sheriff. They'll find them." I stood up. "Miss Etta won't mind if I take a shower?"

"No, but there's only one bathroom."

"I'll be quick. Are you okay with Luke?"

"Yes. We'll be fine."

I took a super-fast shower. The hot water washing over me felt like a hug. By the time I redressed and left the bathroom, I could hear a man talking in the living room.

I discovered the man's voice belonged to a deputy, who had come to take a statement from Miss Etta. I quickly intervened. I really wanted to check her again. "Hi, I'm Jess Cooper. I'm an EMT. Could I take her vitals before you begin?"

"Sure."

I opened my medic bag and knelt down before my patient. "How are you feeling, Miss Etta?"

"Fine. I don't know what all the fuss is about."

"Let me look in your eyes." I clicked on my penlight.

She frowned. "Your hair is wet, chil'!"

"Yes ma'am."

"You're gonna catch your death."

"I hope not, ma'am. Can you follow my finger with your eyes?" I moved my finger across her field of vision and watched her eyes track it. "Good. Now let me check your blood pressure." I attached the cuff to her frail arm and inserted my stethoscope under it. I squeezed the bulb over and over until the cuff grew tight.

"Land, chil'!" she said.

"Hold on." I began releasing the pressure, noted the systolic, then the diastolic pressure. "Looks good, Miss Etta," I said, removing the cuff. I listened to her heart and her lungs. I noted her pulse. Then I closed my bag and rose to my feet. "She's fine."

"I tol' you that afore!" Miss Etta said.

I smiled at her spunk and made room for the deputy. Kathryn Grace and I listened as he began asking questions—her name, age, and address for the record, and then he asked her what had happened that day.

"What do you mean what happened? I got up and ate my breakfast like I always do. Had a cup of tea. Read my Bible."

The deputy looked confused.

"Miss Etta," Kathryn said, crouching down next to her chair, "he means this afternoon. When you saw the men."

"Oh, that." She looked at Kathryn quizzically. "Was that today?"

"Yes, Miss Etta."

The older woman frowned. Pursed her lips. "Okay. That. I like to take a nap when the sun comes 'round right through those windows." She gestured toward the front windows. "Feels right cozy. But there weren't no sun today, 'cause it were clouded up. Looked like snow for sure to me. Smelled like snow. So when I couldn't sleep, I rose up and went over there to see.

"Sure enough, snow coming down like cotton balls fallin' from heaven. Big, fluffy flakes. I went to the back to use the restroom." She held up her hand. "You don't need to put that in your report."

"Yes ma'am."

"When I come back out here, the flakes were fine, comin' down hard, like rice. 'Now that'll last,' I tol' myself. I sat down and took up my sewing. The next time I got up, I looked out, and what do I see? Two men trompin' down the road. And they look like those men I saw afore.

"'Now what are those men up to?' I asked myself. And I determined to watch 'em. I didn't want them circlin' 'round, coming through the woods to my back."

"What'd they look like, ma'am? Can you describe 'em?"

Miss Etta frowned. "One was short, and one was tall. Both of 'em skinny. They could use some meat on their bones. They had on blue jeans and boots and heavy dark coats. And knit hats pulled down hard. I remember one of 'em was bright orange, like a hunting cap. T'other was blue or black.

"The one with the orange hat, he looked like he was carryin' somethin' like this." She cradled her arm. "Like a baby, only I knew it prob'ly weren't no baby, not in that weather. They kept goin' down the road. I decided to keep my eye on 'em by pretendin' to get my mail. I put on my boots and my coat and walked down my lane. Only I forgot my walkin' stick. Or my cane. I made it down all right and was able to see 'em most of the way down the hill. I saw the school bus stop. The two men got on, and somethin' come flying out the door. Maybe Herb.

"Scared me, it did. When I tried to come back up the lane, daggone it, I fell. Hit my head. Musta knocked me out a little.

"Thank God that nosey Miz Warner 'cross the street keeps watchin' me. I think she called you, honey, didn't she?" She patted Kathryn Grace's hand.

"Yes, she did."

Suddenly, there was a knock at the front door. Luke started barking. "I'll get it," I said.

But before I reached it, the door opened and a voice called, "Momma?"

20

MY HEART JUMPED when I heard that voice. Laura! I shot Kathryn Grace a look. She instantly understood.

"Come in!" I said, opening the door wider, my hand on Luke's collar.

Laura walked in, followed by Nate. I kept my eyes on Laura.

"Jess? What are ..." She didn't finish. She'd seen the people in the living room. A look of confusion came over her, then shock.

I took the lead. "Laura, this is Deputy Green. He was taking a statement from Miss Etta. And this ... this is Kathryn Grace McCaskill. She's been a big help to your mom."

You'd have to be blind not to see the resemblance between Laura and Kathryn. They were the same height. They had the same build, same hair and coloring. I felt like I was seeing a miracle unfold right in front of me. Mother and daughter reunited after thirty years.

Laura didn't see it that way. She started to turn, like she was going to go back out the front door. Nate put his arm around her, blocking her move. By the look on his face, he was seeing the miracle too.

"Laura, honey, is that you?" Miss Etta called.

"Yes, Momma."

"Well come here, chil', where I can see you."

Laura had no choice. She moved toward her mother, avoiding eye contact with Kathryn. And Kathryn, wise beyond her years, acted graciously. She left Etta's side, came toward me, and shook Nate's hand. "I'm Kathryn. I'm guessing you're going to spend the night."

"Yes, ma'am." He rubbed Luke's side as my dog, overjoyed, turned circles around him.

Kathryn looked at me. "Well, Miss Etta won't need us then. How about we move up to my house?"

"Perfect. I'll grab my gear."

The deputy left. I briefly explained to Laura about her mother's fall. "I've checked her twice," I said. "Nothing seems broken, and I don't think she has a concussion. I think she'll be fine." Then I turned to her mother. "Goodbye, Miss Etta."

"Goodbye, honey."

I gathered my things. Nate followed me out to the front porch. "Jess, I'm sorry. I been tryin' to help her get through this. It's hard. Her gettin' angry at you, that weren't right. I know it hurt you."

"Not as much as you ignoring me."

He looked down. "I'm sorry. I ain't never seen her like this. Shame's got her by the throat. Long-buried shame. So she's lashing out. But she's my wife. She's touchy 'cause she's hurtin'. I got to help her come to terms with it."

I should have softened, been sympathetic, expressed my forgiveness. I didn't. My heart was an ice ball in my chest.

"I'm your brother, Jess. I love you and I always will. Jus' right now, she needs some space. And she needs me." He hugged my stiff body goodbye. "Why you here, anyway?"

I told him about Kathryn's concerns about a student, about Scott's meeting with the principal, and then about the missing school bus. Nate's face grew serious. Concerned. "Let me know if I can help."

I looked over his shoulder toward his Tahoe. "Did you bring the dogs?"

"No. Amanda's looking after them and the hosses."

Amanda? Another surprise. "I need to go. My hair is freezing up."

"Okay," Nate bent down and patted my dog. "Goodbye, buddy." He straightened up and looked at me, the porch light shining in his bright blue eyes.

I turned and walked away.

I FOLLOWED Kathryn to her house. The still unplowed road remained slippery but passable. I tried to focus on what Kathryn might be feeling so I could be a friend to her when we got to her house. But the image of Nate's bright blue eyes kept intruding, eyes that had searched my heart so many times, eyes that held nothing but compassion and wisdom and grace toward me.

I'd walked away. Now who had the unforgiving heart?

I blamed the cold weather when I sniffed.

Kathryn's home came into view. Decorated by the storm, it looked like a frosted house in a snow globe. Gorgeous.

I parked in her driveway and let Luke out. He immediately rolled in the snow, then stood and shook off.

"Why don't you come in through the back?" Kathryn called out as she unlocked the door.

"Will do!" I grabbed Luke's bag and shut the back. "Come on, buddy." I found the latch to the gate on the short, white fence and let us in. Then I led Luke to the door of the sunroom built onto the back of the house where Kathryn waited for us with a couple of old towels.

"Whew!" I said, walking into the warmth. "There's no sign of that letting up." She didn't respond. I looked at her closely. "How are you doing?"

"I don't know." She shook her head. "Too much going on in my head."

"Let me dry him off. I'll be in shortly."

I hung my jacket up on a hook right inside the door and used a towel to dry Luke off. I removed my boots, set them aside, and pulled Luke's water dish out of his pack. I filled it at the kitchen sink, took it back to him, and told him to lie down on the small rug in the sunroom. "Wait here," I said, and then I went inside.

I found Kathryn in the kitchen. She'd changed out of her teaching clothes, but instead of putting on sweats or lounge wear, she'd dressed in snow gear. She looked at me. "I'm heating up soup for us. And I'm making chili that I can put in the Crock-Pot. We can take it to the sheriff's office for anybody who needs it."

Like Scott.

"Great idea," I said. "How can I help?"

"Open those cans and chop up the onion."

"Got it."

While we worked, we talked about the elephant in the room. "I'd like to tell you," I began, "how I know Nate and Laura, and why I didn't tell you before."

She said okay, so I gave her a short version of our story. "When you told me Etta might be your grandmother, I thought maybe Laura had a sibling who'd had a child. The next time I saw them, I told her that I'd met you. I thought she'd be reassured that this 'Kathryn Grace' who'd been visiting her mother was a safe person. Instead, she was furious—at me!"

"Because her secret had been revealed."

"Yes. I had no idea it was *her* secret."

"I can understand her shock. Thirty years ago there was a lot of shame around unwed pregnancy."

"She was fifteen."

"I know." Kathryn stirred the ground beef browning in the cast-iron pot. "Obviously, that was not the way I'd imagined meeting my mother."

"I thought you handled it well. Graciously."

"I'm not angry. I have been praying about this for a long time. Laura doesn't owe me anything. I grew up with two wonderful parents who loved me very much." She turned back to the food, adding onions to the beef. "Maybe she'll want a relationship. Maybe she won't. Either way, I'm going to trust God with it."

I felt the warm rush of conviction spread over me. I turned so Kathryn wouldn't see me blushing, embarrassed by my own relentless anger at Laura and at Nate. When would I stop demanding people treat me the way I wanted? When would I actually trust God with my relationships?

"Right now," Kathryn went on, "I'm worried about those kids." She tapped the spoon on the side of the pot and added the beans and tomatoes and corn that I'd opened. "This is no simple accident. That bus did not slide off the road into a farm field or down into a ravine like we'd like to believe. They would have found it by now. Those kids—my kids—are in danger. I have to help them. I'll worry about Laura later."

You go, girl.

21

WHEN TWO YOUNG men jumped onto their bus, the kids thought Mr. Herb was giving them a ride in the snow. That perception changed when the men jerked him out of his seat and threw him off the bus. Girls screamed and boys widened their eyes as they saw him fall, hard, in the snow and lie there motionless, a crimson stain pooling around his head.

"You kids sit still and shut up," one of the hijackers yelled, standing in the aisle.

Instinctively, a seventh grader way in the back, Michael "Scout" Jacobson, dove under the seat in front of him. Short and wiry, his ability to scamper over the tops of the playground equipment and climb trees made him famous, as did his willingness to prank substitute teachers by hiding in small places.

Scout's friend, Eric "the Red" Robertson, quietly slipped his jacket over Scout, hiding him.

"Now listen up." The hijacker, who the kids quickly dubbed "Mullet," displayed a handgun. "No one's going to get hurt. As soon as your parents cooperate, we'll let you go. But if you give us any trouble," he said, waving his gun, "I don't mind shootin'."

The bus lurched as the other man put it in gear. Mullet had to grab on to the back of a seat to maintain his balance. "Any you kids got phones?"

Only two girls raised their hands. Phones were too expensive for most families. Plus, cell service in the mountains wasn't reliable.

"Nice. Let me see 'em." They handed them over. "Drop that window, boy," Mullet said to a kid in a red coat. The boy did as he was told, and Mullet threw the phones out. A kid up front who everyone called "Bean" laughed. Eric thought that was mean.

"How many kids are there?" the driver yelled over his shoulder.

"Lemme count. Eight, there's eight kids. Three girls, five boys."

"What are you going to do with us?" an older boy near the front asked.

"Jus' take you for a little ride is all," Mullet answered.

"You can't do that," a small blond-haired boy said.

"Yeah, our parents will be waiting for us," another said.

"They're gonna come look for us!"

"Shut up!" Mullet yelled again.

A girl near Eric started crying. "Shhh, shhh," her brother, sitting next to her, said. "Don't cry. Think." The boy, Jamie, glanced over at Eric, who appeared to be studying. Eric caught his eye, and glanced down hard toward Scout, hidden below the seat. Jamie got it. He gave a slight nod, then yawned and stretched to cover his movement.

The driver was clearly not used to driving a school bus, especially on snow-covered mountain roads. He took a turn too fast, and the bus skidded toward the trees. The kids screamed. A small girl fell into the aisle. The driver had to fight to regain control. Mullet fell hard to the right, nearly losing his gun. He cursed. "Watch it, Kevin!" he yelled.

Eric wrote "Kevin" in the margin of his book, adding it to the detailed descriptions of the men he'd already written there, as well as a timeline and the bus's route. He wrote a note on another page. WE NEED A PLAN. Then he passed the book to Jamie and said, "Here you go."

"Hey! What are you doing?" Mullet yelled.

"We're studying. We have a test tomorrow, sir." Jamie said. He added, "We're in the same class."

They weren't. Jamie was in ninth grade and Eric, who looked older, was in eighth. It was a signal to the other kids on the bus. They were making a plan.

22

IN HALF AN HOUR Kathryn and I were back on the road. Driving carefully, we made it to the sheriff's office in twenty minutes. We'd brought both cars for maximum flexibility. The two of us carried two big boxes of food inside, then we made a second trip for the Crock-Pot and Luke. I don't know which was the bigger hit, the chili or my dog.

The team had turned a large meeting room into a situation room. I suspect that was Scott's idea. Three computers and a printer lined one wall. The dispatch radio squawked from the corner. Maps and notepads covered tables, and a whiteboard with notes hung on a wall.

Scott suggested we make a small adjacent classroom into the food area, so Kathryn and I set that up. The food seemed to brighten the mood.

Luke walked around sniffing everyone, then found a place to lie down next to a wall. Every once in a while, a deputy would walk over to pet him, and his tail would thump. My dog loves cops. Gun oil is near the top of his favorite smells list, right up next to human remains. He's so friendly. I've told him before not to act so much like a golden retriever. It's embarrassing. Here I

have this tough-looking "police dog" who is really just an attention hound.

While they dug into the food, I asked Scott for an update.

"They haven't seen anything like this up here before," he said
in a low voice. "They've got state police on the way. I've encouraged them to use the resources of the FBI. They're not ready to
call in the feds. They're afraid of losing control."

"Was the body the school bus driver?" I asked.

"Yes, we've got a positive ID on that. He had no gunshot or
knife wounds. He apparently hit his head on a rock when he was
thrown out of the bus. It looks like he died of a fractured skull
and exposure. We'll know for sure after the ME has a look."

"How about the bus?" I asked.

"Haven't found it yet. Nor the kids."

"Who would want to take a bunch of students?" Kathryn
asked. "It's not like people up here have money, like they could
demand a big ransom. And you wouldn't traffic that many kids at
once, would you?"

"I wouldn't think so. We haven't seen that anywhere." Scott
ran his hand through his hair. "I don't know what's going on, but
parents are upset and scared. Look, why don't you two go back to
Kathryn's. Get some rest ..." He stopped when he saw the look we
were giving each other. "What?"

"We're not going anywhere," I said.

"Not 'til those kids are safe," Kathryn said. "No one here
knows those kids better than I do. I can help you look for motive
or establish profiles."

"And I doubt that anyone here has searched more than I
have." I raised my chin.

Scott actually blushed. "I'm sorry. I'm a Neanderthal." He
shook his head, grimacing at his own stupidity. He gestured
toward the situation room. "Please. We need your help."

I started to move that direction, but he put a hand on my arm
and stopped me. "I called Mike. Asked him to head this way."

I raised my eyebrows.

"I need someone from the bureau to back me up. I can trust Mike. Right now, I'm acting in an advisory capacity. But if something goes down, I'll need backup."

"Okay, good," I said. "He's a good guy."

"Yeah, he is."

The clock on the wall read 7:04 p.m. as we walked in the room. The bus was now three hours overdue. Parents were driving the roads, looking for the kids themselves. But half of them weren't making it. The roads were slippery, and two-wheel drive pickups were sliding. There was a two-hour wait for a tow countywide. Frustration was mounting. I heard the sheriff on the phone with the Virginia Department of Transportation, VDOT.

"We need plow and salt trucks now!" he said. "I know it's not your usual priority. Half the county's already slid off the road." He clicked off his phone, red-faced.

Within half an hour, Kathryn had created a datasheet listing every missing kid, parents' contact information, and everything she knew about that student. Mr. Chambers, the principal, filled in more. Scott went into profiler mode and began studying each kid. Then he expanded his search to the kid Kathryn had been concerned about to begin with.

"I'd like to talk to him," Scott said.

The sheriff cocked his head. "Hate to see you get stuck out there. How 'bout a phone call?"

Scott shook his head. "It's got to be in person." He'd told me he often could tell more from the nonverbal indications a subject gives than his words. "Give me your best driver and a four-wheel drive vehicle," he said. "I'll take a chance."

I hated that he was going out in the storm. But what could I say? He had to do his job. He had to see this kid to actually get a read on him.

Kathryn had given Scott the notebook that had triggered her concern to begin with. "I'll go with you, if it would help," she said, but Scott declined. "You'll be more help here," he told her, "but thank you."

Scott turned to me. "Mike should be here within the hour. Maybe you could introduce him to the sheriff and give him a tour. He's good with computers if there's a need to check websites or anything online. I'll be back as soon as I can."

"Okay, I can do that."

After checking to be sure the kid was at home, Scott and Deputy Mark Williams, a six-foot, square-jawed, cowboy-looking man, left. They had power bars, water, and blankets with them, as well as sand, a shovel, and a backup radio. I didn't want to even think about Scott shoveling snow. Not with a recent history of chest pains. But I didn't say anything. Scott does not like to be coddled any more than I do.

I did think of one thing. I dug the Garmin InReach out of my pack and gave it to him.

He grinned. "Fair enough." He slipped it in his cargo pocket and kissed me goodbye.

23

DEPUTY MARK WILLIAMS grew up in the county and had worked as a deputy for thirteen years. He knew the roads, hunted in the hills, and knew exactly how to get to Travis Parker's house. "It'd normally be about a fifteen-minute drive," he told Scott. "Today, it'll be more like thirty."

"What do you know about the family?"

Williams shook his head. "Dad walked out on 'em about a year ago. Mom works in the diner in town. Long hours. One kid, Travis. They got other kin scattered up and down these hollows. But they're pretty isolated, the two of them."

"Why'd the dad leave?"

"Who knows? I mean, does anybody really know what goes on inside a family?"

He was right about that, as Scott knew all too well. "Are you married, Mark?"

"Twelve years. My wife's a teacher."

"Kids?"

"Two." He glanced at Scott. "How 'bout you?"

"Married twice. This one's working." He felt a rush of gratitude for that. "Jess is my wife."

"Jess? The searcher?"

"Right. She used to be a deputy in Fairfax. Now she works as a private investigator and does volunteer K-9 search and rescue."

"So both of you in law enforcement?"

Scott grinned. "At least we knew what we were getting into."

The two-lane road they were on twisted left and right as it snaked up the mountain. It had no markings—no centerline and no side stripes. It hadn't been plowed, but the deputy's four-wheel drive SUV was handling it.

"Not many houses out here," Scott said.

"Not many jobs."

"Who owns all this land?"

"A lot of it was taken by the feds for parkland. What's privately owned is often family land, going back to the seventeen hundreds."

"They've kept it all those years?"

"A lot of 'em. As long as they can pay the taxes. They may have jobs in the city— Harrisonburg or Lexington. Staunton. Even DC. They keep the land and come out here and hunt. There's cabins scattered throughout these woods ... roughed in, no electricity. You can't see 'em from the road."

"Not tonight for sure," Scott said, staring at the snow in the headlights. Suddenly, a deer jumped out of the woods and onto the road. "Watch out!" He reached for the grab bar above the SUV door.

Williams downshifted, slowing just barely enough to avoid the doe. She scampered across the road and back into the woods.

"Good job," Scott said. "Whew. If you'd hit the brakes we would have slid."

"This ain't my first rodeo," Williams said. "We get that all the time. I'm always half-watching for 'em." He gestured forward. "About a mile to go, then a long driveway."

"What does it look like out there? Snow's about four inches maybe?"

"Yep. And still coming hard. Up here's our turn." Williams eased into a driveway on the right, a tiny track through the woods.

The SUV bounced on the path, filled with ruts and holes and rocks, rarely maintained and barely passable. And it was a long driveway too. Finally, Scott saw a light. A small house, what looked to be barely more than a trailer, appeared ahead. Williams turned around before he parked so the SUV would face out.

That was smart, Scott thought. Who knew how much more snow would accumulate while they were inside? "I'll want to talk to the boy alone," Scott said.

"Yes, sir." Williams knocked on the door. A thin, haggard-faced woman opened it. "Ms. Parker, Deputy Williams from the sheriff's office. Can we come in please?"

Irene Parker didn't respond, she just opened the door. The two-men stepped inside. Scott closed the door. "Ms. Parker," Deputy Williams said, "this here's Special Agent Cooper from the FBI. He wants to talk to your boy."

Her eyes widened in alarm. "Travis? What for?" She took a step back.

"Ma'am," Scott said, keeping his voice low, "he's not in trouble. I'm not here to arrest him. I only want to talk to him."

"You're not taking my boy!"

"No, ma'am. He's not going anywhere." Scott glanced around. "Are there guns in the house?"

"You think I live out here by myself without a gun? 'Course I got guns."

"Are they secured?"

"They ain't gonna help me locked up somewhere."

"Does he have any in his room?"

"Travis? No."

Scott didn't necessarily believe her. "Is your boy home? Can we talk?"

"Travis! Get out here."

The child that emerged from the back of the house didn't look fourteen. Scott would have guessed eleven. Maybe twelve. Short and wiry, he had brown hair cut close on the sides and long on top, and small, dark eyes that looked like two dots. He had on jeans that were ripped at the knees and an oversized sweatshirt. "Yeah, Mom?" he said, eyeing the two men.

That sweatshirt was big enough to hide a gun. Scott alerted on that right away.

"These men want to talk to you."

"Hi, I'm Scott." He squatted down to get eye-to-eye with the boy. "Can we talk?"

"'Bout what?"

"You're a pretty good artist."

Travis shrugged.

"Would you tell me about some of these drawings?"

The kid shrugged again.

"You're not in trouble. I only want to talk."

Scott shot the deputy a pointed look. "Let's sit over here at the table while Deputy Williams and your mom talk, okay?"

Scott turned to the mom. "Can he have a Coke?" He held up a can he'd brought from the sheriff's office.

"'Course."

Scott joined the kid at the small kitchen table, grabbing two glasses out of the open cupboard first. "You like Coke?"

"Sure."

Scott poured three-quarters of it in the kid's glass. "Someone at your school found your notebook. We were talking about some of your artwork. Can you tell me about this?" Scott pointed first to a picture of a house.

The kid shrugged. "It's just a house."

"I noticed you put a lot of detail in it. That's good." Scott moved on to some of the other drawings—a knife, a deer that had been shot, what looked like a war. Then Scott pointed to something that looked like the earth burning. "What's going on here?"

By that time, the kid had begun to relax, to open up. "Global warming! See, that's the earth, and it's on fire, and everything's burnin' up." He looked at Scott. "On the news it says that we're gonna die from it."

Scott looked serious. "Well, it's true that one day all of us will die, one way or the other."

"My granddad died."

"Did he? How long ago?"

"A little over a year. Right afore my daddy left."

"Have you seen your dad since he left?"

Travis looked away. "Nope."

"That's hard, losing your dad and granddad at the same time."

"I woulda missed the whole hunting season if it hadn't been for Bean."

"Who's Bean?"

"My cousin. I stay with them sometimes when Momma has to work."

"How old is he?"

"Seventeen. When I go there, I have to take a different bus home from school. Then Momma comes and gets me after work."

"So he takes you hunting?"

"Yep. He says as soon as his ship comes in he's gonna buy me my own gun. I don't know about no ship, but he promised me a gun."

"Like this one?" Scott pointed to a drawing of an AR-15.

"Nah. A deer rifle. Like this." The boy pointed to a different picture.

Scott kept talking, asking him about different things. He opened to the page with really violent, almost macabre drawings. He asked about them, and Travis pulled back. "That ain't mine."

"These aren't your drawings?" The kid shook his head. "Then whose are they?"

"Bean. Bean drew that stuff." The kid flipped back a few pages and found a torn-out sheet that was folded. "And this too." The picture showed a school bus and kids. The bus was tilting, like it was going off the road. And kids were flying everywhere.

Scott stiffened. "What's going on here?"

"I dunno. Bean drew it while he was talking."

"On his phone?"

"Nah. On the computer."

"Tell me about that."

"I was at Aunt Mina's one day. And Bean was talking to somebody on the computer. He had a headset on. I couldn't hear the other people. Only him. He was saying something about the school bus. And he was laughin' and saying, 'yeah, man' and stuff like that." Travis shook his head. "I was waitin' for him to get off, 'cause we were going to play on the Switch. I don't know what he was talkin' about. But kids get mean on the bus sometimes. Bean's mean too."

"How? How is he mean?"

"He picks on younger kids. Pulls their hats over their face. Gives them wedgies. He doesn't do it to me because we're kin."

"What do you think about that?"

"Kids don't like sittin' with him."

"You have a computer?"

The kid snorted. "No. We don't even got Internet."

Scott took a deep breath. "What's Bean's real name?"

"Thomas. Thomas Jones."

"What bus does he ride?"

"Bus 16."

24

MIKE ARRIVED while Scott was gone. He gave me a hug, and I introduced him to Kathryn Grace.

"Kathryn Grace," he said, savoring the name, his eyes twinkling. She blushed, disarmed by his easy charm. I have to admit, Mike is a good-looking guy in a Tom Cruise kind of way.

"Come on, I'll introduce you to the sheriff," I said, diverting him. We walked across the situation room. "Sheriff McCormick, this is Special Agent Mike Perez. Scott's friend. He's a terrific investigator, and Scott says he's good with computers."

McCormick looked him up and down and extended his hand. "'Preciate you comin' all the way up here," he said.

"How can I help?"

The two of them went off to confer in the sheriff's office. I could tell Mike was exercising his investigative skills—discreetly —when they emerged, and the sheriff asked, "What's the ground clearance on those buses?"

For the record, I'd asked the same thing but had gotten shrugs all around.

"It varies. I'd say no more than seventeen inches. I think this one's one of the shorter buses," a deputy named Chet Graves responded, "but I'm not sure."

"Can we get an exact description, make, model, year, height, length, and ground clearance on Bus 16?" Mike asked.

"Yes, sir," Graves said. "My cousin runs the bus garage. Let me see if I can get ahold of him."

"I'd like to go over the maps," Mike said.

"Sure," the sheriff responded. "The girls been working on them."

"Come on, girls," Mike said, fighting back a grin. "Show me where we are."

So Mike, Kathryn, and I began pouring over the street maps and the topographic maps. Mike was logical, and Kathryn had lived in the area long enough that she could picture some of the areas we were talking about. I was used to dealing with topo maps, so we made a good team.

We highlighted every possible place we could see where a bus could leave the road. Then we talked about breaking the area into searchable sections. At that point, I wished Nate were there. He had more experience at this than I did.

Deputy Graves came back with the details on the bus as well as a stock photo of that model. He looked at our search maps and made a few suggestions. So did the sheriff. Soon we had a plan mapped out.

Then the door opened, and two state troopers walked in, snow on their hats and shoulders. "Got here as soon as we could, Sheriff," one of them said. "Those roads are rough."

"Glad you're here. Come over here, and I'll tell you what we got goin' on."

I looked at Mike and Kathryn. "I'm going to take Luke outside. I'll be back in a little while."

. . .

I PUT on my coat and leashed up my dog. Outside the snow was still falling, sheets of it dropping from the bleak winter sky. The soft lights of downtown plus the snow made the town look like a Christmas village.

No one else was around. I let Luke off-leash and he watered the bushes, then went running around, plowing through the snow with his nose, eating some in big chomps. We walked a few blocks. He roamed freely while I thought and prayed about the missing kids, the family of the deceased driver, my husband, and then all of us working on the search.

I couldn't say or even think the word "search" without thinking of Nate. He'd taught me virtually everything I know about SAR. He'd been a steady friend, a trusted confidant, for years. In my anger at Laura, I'd tossed all that out like it was nothing.

How many times had he forgiven my stubbornness, my self-centeredness, my irritability? How often had he given me grace for the sake of our relationship? Could I do the same for Laura, who had acted badly because she was drowning in emotions from her own trauma?

I pulled out my phone. On Main Street, on a slight knoll next to the library, I caught a signal. One bar. I pressed his number.

"Hey," I said when he answered. "It's me."

"Hey."

"I'm sorry I was angry."

"I understand. I really do," he said.

"I know Laura's struggling right now. I hope we can get back on sure footing."

"I hope so too," he said. "How's it going up there?"

I told him what we'd done and the plan we'd made. "I'm worried I'm missing something," I confessed. "I work better with you."

He asked me some questions. I gave him my best answers. Then there was silence. "Can you come get me?" he said. "I won't leave Laura here without a car, but if I can hitch a ride, I'll come help."

My heart jumped. "Yes! How soon can you be ready?"

"Fifteen minutes."

I GAVE HIM TWENTY. I was surprised to see him emerge from Miss Etta's house with his SAR pack in hand. "Yeah, I brought it with me, even without the dogs. It's easy enough to throw in the car. You never know when you'll need it."

"And your dogs don't eat your house when they see you leaving with it?" I asked. We both grinned at the memory. The first time I did that, Luke scratched up the door, chewed the carpet, and ate half the doorframe of my landlord's house. Nate helped me fix the damage.

"How's Scott doing?" Nate asked.

I glanced over at him.

"Chest pain?" he asked.

"Not having it as far as I know."

"And you?"

"I'm okay."

"What happened to your face?"

"I fell on a rock."

He was silent for a few minutes. Then he said, "You know, I think the pandemic did a lot more to us than we realize."

"What do you mean?"

"All the mask wearing. The isolation. The stress. Working from home. Fightin' each other over vaccines or no vaccines. I think in some ways we forgot how to be a people living together." He shifted his weight in the seat.

My Jeep climbed the hill on the way back to town. I drove gently, trying hard not to spin the tires. At the same time, I was wondering what prompted Nate's philosophizing. His next words were a clue.

"I seen it when I lived up here." He gestured. "People livin' in the hollers. You could grow up two hills over and never know each other. You don't learn how to get along. The isolation caused splits, fragmentation. Like the Hatfields and McCoys. All that fightin' and ain't nobody can remember how it started. I think that's what we're seein' now. A fragmented society. Everybody livin' in their own holler. We've forgotten how to get along." He paused again. "That trickles down, even to friendships."

Ah, got it. He was talking about me and Laura.

"The one thing that does spread easy in these hills is gossip, and along with it, shame. Shame's toxic. Like jimsonweed."

I had no idea what jimsonweed was, but I got the picture. "How is it toxic?"

"The devil uses it to hurt us. Demoralize us. Split us from each other. What we need to remember is there's a remedy. Jesus bore our shame, along with our sin. Carried it for us on the cross. We don't need to carry it no more."

... he made him to be sin who knew no sin ... I glanced at Nate.

"Shame's like sin. If you don't process it right, it festers in you. Makes you touchy."

"Everybody seems touchy right now," I said.

"Even when we're all touchy we got to figure out how to be a people again." Nate let that comment ride for a minute. Then he said, "When I was a kid, I couldn't never figure out how porcupines made love." He rubbed his jaw.

I burst out laughing.

"What?" Nate said.

I shook my head, grinning. "I've missed you."

We arrived at the sheriff's office. As I put the Jeep in PARK, Nate reached over and put his hand over mine. I turned to look at him and saw his eyes shining in the building's lights.

"This ain't my story, it's Laura's, but I'll tell you a little," he said, his voice serious. A band of tension tightened over my shoulders. "She was fifteen, young and innocent. Nobody talked about sex in those days. Her daddy had left her and Miss Etta a couple years afore. She had a new stepfather takin' Miss Etta's attention. In a way, she felt like she'd lost both parents.

"An older boy, already graduated, started courtin' her. Treatin' her like a queen. Tellin' her she was beautiful. Takin' her places, to parties and such. She was thirsty and she fell for it. Afore you know it, she was pregnant. Didn't even know what was goin' on." He paused and took his hand off mine, closing his eyes and shaking his head as he processed once again this apparently familiar story.

"How'd they handle it? Her parents?"

Nate's jaw tightened. He stared forward. "The way most folks back then did. Laura got sent to a home for unwed mothers, over in West Virginia somewhere. Didn't know nobody. Didn't know nothin' about birthin'. The people there took care of her physical needs, but didn't care a spit about her loneliness, her fear, nothin'. Anything she learned she got from the other girls, and half of it weren't true.

"She spent five months there absorbin' the shame 'til it got into her bones, into her marrow, and became part of her. "Goin' through labor was painful, terrifying, but she says the minute she saw that baby, she fell in love. She got to see her right after she was born, got to hold her and look in her eyes, but that was it. They took that baby right out of her arms, and the next day, that baby was gone, adopted out, and Laura was left alone, consumed by grief."

My Jeep was cooling off but the shivering in my body was from Laura's story, not the cold. "Did she get to approve the adoptive parents? Or meet them?" I asked.

"None of that. The onliest thing is, she asked that they be believers, and the social worker promised he'd try."

"Well, he was true to his word," I said, "from what Kathryn told me. Oh, Nate! What a horrible story! No wonder she's so sensitive!"

"And shocked to her core. I been prayin' she'll trust the Lord that Kathryn showin' up is for the good. I'd 'preciate it if you would, too."

"Of course!" I said. Then I asked the question that had been nagging at me. "Did you know all this, back then?"

"I were a couple years ahead of her in school. When she disappeared, I guessed what was goin' on. When she came back, she was quiet, shy. I dated her in my senior year. Was real careful with her, you know?"

I nodded. I could easily imagine he would be.

"But then my own life took a turn. I left home and joined the Marine Corps. Heard she got married. And you know the rest." He put his hand on my shoulder. "Thank you for bringin' us together again. That was your doin'."

"God's, I think."

He grinned. "Preach it, sister! Now we'd better get on with this." Nate hesitated, his hand on the car door. "Keep this to yourself for now, okay?"

I nodded. "I will."

I got Luke out of the back and we walked inside, my knees wobbly from Laura's story. I introduced Nate to the sheriff. "He's better at figuring out how much time each search segment should take," I explained. "Plus he grew up around here."

That led to a three- or four-minute discussion of where Nate grew up, who his kin were, and how all that related to the sheriff's background. Then Nate asked to see the topographic maps. As I watched Kathryn pointed out the search sections we'd done, I couldn't shake Laura's story and I prayed silently for their reconciliation.

Soon after, Scott returned, and I could tell by the look on his face, he knew his next move. Surprised Nate there, he greeted him with a strong handshake. He thanked Mike for coming, gave me a quick hug, then disappeared into the sheriff's personal office.

When he came back out, he had a typed affidavit in his hand. He gave it to a deputy to take to the local magistrate. The deputy returned with a search warrant for Thomas "Bean" Jones's home, computer, and cell phone, if any. Soon, he and another deputy were on their way to execute it.

"Travis isn't directly involved," Scott explained to us. "He's immature. His home doesn't have Internet, much less a computer. He doesn't have means or opportunity to be part of a bus hijacking. Most of those violent images were drawn by his cousin."

The sheriff approached us with two state troopers in tow. "Scott, introduce your colleagues."

Scott said, "This is Special Agent Mike Perez, FBI. He's a sharp investigator and works with me at BAU. And this is Nathan Tanner. He's an expert at K-9 search and rescue, plus he grew up around here."

"How'd you get involved with this?" a trooper asked Scott.

"Miss McCaskill here is a teacher. She got concerned when she found this notebook in school and called me." He showed them the notebook. "Mass shootings are my specialty. The FBI emphasizes prevention when it comes to school violence, and I had to agree with her; these drawings and essays indicate a lot of anger." Scott specifically didn't mention his interest in the climate change pictures Travis had drawn. "The school bus disappearance was coincidental to our visit. But I interviewed this kid. He's not the mastermind behind the bus disappearance, but his cousin may be involved. The sheriff's deputies are out executing a search warrant for his room and computer now."

"So, what? You think this bus has been hijacked?" a trooper asked.

"Yes."

"It didn't run off the road?"

"The driver was violently ejected from the bus. He died. We haven't found the bus yet, and it's now almost four hours overdue."

One of the troopers looked at me. "And you are ..."

The way he said it took me aback, like I was intruding in the boys' club and about to be kicked out. "I'm Jessica Cooper, Scott's wife," I said, like I needed his protection. What was wrong with me?

"She's a former detective and also an expert in search and rescue techniques," Scott added. "That's her dog over there." He gestured toward Luke, lying on the floor up against a wall.

"Wait, I know you," another trooper said. He was short but muscular, dark-haired with brown eyes. "You saved my nephew!"

Surprised, I looked from him to Scott and back again.

"Brody! He's my brother's boy."

That's when I noticed the name on his breastplate: Ward.

He stuck out his hand. "Dave Ward. Glad to meet you." I took his hand, and he pulled me into a hug. "Thank you! We love that boy."

"What'd she do?" the sheriff said.

Suddenly, we heard a loud pounding at the door.

"I'll tell you later," I said.

A deputy opened the door, and five angry fathers walked into the room. Some had rifles.

Every officer's hand went to his sidearm. My heart started pounding. I glanced at Scott. His face was taut. Instinctively, I looked for Kathryn. I edged toward her. I wasn't carrying, but I'd protect her if I could.

"Hold on, hold on here, boys," the sheriff said, walking toward them, hands raised. "What's going on?"

"We wanna know," a man with a red beard said, stepping forward, "what you're doing to find our kids!"

"You can't just come walking in here carrying weapons! You know that." The sheriff shook his head. "Now you put those guns back in your vehicles and then we'll talk."

"We don't want talk, we want action!" a dark-haired man yelled.

"I'll tell you what action we're taking *after* you put the guns down."

The tension in the room gripped all of us.

The sheriff lowered his hands. "After I tell you what we're doing, I'd like to hear your ideas. But I can't do that staring at a bunch of guns."

After a few minutes, the red-haired leader turned to the others. "Let's do it, boys. We want our kids, not a war."

With the guns stowed, the sheriff took the men into the room holding the food. He closed the door so I couldn't hear him, but I could imagine what he was telling them.

The tension quickly diffused. "That was scary," Kathryn said quietly.

"That could have been bad. The sheriff handled it perfectly."

"He's pretty popular from what I've heard."

With that situation under control, at least for now, I heard Scott ask a general question to the deputies and others near him. "If we found the kids right now," Scott asked, "what would we want done with them? Where would we take them, what would they need?"

Kathryn and I joined the group.

"Give 'em to their parents," a deputy said.

"Okay."

"Medical checks."

"Food."

"They'll need to get warm."

"They'll be scared," Kathryn said.

"All right. Medical care, food, warmth, trauma care, and their parents. Plus they'll need to be interviewed by deputies," Scott said. He looked at the school principal. "Mr. Chambers, how about you work with someone and figure out how and where to do that?"

"On it," Chambers responded.

"I can help with that," a deputy said, raising her hand. She was the only woman on the force that I'd seen, but I was glad they at least had one.

"Good," Scott said. "Now, you may not have news media in this town, but word's out, and we need to get information out to the community without revealing evidence we'll need if this goes to court. Plus, we need to interface with whatever reporter gets on this story as time goes on. There's a newspaper where? Staunton? Harrisonburg?"

A young, fair-haired deputy raised his hand. "Harrisonburg, sir. I've played that role before. I can handle that."

"Good." Scott looked around. "What else?"

"Tips," Kathryn said. "Somebody needs to handle tips from the public."

"Good point. I'll see if the sheriff can call in an extra dispatcher." Scott turned to me. "Jess, what do you suggest search wise?"

I straightened my back and addressed the group. "You've already done what we would call a hasty search. You've checked the school bus route and looked in the most likely places. Now it's time to dig in deeper. We need to find out exactly where the bus left the road. So let's start with the last known position. Where is the last place we know the bus was?"

"The place where the driver's body was found."

"Right. Now, we have to check every possible place the bus could have left the road from there. If the road branches off, we have to follow both branches."

A deputy raised his hand.

"Yes?"

"Ma'am, the snow's covered whatever tracks that bus left."

Of course. My mind went blank.

Nate picked it up. "So you'll need to look higher—at branches that have been broken or tree trunks gashed by the bus."

"Thanks, Nate. Got that?" I asked. I got some general nods in response. "Okay. We've broken the roads into segments. Study your segment. You need to check every lane, every power-line easement, every path in your segment that the bus could have been driven down. Could it be hidden in a barn? Or behind a barn? An old house? In a ditch? In the woods? If no one's checked the bridges, or looked down at the creeks, we need to do that. And you need to document everything."

"I can help with that," Kathryn said. "Do y'all use a spreadsheet for collecting data in complicated cases?" she asked the deputies.

They looked at each other. "No ma'am. The sheriff keeps track."

"We need a spreadsheet," I said.

"I'll set that up," Kathryn said.

I looked at Scott. "Those men the sheriff is talking to are not just going to sit and wait. What would you say if we pair each of them up with an officer, assign them an area, and send them out? That way we can use the manpower without risking an overreaction if they find the kids or if they get into a confrontation."

"Sounds good. But they leave their guns here."

The sheriff stuck his head out of the door. "Scott?"

My husband walked over to him. The sheriff said something to him in a voice too low for me to hear. I saw them going back and forth, conversing in low tones.

Scott came back to the group. "The sheriff wants help from the FBI. In the meantime, I like Jess's idea and so does the sheriff. Let's get going on that."

Everybody got busy. Out of the corner of my eye I saw Scott on the phone. I knew he'd call his immediate boss. I didn't expect him to also call Marcus Walker, the head of the Critical Incident Response Group. "I've got to cover my back," he told me later. "Plus, he'd be the one to get authorization for bringing in other field offices and RAs."

About that time, the sheriff emerged with the fathers from the back room. He assigned a deputy to each civilian. There was one extra deputy. Nate volunteered to go with him. The sheriff, after consulting with us, gave each team a section to search. We passed out packets—the description and stock photos of the bus, the description of the suspects, and the maps. "Be sure you look high for broken branches, skinned tree bark, or other indications a bus might have passed by," I reminded them.

The teams left, and we all took a deep breath. "I need a cup of coffee," Sheriff McCormick said.

Scott and I followed him into the back room. "Hostage Rescue is on a practice run in Northern California, but we're getting SWAT-trained agents from Northern Virginia and Richmond," he told the sheriff. "I told them we did not want an overwhelming show of force, sir. This is still your show. We're coming in to support you."

"How about equipment?" he asked.

"We can't use a plane or helicopters or even drones until the weather lifts."

"Hostage negotiators?"

"I can help you with that for now."

"I'm prepared to search on foot if we get indications of where the bus may have gone off the road," I said. The sheriff looked at me skeptically. "I'm used to searching in the mountains, and I have confidence in my dog."

Scott nodded. "I hope it doesn't come to that."

I looked at the sheriff. "You should notify the Virginia Department of Emergency Management. They'll call out SAR volunteers."

He frowned. "Tonight? In this weather?"

"Maybe they won't get here 'til morning, but I'd notify VDEM anyway and get them started in this direction."

"Does anybody around here have snowmobiles?" Mike asked.

"We don't, but some folks do. I'll see if I can gather some."

"Sheriff!" someone called from the outer room.

"I'd better see what that's about," he said, and he walked out.

"How are you holding up?" I asked my husband when we were alone.

"I'm okay."

"Chest pain?"

"No. How are you feeling?"

"I'm a little tired, but I'm ready to go if we need to search on foot."

"Did you eat?"

"I had some soup at Kathryn's." I didn't feel like eating, but I didn't want to tell him that.

"Better get something else down in case we need you." He hugged me.

The sheriff stuck his head in. Mike stood right behind him. "Scott, Thomas Jones's mother confirmed he's on that bus. We have his computer."

"Great! Can we get into it?"

"She was cooperative. We have what we need."

"Good. Mike, take over that job, okay?"

The men walked out, and I was left alone in a room that smelled of chili.

25

By the time the bus turned on to the nearly hidden farm lane, Eric had drawn a map of its route on a blank page in the front of his history book. He'd made note of the time spent on each road, before each turn, and of landmarks along the way. He'd carefully listed the mailbox numbers they'd passed, drawn the churches and houses in appropriate places, and had even depicted the gate they'd passed through at the top of the lane.

The lane went down a hill. The driver barely kept control, the bus lurching and sliding, shuddering to a stop, then starting again. The man cursed and swore as he fought the slippery hill. Three-quarters of the way down, he lost control. Kids screamed. Men yelled, and the bus slid sideways and slammed into a tree. Kids, backpacks, and books went flying. The sudden stop threw the man the kids called "Mullet" to the floor. He dropped his gun, and two boys went scrambling for it.

But Mullet recovered his fumble. He scrambled to his feet and screamed at the kids. "Sit down! Sit down every one of you!"

Four kids were crying, two girls and two boys. "Hey, she's bleeding!" a boy said, pointing to a girl across from him. She'd hit her head and had a good-sized gash.

Jamie pulled a T-shirt out of his backpack. "Here. Press this against the cut." He passed it forward. Then he addressed Mullet. "Hey, where are we?"

"What are you doing with us?" someone yelled.

"I gotta pee," another kid said.

They kept their voices loud while Eric quietly tore the pages out of his book and passed them to Scout, still hiding under the seat.

"In the barn, kids, and don't try anything funny!" the driver yelled.

"Should we bring our backpacks?" Jamie asked.

"Bring what you want. I don't care," Mullet answered. "Move!"

The driver turned off the engine. Immediately, the "kid-minder alarm," designed to make sure no kids were left on the bus at the end of a run, went off. "What the ..." the driver yelled, cursing.

"I got it!" Jamie said. Quickly, he went to the back of the bus and hit the alarm reset button near the emergency exit. "All good!" he said, turning back toward the front. He pretended to stumble and dropped something.

Scout stayed still, his heart pounding. Jamie had dropped a small flashlight almost within his reach. Scout recognized the light. It belonged to a girl who was always reading, even in winter when their bus run was in the dark. The kids, his friends, knew he was hiding, knew he was part of the plan to save them. His friends were depending on him!

Scout listened as the students left the bus, some still crying, some silent. He held his breath when heavy footsteps told him one of the men was walking down the aisle, checking to be sure everyone was out. He peeked out through a fold in his jacket. The man had a flashlight, and in that light, Scout saw what looked like blood on the floor. Then a voice cried out. "Tony, get out here. Help me with these kids," and the footsteps retreated.

The door of the bus closed. Scout remained quiet, working

over the plan in his mind. He was no stranger to the woods. He'd gone hunting with his dad and older brother practically since he could walk. Camping too. Even in the snow once when an early storm caught them. He had good boots. A warm coat. Plus, he wasn't afraid of being cold and wet.

Scout knew how to open the emergency doors on the bus. He could imagine himself walking through this storm, finding a house, getting some help. He only had to slip out of the bus and up the hill without the men seeing him.

Scout didn't have a watch, and he wasn't sure how long to wait. He finally decided to go for it. He folded the papers Eric had given him and stuffed them in the pocket of his jeans. He reached for the small flashlight and put it in another pocket. Then he pushed the jacket and the backpack aside and crawled out of his hiding place. He raised his head slowly. No one was in sight.

Quickly, he slid on his coat and zipped it up. Did he need his backpack? He decided he didn't. Except for the candy bar. He always kept a candy bar in the small pocket. He could use that.

Time to go. Scout kept low and walked to the door of the bus. He raised the red handle on the emergency exit and slipped out into the night.

26

NATE HAD GONE out to search a segment teamed up with the sixth deputy. I wondered how he'd do in the snow with his artificial leg, but he probably wouldn't be going far on foot.

His absence gave me time to talk to Kathryn about him and Laura. I told her about how he lost his leg, how we'd found his long-lost love, Laura, and reunited them in the hospital. It was a sweet story, it really was, and her smile said she recognized that.

I also told her about Laura's love for horses and about her helping little Harper Lee, the motherless child who'd stopped speaking. Laura used her horse to help Harper learn to trust again. "I think she and Scott would like to set up a therapeutic horse program eventually," I said.

As I shared these stories, I felt my heart toward Laura changing. My anger and hurt began to dissipate. Forgiveness flowed into the gap. God started doing a work in me.

Bearing with one another... what was that verse? I pulled out my phone quickly. "*...bearing with one another in love, eager to maintain the unity of the Spirit in the bond of peace.*" Ephesians 4:2-3

"Jess?"

Kathryn's voice snapped me back to the present.

"Look," she said, gesturing toward the cluster of men that had formed across the room. Scott, Mike, the sheriff, and Mark Williams were engaged in an animated discussion about something.

Right then we heard a deputy on the radio, checking in. "Segment two-dash-one is clear," the voice said.

"I need to document that," Kathryn said. She moved to the computer where she'd set up a spreadsheet. I marked the map with a symbol indicating that segment was clear. Then others began calling in. The two of us worked side by side, annotating the records, updating the assignments as deputies called in with new information. A logging operation had cut an access road that wasn't on the map. A tree fallen across a lane, preventing any vehicle from passing. Documenting these details was tedious work, but we were beginning to get a picture of the county from the boots on the ground

Meanwhile, I saw Mike and Scott huddled over another computer. The tension on Scott's face showed. He was leaning over Mike, pointing to the screen, and Mike was using the keyboard. They were searching out something, but I had no idea what.

A noise behind me made me turn around. A deputy held the door open as two women walked in carrying boxes of what I would later discover was fresh food for everyone. They laid out sandwiches and plugged in Crock-Pots full of soup, a good thing since Kathryn's chili was long gone. Trays of cookies and bags of chips, apples, pears, sodas, water, brownies—they'd gathered food from friends and neighbors to support the search.

At the school, they told us, cafeteria workers were cooking up a feast of the kids' favorite foods. Pizza. Mac 'n cheese. Hot dogs. Hamburgers. They'd be ready for them when the kids were found.

Two pastors showed up, too, a Methodist and a Baptist minister. "We're here to pray for you," they said, "and listen if you want

to talk. And if we can help some other way, tell us what to do."
The community was banding together, even in this storm. The
dichotomy struck me. Inside was warmth, light, teamwork, a
common purpose, determination, hope. Outside was cold, darkness, swirling snow, danger, and maybe despair. Who or what
would bridge that gap?

27

SCOUT STAYED LOW, crouching down as he moved away from the bus and up the hill. His father had taught him to move quietly through the forest, to strike the ground with the outer part of his foot before rolling his foot flat. He'd showed him how to use trees and thick underbrush to camouflage his movements, and how to make use of ravines and ridgelines to hide from the whitetail deer he was stalking.

Scout had gotten his first deer using those techniques. It seemed like they'd work for kidnappers too. So Scout took his time, carefully making his way back up to the road, paying attention to what anyone below could see if they looked his way, hiding himself by staying behind trees.

What should he do when he reached the road? He'd thought about that, hiding under that bus seat, mapping out his plan. He couldn't trust anybody right now. Flagging down the first car that came along seemed stupid. The kidnappers could have friends.

So he couldn't walk *on* the road. That wouldn't be safe. He'd have to parallel it, staying out of sight, in the woods, until he saw a house or a driveway or a vehicle that he recognized.

Worse came to worse, he'd walk all the way home.

First, he had to get to the road. The snow complicated things. He thought the falling snow might hide his movements, and maybe it did. But it also made him slip and fall a number of times climbing up that hill. His knees were wet and probably bruised. His right wrist hurt. Snow collected on his eyelashes and made it hard to see.

Ten minutes into his climb, Scout hit an impasse. A sheer wall, a rock outcropping, stood before him. He'd have to go around it. But which way? Because he'd been hiding under the seat, he hadn't seen how they'd moved down the driveway, what twists and turns the farm lane made on its way down to the barn. He was disoriented. He didn't know which direction the driveway was in.

So Scout made a guess. He turned right. It was a shot in the dark. It was wrong.

By the time Scout worked his way back to where he'd run into the rock outcropping, he was tired and discouraged. His legs felt leaden. He wanted to cry.

But he thought about his dad, and what his dad would say to him. His friends were counting on him. He had to get help. He wanted his dad to be proud of him. So Scout took a deep breath and soldiered on.

Scout finally found the driveway. He moved parallel to it, uphill, until he came to the gate, which stood open. He moved through it, then turned around and studied it. That was another thing his dad taught him. Turn around and make note of the path you've been on, so when you return, you'll know what it looks like, which way to go.

Once he found the road, Scout had another decision to make. Which way to turn? In the snow and the dark, he didn't quite know where he was. Was his house to the left or right? Then he remembered Eric's map. Finding a clump of dense underbrush, Scout squatted down and took the small flashlight and the papers from his pockets. He didn't want to keep them out long. They'd get wet.

He shuffled through them, dropped one, retrieved it, and then found Eric's map. According to it, the gate he'd just gone through was on the north side of the road, west of Paul's house. Which meant his home was further up the road to the right.

Satisfied, he returned the papers to his pocket and the flashlight to his other pocket. He'd parallel the road, keeping to the woods so he wouldn't be seen, and walk to the right until he was home. Once home, he'd tell his mom and dad what happened, give them the map, and they'd get help.

Were they worried about him? His mom would be, for sure. His dad would be mad.

Picking a path on the north side of the road, Scout began walking toward home, or what he hoped was toward home, if he'd read Eric's map right. He didn't have a watch, so he had no idea what time it was or how long it had been since he left the bus. But it was dark and cold, and he was hungry, and the snow was blowing hard.

One pickup went by. Scout crouched down and watched it slowly making its way through the storm. He didn't recognize it. It, for sure, wasn't his dad's. He hid low behind a tree and watched it go by. Was it someone looking for them? Was anyone looking?

Once the truck was gone, he resumed walking. He tripped on a bramble and fell headfirst, bruising his arm on a rock. He got back on his feet and continued. Then he got scared when he heard loud crashing in the forest. It was only a buck, but it stopped and stared at him, and for a minute, Scout was afraid it would charge him. "Go on! Git!" he yelled, raising his arms to make himself look bigger, and the deer ran off.

Scout's legs ached. He felt tired. He scooped up some snow as he walked and rubbed it on his face to wake himself up. He let some melt in his mouth. He wondered what his friends were doing and if they had anything to eat. He remembered his candy bar and found it in his pocket, a little smashed but still edible. Maybe he'd sit for a minute and eat it.

He found a log and he sat and took one bite, then another, and another. He didn't know how long he sat there. The snow continued to fall, turning his knees white, covering his boots.

Staring at the collecting snow, he remembered a story they'd read in school—what was it called?—about a man hiking alone in Alaska in bitter cold weather. As he walked, he grew colder and colder. Night was falling. He tried to build a fire but kept failing. The man remembered a story of someone killing a big animal and sleeping in its carcass to keep from dying, but all the man had was a wolfdog, and by the time he thought of killing it, he couldn't move his hands. Couldn't grip his knife. His arms were like frozen logs.

"To Build A Fire." That was the story. The guy died in the end, freezing to death little by little, until he finally sat down, went to sleep, and died.

The thought of it drove Scout to his feet. "No!" he said out loud. "I've got to move."

He started out again walking in the woods until the terrain began a steep rise. He knew this place. They called it the "one-mile hill." He pushed his way up and tripped again in the woods, this time on a fallen branch covered by snow. Discouraged, he forced himself forward.

Then he heard a sound. An engine. Coming from behind him. Scout hid behind a thick oak and watched as an SUV crawled up the hill. He blinked. He saw black. White. A seal on the door. It was a sheriff's car. A deputy!

Scout stepped into the road and waved his arms.

28

"We need a Plan B," Kathryn said, as she logged another entry. "Everything's coming up clear so far."

"That's good and bad," I said. "I mean, I'm glad we're not finding them wrecked somewhere, but where could they be?"

I took my question to Deputy Hitchens, who was handling public information. "You busy?"

"No, ma'am, not right this second."

"If I have the ground clearance on Bus 16, how would I find out how steep a grade that bus could handle?"

The deputy frowned. "I don't know, ma'am, but I'll make some phone calls and see if I can find out."

"Let me know if you do," I said. "Thanks."

Why did I want to know? The deputies searching the segments were radioing in comments like, "I don't see how they could make it up that hill," or "road's too steep there." I'd marked on the map the areas that had prompted those comments, specifically so we could go back if Plan A didn't yield results. Maybe a bus could handle a steeper grade than they thought, especially if the driver didn't care about damaging the underbelly.

Luke had expressed a lot of interest when the new food came

in through the door. He'd walked over to the ladies, tail wagging, head high, sniffing, looking as charming and handsome as he could. I was ready to jump up and stop them if one of them started to feed the beggar, but his silent pleas fell on deaf ears. Now he was lying against the wall again. I could see his nose still twitching.

Two of the six search teams returned. They immediately went into the room where the food was. With steaming cups of soup in their hands, they reported on the roads. "Barely passable" was the consensus. "Most aren't plowed, and there's about eight inches of snow on 'em."

That prompted the sheriff to get back on the phone with VDOT. I imagine that conversation was as heated as the soup.

"We have another assignment for you when you're ready," I said.

The deputy and the civilian dad looked at each other. "We're ready," the deputy said.

Kathryn had already put together the next five packets. She handed them one and explained the location. The deputy looked up at her. "This is a pretty remote hollow," he said.

"Yes, sir, we know that. Might be a good place to hide a school bus."

The deputy pursed his lips. "We'll give it a shot."

Then the deputy paired with Nate radioed the dispatcher with a message for me. They'd found a potential clue, footprints in the snow, and Nate wanted to know if I wanted to try Luke on them.

"Sure!" I told the dispatcher to reply. I was ready for some more action, and I was positive Luke was too.

I'd seen Scott, Mike, the sheriff, and Deputy Mark Williams go into the food room and shut the door. Through the large window between the two rooms, I'd seen them huddling over some issue. I wondered what it was. Deputy Williams left. Scott,

Mike, and the sheriff were still talking. There was some intense conversation going on.

I wanted to say goodbye to Scott, to tell him where I was going, to extend to him the same courtesy I would want from him. But the food room court was still in session. I checked my watch. I had about fifteen minutes before Nate and Deputy Gibson picked me up.

I started to gather my things. Luke raised his head. "I'll be right back," I said. "You stay."

29

I LEFT the room and walked down the hall to the ladies' room. When I emerged a few minutes later, Scott was coming down the hall, his grip in his hand.

"Oh, good!" he said, seeing me. He glanced around. "Come here." He took my elbow and guided me into a small storage room. He clicked on the overhead light and shut the door.

"What's up?" I asked. His grip was how he carried his extra clothes, extra guns, and extra ammunition.

"Look," he said, in a low voice. "What I'm about to tell you can't go anywhere else, not even to Kathryn or Nate."

"Okay." My stomach clenched. I was already a bit nauseated. What was up?

"The only people who are in on this are Mike, the sheriff, and Mark Williams, got it?"

I nodded.

"You know the reason I bothered with that kid's notebook was the global warming stuff."

"Right."

"I thought it might indicate there really is a conspiracy with widespread planning, violent climate change demonstrations. Like what we uncovered in Montana."

"Right." I was tracking with him. I'd rarely seen him this intense.

"Okay, so first, Mike finds messages on this kid Thomas "Bean" Jones's computer with some guy calling himself Pale Rider. When Mike dug down in, he found many references to something called PoDoX and Maple View. These people are linked to Contra2+, the group targeting the kid in Montana."

"What's PoDoX?" I frowned.

"We think it means 'power down extreme.'" He took a deep breath. "Anyway, I called the tech analyst, the one who'd helped me with the Montana case? He spent a good part of the evening looking deep into the dark web. And he found some chatter about a new section of power grid being built in the area, high-voltage lines carrying power to DC and other parts of the East Coast. The project is called Maple View Power Transfer Station." He swallowed hard. "They may be ecoterrorists, and they may be planning something. He found today's date and midnight encrypted in the messages."

"What? What does that have to do with—"

"The kids. I know. Here's what I'm thinking. I think the kids are a diversion. I think these ecoterrorists want all the attention going toward these kids so they can pull something off on this power installation."

"It's online?"

"Scheduled to go online. Tonight. At midnight."

My stomach rolled. I thought I was going to throw up. "Oh, Scott."

"We don't want word to get out about this. Nothing."

"Okay."

"Mark Williams is familiar with the power project. He says he can get me to an overlook, close enough to see the facility. We may have to watch it for a while."

"Why not just send people there?"

"Politics. The deputy AD, remember? I'm not supposed to suggest anything about ecoterrorism."

"Yes."

"Jess, I could lose my job over this."

I raised my chin. "You do what's right, Scott. Follow your conscience."

He nodded.

"Don't worry about your job."

His chest heaved. "Thank you. Mark's gone to get his truck. He thinks it'll handle the snow better. When he gets back, we're leaving."

"Okay, I'm going out too. Nate found some tracks he thinks Luke should check out."

Scott's eyes softened. He wrapped his arms around me. "I love you. Find those kids, okay?"

"While you're saving the world? You bet, Superman!" I poked him gently in the ribs. He kissed me on the mouth. "You're the best. I love you so much."

"I can't wait to get through this and get a shower and a good night's sleep with you." Scott opened the door. "I'll see you in a couple of hours."

"Don't stay out too long! I don't want to go to bed with a frozen husband."

He turned around and grinned at me.

I watched him stride down the hall, broad-shouldered, strong. *God protect him,* I thought. *Please protect him.*

30

"WHAT ARE you doing out here, son?" the deputy asked. He'd stopped his SUV, activated his lights, and gotten out. "Get in my vehicle. Here." The deputy opened the back door, and Scout climbed in.

Scout stared in awe at the equipment in the front—the radio with its blinking lights, the laptop, the shotgun. The deputy got back in the driver's seat, and when he did, his sidearm was in plain view. He turned toward Scout. "What are you doing walking in this storm?"

Scout told him the whole story, from Mr. Nowers being shoved off the bus to him hiding and then escaping. The deputy listened, frowning and nodding his head. It bothered Scout a little that the deputy didn't already know all this. Wasn't anyone looking for them? But maybe he just wanted Scout to talk. Or maybe the guy was from a different county. Scout hadn't looked at the seal carefully, he was so excited about getting help.

"My friends, they're still stuck, eight of them, with two kidnappers. And look," Scout said pulling out his papers. "My friend Eric drew this map so you can see exactly where this place is, and he described these guys and everything." The heat in the SUV felt so good.

The deputy nodded as he looked at the papers. He'd stopped his SUV in the middle of the road, but it didn't matter. They were alone out there. "This is great. I'll get some of my buddies to go get them. Right away." The deputy put the papers in his coat pocket.

"That would be awesome, sir."

"Where do you live, son? I'll take you home."

"Up here, sir," Scout said. "Maybe a mile or so."

The deputy put the SUV in gear and started moving up the hill. Scout was so glad he wasn't walking, so happy to be out of the cold. The heat was actually making him a little sleepy.

The deputy picked up his phone. He called somebody, Scout didn't know who, and reported what Scout had told him. "Yeah, I'm taking him home now," the deputy said, "then I'll meet you over there."

"This is it! Turn right here," Scout said when they reached his driveway.

"Okay, kid. You think your momma kept dinner for you?" The deputy grinned.

"Yeah! For sure." Or she'd make him grilled cheese. Or a hamburger. His stomach growled thinking about it.

Where was his dad's truck? He didn't see it. Maybe Dad had been hauling wood or something and had left it out back. Maybe he'd been called into work.

The deputy parked his SUV, got out, came around, and let Scout out of the back seat. Then they walked up to the house. The front door flew open before they stepped on the porch, and Scout's mother came out. "Scout! Oh, thank God." She wrapped her arms around him. Scout felt his face grow warm. "Are you all right?"

"I'm fine, Mom," Scout said. "Where's Dad?"

"He's out looking for you!"

"With Bobby?"

"Yes. Your brother went with him. Now come inside."

The deputy followed them into the warm home. "You got a tough kid, there, Mrs. ..."

"Jacobson. Heather Jacobson." She extended her hand. "Can I get you something to drink? Coffee?"

"No ma'am. I need to get back on the road. But thank you."

She looked at Scout. "Where were you? What happened to your bus?"

Scout started telling her the whole story. The deputy interrupted him. "It seems like a couple of older teenagers thought they'd play a prank and take the bus for a joyride. One of those stupid things kids do. They're in big trouble, but the kids are fine. My boys are picking them up now. They'll all be home soon."

Scout stared at him, open-mouthed. "One of them had a gun."

The deputy frowned. "You can't tell a toy gun from a real gun?" He unsnapped his holster and lifted his weapon out. "Now this here, this is a real gun."

Scout's eyes widened. A shimmer of fear went through him.

The deputy grinned. He dropped his gun back in the holster and snapped it shut.

"Come on, honey. I saved you some dinner," Mrs. Jacobson said. "Thank you, Deputy, for bringing my son home."

"Sure. You got a real fine boy there. Good night, ma'am."

31

SCOUT LAY IN BED, tears dripping quietly onto his pillow, a sour feeling in his stomach. He'd had a hard time forcing food down, even though it was his favorite, mac 'n' cheese. Concerned he was coming down with something, his mom made him take a shower and go to bed. He wanted to stay up until his father got home. For sure, Dad would listen to him. But that was a no-go with Mom.

So he lay in bed in the dark, exhausted but unable to sleep. When he thought about his friends he felt sick. He actually thought about running away, leaving the house, finding someone else who would help.

But who? Who could he trust?

No, his best bet would be wait for Dad. So he'd left his bedroom door open a crack, hoping he'd hear his dad when he got home. Now, lying in bed, he saw it push open wider and his dog, Tuck, slipped in. Tuck wasn't allowed on the bed, but he jumped up anyway, and Scout didn't correct him. Not tonight.

Scout's dad had bought Tuck, a black-and-white border collie, as a puppy from a neighbor who had sheep. Paying money for a pet was an extravagance, but Tuck was a special birthday present for Scout.

He could still remember the day his dad brought him home, an eight-week-old bundle of black-and-white energy. Scout named him Tuck for the way he'd tuck his little head under Scout's arm when he held him.

Scout rolled over in bed and began stroking Tuck's head. The light from the hallway caught in the dog's eyes. Tuck sniffed Scout's face and licked his tears away. Scout put his arm around his dog and closed his eyes.

32

WITH SCOTT GONE, I refocused on my job: take Luke and check out the area Nate found. I finished getting my stuff together as Deputy Sam Gibson and Nate came inside. They got some coffee and reported to Kathryn what they'd found. I saw her asking questions and taking notes. When they were finished, they came over to me.

"How is it out there?" I asked, nodding toward the door.

"Roads are pretty rough," Deputy Gibson said.

"Reminds me of why I moved to the flat," Nate said, grinning.

"It's not that flat," I said. Nate had a 'right good-sized hill', almost a mountain in my books, behind his house. "You ready to go again?"

"Yes ma'am," the deputy said.

The snowfall had slowed down quite a bit since the last time I'd been out. Visibility was better. Maybe the storm was moving off.

Nate suggested I leave my Jeep and ride with them. "Ain't no sense in risking two vehicles getting stuck."

So I threw my gear in the back of the deputy's small SUV and told Luke to jump up there as well. "I apologize in advance for the dog hair," I said to the deputy as I climbed in the back seat.

"No problem, ma'am. I'm used to it. I got dogs of my own."

Of course, I had to ask him what kind of dogs he had. "Great Pyrenees, ma'am. Two of 'em. Guard dogs for my wife's sheep."

"Two Great Pyrenees!" I said. "Then you really do know dog hair." The three of us got talking about dogs, and it was like releasing the valve on the pressure cooker, for me anyway. Stress over the kids and stress over Scott came streaming out in stories about Luke and Sprite and Ember and the deputy's dogs.

"So why does your wife have sheep?" I asked.

He threw a grin my direction. "God only knows. Ain't no money in 'em. She loves 'em that's all. Says they remind her of the Bible." He glanced in the rearview mirror at me. "You know that verse that says, 'Why are you cast down, O my soul?'"

"Yes."

"First time I ever saw a sheep shearin' I understood what that meant. The shearer stands at the sheep's head and kinda throws the sheep on its back, and when he does, it freezes. They act like they're helpless. Don't even try to get away. They lie there while he takes his clippers and brings that wool off like it's a coat."

Nate piped up. "Happens in the field too. They fall and roll on their backs and cain't get up. Least they think they cain't."

"So they're easy prey for wolves or coyotes," I suggested.

"Right."

"Does your wife shear them?" I asked the deputy.

"No ma'am. She helps, but she's a bitty thing, my wife. The ewes weigh up to two-hundred pounds and rams even more. So flippin' 'em is right hard." He glanced back again. "You should come watch sometime. May or June is when we shear 'em."

"This is the place," Nate said, pointing.

The deputy stopped his vehicle, and we got out. Nate shined his light on the ground near the side of the road illuminating footprints that trailed off in the woods. "They're kind of small," I said.

"Kinda like what a kid might leave. Want to let Luke have a go at it?" Nate said.

"Sure." This wasn't going to be easy. Going uphill in the woods is hard enough, but add snow and it's real hard. While it's true that when it's cold there are fewer scents around to confuse the dog, Luke hadn't done much searching in the snow. How was this going to work?

It's not your job to succeed, a voice in my head said. *It's your job to try.*

I took a deep breath and opened the back of the SUV. I let Luke out, then rummaged in my pack and found his SAR vest and put it on, along with the blinking light I used to keep track of him at night. I put on my headlamp, tugging a knit cap over it. Then I shouldered my pack and closed up the back of the SUV.

I turned back to the men. Nate had a walking stick in his hand. "What are you doing?"

"You need a walker. I'm it. The deputy here will stay with his vehicle with his lights running."

"I can do this myself."

"Nope. I'm with you."

Remember all that stuff I said about "going uphill" and "snow"? Add "with an artificial leg." I really didn't see how Nate was going to do this. But there was no point arguing with the man. He can be stubborn.

I called Luke over to the place where the footsteps seemed to go uphill. I brought him to heel. His tail swept the snow, his eyes fixed on me, anticipating my command. "Seek, Luke! Seek!" I gestured uphill.

"Got it," Nate said, as he marked our start on the GPS.

Luke took off, sweeping left and right a little before honing in on the track. His nose, not his eyes, was his primary sense organ. At first it wasn't too bad. I kept Luke in sight. I could hear Nate behind me. And the hill moderated about fifty yards up, the incline becoming less steep. But then about a hundred yards beyond that, Luke seemed to lose the track. He doubled back, then tried circling, then stopped and looked at me like, *What now, boss?*

"Call him in," Nate said.

I rolled my eyes. He was the only walker bold enough to tell me what to do. He was also the only one I'd listen to. "Luke, come!"

My dog came running. He sat in front of me and looked at me, asking with his eyes if he got to play now.

Nate came past me and walked up to where Luke had lost the scent. I could see then how awkward this walk was for him, and I had more sympathy with his idea to learn to search on horseback. He used his flashlight to check for footprints in the snow, moving left ten yards and right ten yards, then walking in a big circle. As he came back to me he was shaking his head. "Trail disappears."

"How can that be?"

He looked upward. "Maybe a big chunk of snow came off of a pine tree and covered it up. I don't know."

"Can we pick it up again?"

Nate's mouth twisted at his thought. "We could go off at a forty-five degree angle one way, then t'other." He extended his arm, demonstrating. "That might do it."

I didn't want to give up yet. On the other hand, it was one set of footprints. Not nine. On another hand ... it was something.

So we marked the tree where we lost the trail, set our angle, and started out. "Seek, Luke! Seek!" We knocked around those woods for another forty-five minutes before I looked at Nate and he looked at me, and we mutually gave it up.

"I'll go hide," he said.

This was the capper on a fruitless search—somebody had to hide, give the dog someone to "find" so he'd stay interested in the game. I watched Nate walk down the hill, watched him fall and get up awkwardly, then watched him disappear. I gave him five more minutes before I sent Luke.

I walked downhill, following my dog, but thinking about the kids. Scott's theory, that taking them was a diversion, made more sense than anything else. Still, would an ecoterrorist group really come all the way out here in the snow to disrupt something?

I guess we'd know soon enough. Midnight was only a few hours away.

33

"WAKE UP, SON!" His father's big hands jostled the boy.

Scout opened his eyes. The clock on his bedside table read 9:52. He sat up quickly. "Dad?" Tuck jumped onto the floor.

Charlie Jacobson hugged his son. He sat down on the edge of the bed and put his arm around the boy.

"Are they safe? My friends?" Scout asked.

"Tell me what happened."

And so he did, the story rolling out easier this time, the drama of it sending little shocks of adrenaline all through him, jolting every cell in his body awake. Then he got to the part where the deputy brought him home. "He was lying, Dad, I know it!" Scout said, and then he burst into tears.

His dad held him close, the warmth of the big man's body comforting him. "It's all right. Get dressed, son," Charlie said. "We're gonna fix this."

Scout jumped into his clothes—clean jeans, a pullover shirt, a sweatshirt, and thick socks. When he walked into the living room, his parents were arguing. Scout's older brother stood off to the side, arms crossed, listening.

"Charlie, you can't take him out in this! Not after what he's been through," his mother was saying.

"That man, whoever he was, told you two hours ago they were picking up the kids. I left Jack Miller's house ten minutes ago, and his girl wasn't home yet. No phone call. Nothing! I'm telling you something's going on."

Scout set his jaw. "I'm ready, Dad." Both parents turned toward him. He looked at his mother. "Mom, I'll be fine. I need to do this."

Something in his tone of voice, or her husband's, made his mother back down. She walked over, kissed his forehead, and said, "I love you."

Scout nodded and said, "Let's go, Dad."

34

By the time we got back to the sheriff's office the snow had picked up again. I checked my watch. The temperature was twenty-four degrees. I felt it in my bones.

Inside, I looked around. "Scott's not back?" I asked.

"Not yet," Mike responded.

Fatigue and frustration drained my energy. I took care of Luke, making sure he had water and a snack. He found his place along the wall and laid down, his chin on the floor. Kathryn urged me to eat something. I walked into the food room and looked at what was left. Nothing appealed to me. I picked up a cookie, chocolate chip, homemade, and ate half of it.

For the first time, I thought about finding a place to sleep for a while. I looked over at Luke. Maybe I'd stretch out on the floor by him. Why not? I'd slept in all kinds of crazy places.

"You doin' okay?" Nate asked.

"I'm tired. Frustrated, too, that we didn't find anything." I looked at him. "How's your leg?"

"Not bad." He stretched and yawned. "I think I'm gonna find a place to sit for a bit."

Before I could respond, the door opened, and a man walked

in. He had two boys with him, no doubt his sons. Instinctively, I looked at Kathryn. Her eyes were wide.

"Sheriff," I heard the man say, "we need to talk."

I moved over to Kathryn. "What's going on?"

"That's Scout!" she said. "One of my students."

"Wait, what?" I had trouble absorbing what she said.

"He was on the bus! What's he doing here?"

"Which one is he?"

"Michael Jacobson. They call him Scout."

"What's happening?" Mike asked, moving close. Nate joined us as well.

Kathryn repeated what she'd said. "He's one of my students. He was on the bus."

The sheriff took the man and his boys into his inner office. The four of us spoke in low voices, trying to guess what was going on. My heart rate had elevated. I felt a quiver in my stomach.

Not five minutes later, the sheriff opened the door and yelled for two of his deputies. Gibson and Sawyer joined them inside the office.

Then the door opened again, and the sheriff and the others emerged. They walked toward the maps. The younger boy spotted Kathryn. He broke away and gave her a hug. "Scout," she whispered, "I'm so glad to see you." I could see tears shining in her eyes.

The sheriff and the others looked at the map for a few minutes, then the sheriff turned to the room and yelled for everyone to gather. Fatigue took a hike. Officers stopped what they were doing and moved close. Excitement charged the air in the room. Even Luke got up from where he'd been sleeping and sat at my side, ears pricked, waiting.

"This here's Scout," the sheriff said, putting his arm around the young student. "He was on Bus 16. He escaped and was walking home when a deputy picked him up. If that was you, I want to know about it now."

His tone of voice conveyed authority. I had a sense he was making eye contact with every officer in that room, one at a time.

No one responded. "Who's missing?" he asked.

"Deputies Wilson and McGee, sir," Kathryn responded, looking at her notes.

"And Mark Williams," someone added.

A tendon in the sheriff's jaw tightened and released. "Scout says the bus is pushed up next to a barn, down off the road. He's gonna take me back to where he thinks it is. I want every one of you locked and loaded, ready to go when I call you." He looked at me. "Miss Jessica, I'd like you and your dog to come with us. Deputy Gibson can drive you."

I nodded my assent. "Yes, sir." Luke nudged my leg. Finally! A breakthrough.

FIVE MINUTES later we loaded up in the parking lot. The snow had almost stopped. I gave Luke a chance to relieve himself, then asked him to jump in the back of Deputy Gibson's SUV. Nate decided to come, too, and climbed in at shotgun. The sheriff came over as the deputy and I were about to get in. At the last minute, I grabbed my first-aid kit out of the Jeep.

"Scout was hiding and didn't see the route the bus took after hijackers took over. But when he escaped he climbed a hill, found a road, and started walking home."

"How'd he know which way to go?" I asked.

The sheriff told us about the map another kid drew. "He gave that map to this alleged deputy ... whoever he was," the sheriff said. Anger darkened his voice.

"Fake cop?" I asked.

"Better be."

That added another layer to the mystery, I thought as I climbed into the deputy's vehicle. Maybe Scott was right. Maybe the bus hijacking was a diversion. That could be good news as far as the kids were concerned, if the primary intent was not to hurt them, but simply draw the cops' attention. There'd been no ransom demand, no contact with the perpetrators at all.

Hmmm.

We followed the sheriff's vehicle to a driveway leading to what I guessed was Scout's house. I was happy sitting in the back, listening to Nate and the deputy talk. I prayed, then, for the kids, for us, for Scott, for success in bringing those kids home. Little gusts of wind occasionally buffeted the SUV. The storm was definitely moving off.

From Scout's driveway, we drove east slowly, following the sheriff, until suddenly his vehicle stopped, and the young boy, his father, and his brother got out. The sheriff emerged, too, with a big flashlight, and together they studied an area up in the woods, fifteen, maybe twenty feet off the road.

After a few minutes, the boy's brother came jogging back to our SUV. "The sheriff wants to know if maybe your dog can help us follow the track my brother made in the snow."

This was not the right time to explain that Luke was an air scent dog, not a tracking dog. He wasn't trained to follow a specific person's scent, but instead to find "any person" in a given area by catching the scent of "human" drifting in the air.

"Hang on. Let me see if I can help," Nate said, getting out of the vehicle.

The deputy looked back at me. I shrugged. "Nate knows all kinds of stuff."

I saw Nate shining his night-vision flashlight on the ground as he squatted down. He moved to get different angles. Then he switched it to the standard white light and shined it in the trees and bushes. He began walking through the woods, paralleling the road, carefully following the track. After about fifty feet, he stopped.

Whatever he did satisfied the sheriff, who returned to his vehicle with the Jacobsons. Nate climbed back in the front passenger seat of our car. "The boy got confused," he said, "about how far he'd gone. Felt like we'd missed the gate he was looking for. But I was able to show 'em footprints in the snow, even though they'd been covered by more snow. Plus you could see where he brushed against the bushes and low shrubs. He'd knocked off the snow. More had fallen, but it obviously weren't as thick as the snow on the brush that hadn't been touched. I followed his trail far enough to convince Scout we were still on track."

Deputy Gibson stared at Nate like he was some kind of magician. Nate grinned. "We didn't have video games when I was a kid. We didn't even have TV."

Another mile down the road, Scout spotted the gate he was looking for, now covered in snow. I could see his excitement even riding in the car behind.

We all got out. Overhead, I saw a patch of clear black in the sky. The clouds were breaking up.

"This is it!" he exclaimed. "They're down there."

"You sure?" the sheriff asked.

"Yes, sir! I remember that gate. Eric even drew it on the map!"

Nate walked over, shined his red light on the snow, and asked, "Did you walk up this side of the lane?" he pointed.

"Yes, sir!"

"I'm calling in my deputies," the sheriff said. He used the radio in his vehicle to call the dispatchers. Then he returned. "They're coming. I want to walk partway down this hill and see what I can see. Tell me, son, what am I lookin' for?"

"A big old barn, sir, and the bus."

"It's on this side of the barn?"

"Yes, sir. Slammed into a tree."

"Gibson, you stay here and have my people park on the sides of the road. I told 'em to come in cold. Mr. Jacobson, how about you come with me. Boys, get in the car. Don't touch anything. Mr. Nate, I could use your input if you can navigate this hill."

"Yes, sir." He retrieved his walking stick from Deputy Gibson's SUV.

I didn't have a role to play in this part of the search, and that was okay. I was already starting to think ahead to the end of this crisis, to when Scott and I could be together. Maybe he'd take a few days off. We could have some time together around the house, probably playing with horses. I wondered how much snow we'd gotten at home.

Then I thought about Laura and Kathryn and how that might play out. I liked Kathryn. I really did. I hoped Laura would accept her.

Which led me to think about grace ... not just the grace God had given me, despite my sin, but the grace I'd experienced from Nate. Not tolerance, as if my sin didn't matter, but a patient forbearance while God's love worked in me.

When someone sees your scars and loves you anyway, they almost disappear over time. I had read that somewhere. Laura's scars had been hidden deep. They were now in the open, and she'd lashed out at me. I'd been angry in return.

I could see how evil uses our shame to divide us. Defeat us. Cause disorder and chaos.

I let go of my last bits of anger toward Laura right there and then, hoping love would do its work.

IT DIDN'T TAKE LONG for the deputies' cars to start arriving, coming in cold with no lights or sirens, as the sheriff had ordered. I got out of the car. I wanted to see how this would play out.

The sheriff came back up the hill a few minutes later. Deputy Gibson had counted the vehicles, and everyone was there, including the two state police officers. Mike had stayed back at the sheriff's office waiting for the SWAT agents.

"Okay, listen up," the sheriff said. "What we got is an old barn with a few trees around it. Mostly in the open. Not much cover.

The school bus is there, right upside it. It's not goin' anywhere. It'd never make it up the hill."

"What about the SWAT team on the way?"

"I ain't waitin' for them. We can do this, boys. Charlie here, he snuck down that hill and got a look through a crack in the barn." He turned to Scout's dad. "Tell 'em what you saw."

"The kids, they're all in the back of the barn, huddled up together. They're quiet, just waiting. There's two men near the front double door. On the downhill side. One's got a pistol. I can't guarantee what else. There's one other smaller door on the left side."

Sheriff McCormick took over. "Now here's what we're gonna do. We're gonna surround that barn and treat it like a barricade with hostages. In other words, I will try to negotiate with these men. In the meantime, I want three volunteers. One needs to get set up behind the barn, and one on the right side. The barn's old and full of holes. See if there's a way to take a shot without puttin' the kids in danger, but only if I give you the go-ahead, got it? No shootin' without me saying so. My third volunteer I want on the left side, ready to pull that single door open and get them kids out. Who's in? All the deputies raised their hands. The sheriff picked three.

Talking to the three volunteers, the sheriff said, "You are gonna ride with me down the hill. You get around the barn to where you can see. If we need to, we take those men out, got it? But don't shoot unless I say so. We don't need to traumatize those kids further.

"When we get those kids out, and we will get them out, I want them taken to the school. That's where we've got food and medical care for them, and that's where their parents can pick them up."

He addressed the five dads who'd joined the deputies in the search. "You men, listen up. I am not deputizing you, but if these men start a war, you help finish it. Stay behind us twenty feet unless it goes bad. Got it?"

A chorus of "yes sirs" followed.

"Sir," a deputy asked, "will our vehicles make it down that hill in the snow?"

"It's more important that they make it back up," the sheriff said. "I'll take mine down so I can use the loudspeaker. The rest of you should walk."

"How about tractors?" one of the dad's said.

"You tell me. I don't plow."

"A good tractor should be able to get up that hill."

"If one shows up, we'll use it. Miss McCaskill, are you here?"

"Yes, Sheriff." I was surprised. Kathryn must have ridden over with a deputy.

"Tell the men the system you've worked out for the kids."

"Okay," she said. "When the kids arrive on the road, if any of them need immediate medical care, bring them to the ambulance that will be here. Otherwise, deputies will take two in each car to the elementary school. Don't leave before I get your name and the kids' names on my record." She held up a clipboard. "Go straight to the elementary school and check them in there with Carol Langley." She looked around. "Any questions?"

No questions. The men were getting restless. I was getting restless. I raised my hand. "Sheriff?"

"Yes?"

"How about if Luke and I ride down with you?"

"No."

"I'm a certified EMT. I could offer immediate help if someone is hurt."

"You got your gear with you?"

"Yes, sir."

"Then fine. But leave the dog."

I started to protest, but he went on. "Boys, let's get those kids!" the sheriff said.

I quickly grabbed my first-aid kit from Gibson's police SUV. "You got Luke!" I said to Nate, and I jumped in the back of the sheriff's Interceptor before he could change his mind about me coming.

We part-drove, part-slid down the hill through eight inches of snow. The sheriff downshifted and used engine braking to control his speed. We still slid a lot. I could feel the ruts on the path and deep potholes as we descended. Emerging from the woods, I saw the barn down to the left, with the school bus right next to it. I leaned forward, excited and anxious all in one.

The barn was a big, two-story, traditional barn, missing planks here and there but overall in pretty good shape with no doors on this side. I wondered if the kidnappers or kids could see or hear us. The sheriff only had his parking lights on, and I hoped the snow muffled the noise of his tires.

He pulled around to the front of the barn and stopped about thirty feet away from the large, double-sliding doors. The sheriff had moved slowly enough coming down the hill that his deputies on foot were able to keep up. He shot a look my way. "Stay in the Interceptor," he warned. "I don't want you getting hurt."

"Yes, sir."

He rolled down his window and pulled the mic off his dashboard. The cold night air poured into the car. Adjusting a knob, he spoke. "Attention in the barn. This is the sheriff. You are surrounded. Come out with—"

He hadn't finished when two men emerged, raced across the snow, jumped down an embankment, and ran toward the creek. The sheriff flipped on his lights and siren and hit the accelerator. Too hard! His wheels spun. The SUV struggled for traction. He cursed up a blue streak, threw the SUV in reverse, and started again, only to be stuck once more.

"Sheriff, look!" I said. Leaning forward, I pointed to three deputies running, following the men. Two more joined the chase.

I wished I had Luke with me. He wouldn't have taken the

suspects down like a tactical dog, but he might have scared them into surrendering.

The sheriff tried again to move, but he'd dug himself in. That turned out to be a good thing. You couldn't see it in the dark, but there was a three-foot drop around most of the barnyard, too much for his SUV to navigate safely.

Then the double door slid partway open and a boy came out with his hands raised. "We're safe!" the kid said. He looked tall and scrawny, older than middle-school aged. Other kids came from around the side.

I watched, moved by the real-life replay of what had become a common image after a school shooting—a line of kids emerging with their hands on their heads under the watchful eyes of armed deputies.

But they were alive! "Is anybody hurt?" I called out.

"Just her," a boy said, pointing to a girl with a cut on her head.

"Let me look at that, honey." I shined my flashlight on her forehead. The bleeding had stopped. "Do you feel dizzy?"

She shook her head. "I'm okay."

"You did a great job stopping the bleeding. Let's get you up the hill."

She stopped me. "He helped them. The bad men. Bean was with them." She pointed to the scrawny kid who'd come out first.

He must have heard her and started to run. "Oh, no, you don't!" I said. I chased after him and tackled him, the snow softening our fall.

Two deputies saw us and came running. "He may be part of it," I said, slightly out of breath.

"Come on, boy," a deputy said, hauling Bean to his feet.

The other deputy gave me a hand up. Above us I saw the clouds streaming north. Patches of black sky grew bigger, and here and there I could see a star. The storm was lifting. I silently gave thanks to God.

35

"MAN, I'm sure glad you know where you are going!" Scott said. Mark Williams had traded in his sheriff's office Interceptor for his own four-wheel-drive pickup. They were bouncing through a field, headed for an overlook, which Mark said would give him a good view of the new power transfer station. If ecoterrorists were targeting it, he'd know in a few minutes.

If he was right, he could potentially thwart what would be a devastating blow to the power grid in the Mid-Atlantic. He had already started planning how he would use the SWAT-trained agents to confront the terrorists. He'd looked up the planners' drawings of the facility online so he could figure out how best to approach it and how to deploy agents. He had the names of the project managers and their cell phone numbers.

He'd need that information if he was right. If he was wrong, well, he could lose his job.

Maybe, if he was wrong *and* lucky, Washington wouldn't find out. But if he was wrong, that left the motive for the bus hijacking in question. Why would anyone do that?

The storm had moved off, the clouds breaking apart like icebergs, streaming north. They were driving through about eight inches of snow. The temperature on Mark's dashboard read twenty-three degrees, cold enough to keep the snow from turning to slush. The pickup was handling it fine, its tires chewing through the snow like four hungry beasts.

"So this is your land out here?"

"Yep. Two hundred acres and a little more."

"You raise cattle?"

"Black Angus."

"Hard to see in the dark."

"I move 'em around. This field's empty right now. Might see a deer is all." They hit a hard bump. Scott grabbed the bar over the door. Mark looked over at him and grinned. "Almost there."

"My bones appreciate that." In the bouncing light of the truck's headlights, Scott could see a stand of trees to the right and blackness straight ahead and to the left. "Tell me how this is going to work, Mark. What will I need to do to see down to the power station?"

"To the left of those trees there's a rock outcropping. We'll have to get out on it a little bit, then look down and to the right. We're about a mile from the facility, but it'll be a clear shot."

"Have you been watching for activity down there? Do you know what normal looks like?"

Mark shook his head. "Not a clue. Hasn't been on my radar."

He brought his truck to a stop about twenty feet back from the rocks and turned it around, so it was facing out. *A cop habit,* Scott thought.

Scott stepped out of the truck and pulled his backpack out of the back. Retrieving his good binoculars, he zipped it back up and shouldered the pack.

"You won't need that," Mark said.

Scott shrugged. "I'll take it with me. It's got a good scope and some other stuff I might want."

"Suit yourself."

The snow crunched under their boots as they walked toward

the rocks. Scott was already imagining in his head what he wanted to look for. If he couldn't see well from this location, he'd ask Mark to drive him closer, down to the facility itself.

He wondered how Jess and the others were doing, whether they'd found the kids, or what was going on. Mark had brought his portable police radio with him in the truck. Scott had heard chatter on the way here, but the volume was too low for him to tell what was happening.

It had been a long day. His adrenaline had been running on and off, and now it was spiking again.

Out of the corner of his eye, he saw Mark stop. "Daggone," Mark said, "I forgot something. I'll catch up with you. Go about a dozen feet out on those rocks. Be careful. I'll be right with you." He jogged back to the truck.

Okay, Scott thought, and he kept walking. The cold air smelled good, like pine and oak, and he thought about how much he enjoyed being outside. He considered dropping his backpack at the edge of the rock outcropping but decided not to for some reason. He started moving forward, testing the footing. There was loose rock on the surface, but underneath was solid rock. Granite, he figured, considering where he was, covered in snow and ice. The outcropping was not a sheer cliff. Instead, there was about a twenty-foot drop, then a rocky slope going down to where it leveled off.

He moved to the edge and looked down to the right as Mark had instructed. He saw nothing but blackness. He raised his binoculars and played with the focus. Still nothing. Confused, he leaned out a little to get a different angle and scanned the valley below. The clouds moved enough for the full moon to break through, and Scott used that additional light to look again. Nothing. "Hey, Mark," he called out, as the moon hid behind clouds again.

When he didn't get an answer, he lowered his binoculars and turned around to look. Mark stood fifteen feet away, his Glock pointed right at Scott's chest. Adrenaline surged through Scott's body. His binoculars hit the snow with a thud. He extended his hands. "Mark, man, what are you doing?"

"You had to get involved, didn't you?" Mark said, and without further warning, he fired three times.

The first shot hit Scott square in the center of his chest. Instinctively, he twisted and dove away from the gun. He felt a jolt in his right shoulder. He hit the ground and slid off the cliff. He bounced off some rocks, and landed on his back, his head hitting hard. He kept tumbling down, twisting his body as more shots pinged off the rocks around him. Then he lay perfectly still on his belly, hiding his breath.

He laid that way until he heard Mark yell something. Then he heard the truck start up. He heard the tires spin on the ice. Then the sound of the engine moved farther away, until finally Scott couldn't hear it any more.

Part of him wanted to close his eyes. Go to sleep. Drift off. *If you move, it's going to hurt. Why not close your eyes? Just for a while.*

No! he told himself. Move. Assess. Survive.

Scott forced himself to a sitting position. He couldn't move his right arm for some reason. He reached over with his left hand and pulled his right arm across his lap. The white-hot pain made him cry out. His head spun.

Jess. Call Jess. He groped for his phone. It was gone. *Oh, God!* He felt for it on the rocks nearby, felt everywhere. His hand brushed the cargo pocket on his left leg. *Jess!* That's when he remembered. The Garmin InReach. She'd given him that emergency beacon.

He pulled out the Garmin, turned it on, and tucked it into his clothes, next to his body, to warm up the batteries.

Every movement hurt. His whole body ached. His chest felt like he'd been punched by a gorilla. His arm, though ... why wasn't his arm working? He felt his right shoulder with his left hand. He pulled his hand away and stared at it. Blood. It was wet with blood.

He either had a compound fracture or he'd been shot.

Think, Scott. Assess. He'd fallen hard, but his backpack had absorbed some of the blow. He needed to stop the bleeding. Maintain body temperature. Avoid going into shock.

Mark Williams had left him for dead. He hadn't reckoned on the fact that Scott had been raised in Colorado and knew cold-weather survival techniques.

Step 1: Stop the bleeding. Scott found the hole in the shoulder of his parka. A bullet-sized hole. He'd been shot. That was where the bullet had entered. There was no way to place a tourniquet above the wound. So direct pressure. Cold.

He grabbed a handful of snow and pressed it on the spot. He held it there until his left arm ached and then he held it some more. He prayed while he held it, prayed little chunky prayers for help. For him. For Jess. *Help me, please.*

Step 2: Heat. Scott could already feel the heat leaving his body. He needed shelter. Maybe a fire.

First, get the backpack off. Easier said than done. He slipped it off his left shoulder but taking it off his right was excruciating. Tears came to his eyes. He nearly passed out. He grabbed more snow and pressed it against the pain.

Now, could he walk? He expected after that fall for his hip to be broken, the hip where he'd been shot a few years ago. Was it? He forced himself to his feet. He gingerly put weight on his hip.

It was okay. A miracle, practically.

Encouraged, Scott reached down and grabbed his spare flashlight from his pack. It wasn't very strong, but he cast its light around, looking for resources. He saw lots of snow. Rocks. Some trees. Some evergreens in the trees ... pines, which were sappy and good for fires, and cedars with heavier boughs. Good for cover.

Honestly, he wanted to rest. But he knew one thing—to

survive, he needed heat, and he had to make that happen before he'd lost so much blood he couldn't function anymore.

Wait. First, the Garmin. He felt for it in his clothes. Tried to remember how it worked. Put the flashlight on it. Found the cover over the emergency button. Opened it. Pressed the button.

Then he shoved it in his pocket, picked up his backpack with his left hand and began moving across the snow-covered rock field toward the woods. *Help me, please. Help me.*

36

THE TWO MEN who'd hijacked the bus eluded the deputies chasing them. Sheriff McCormick wasn't concerned. He figured they wouldn't get far. His priority now was the kids. Several of them had said the tall, lanky boy that had been the first one out had helped the hijackers. He needed to get to the bottom of that.

We made the long walk up that hill, and Kathryn Grace's plan went into effect. The little girl with a gash was the only child injured. Quick thinking on the part of the kids had minimized even that.

The school buzzed with excitement as the kids began arriving. Parents could hardly wait to get their hands on them, but they cooperated with the authorities and followed the plan Mr. Chambers had laid out. The kids were checked by the doctor and nurses on site first. Then they reconnected with their parents and ate.

Hungry, scared, but mostly unhurt, they pounded their hero, Scout, on the back and asked what took him so long.

"My mother," he said. "She didn't believe me! She made me go to bed."

Mrs. Jacobson, who'd arrived courtesy of her husband, blushed and took the blame.

I watched the celebration, smiling along with everyone in the room, but expecting to see Scott walk in the door any moment. I couldn't wait for him to experience the positive vibes, to know that the lack of sleep, lack of food, and all the stress had been worth it. Tired as I was, I could hardly keep the grin off my face.

When this night finally came to an end, I knew what he'd want. A steak, a hot shower, and a good night's sleep. Those were his go-to requirements for recovery after a hard case. I wondered where we'd get a steak around here.

Kathryn brought me some hot cider and urged me to eat a little. Someone had made chicken salad sandwiches using little, sweet rolls. I got one down, but I still felt sick. I wondered if I was coming down with something.

Luke, even though he was not the hero in this case, had managed to turn himself into a therapy dog. He was getting more than his share of attention as kids came over to pet him. A couple of them hugged him. One little girl took his paw and seemed to be telling him her story. He soaked it all up. "He'll be insufferable for days after this," I joked to Kathryn.

Across the room, Nate sat at a table talking with someone. He was about Nate's age, and I wondered if Nate knew him from when he lived up here.

The eight FBI SWAT team members were gathered in another room, waiting for Scott to release them. Even if he didn't find anything at the power transfer station, I wondered if Scott would have them standby until it was activated at midnight.

Then the door opened, and Sheriff McCormick walked in. He didn't look good. He looked gray, and I wondered for a minute if he was having a heart attack. It wouldn't have surprised me with all the stress.

Mike was right behind him, looking uncharacteristically serious. As they walked past Nate, the sheriff tapped him on the shoulder and gestured for him to follow. "Miss Jessica, can we talk for a minute?" He led us into the teachers' room. Kathryn joined us.

What was going on? Scott's been in an accident, I thought. I braced myself.

When we were all gathered, the sheriff said, "Close the door." He took a deep breath. "Earlier today I got a call from Mark Williams's ex-wife."

"Ex-wife?" I blurted out. "He told me he was married."

"Ex-wife," the sheriff repeated. "Joanie said she got a text from him this morning saying *Watch the news.* Now I don't like to get involved in marriage fights. But Joanie Williams claims Mark was abusive. She left him, and they divorced six months ago. She said he's been pretty angry about that and also because some of his land had been taken by the state for this power project. Land that had been in his family for generations.

"I didn't know about any of that. This boy, Scout, talked about being picked up by a deputy. The actions he described that deputy taking, well, they didn't make sense. He lied to Scout's mother, saying the kids were being picked up. He didn't turn in the map another kid drew along with a description of them men. Scout says the deputy wasn't wearing a name badge, but the way he and his mother described him fit Mark Williams."

What does this have to do with Scott, I wondered.

"Now Mark's been my deputy for mor'n three years," the sheriff said, continuing.

"Three? He told me thirteen!" I said, interrupting again.

The sheriff took another deep breath. "He's been a deputy for thirteen, but on my staff for three. He worked in another county first." He looked straight at Mike. "I got to face the fact he may be involved in this whole business, and that Scott may be in danger."

Scott in danger? Oh, no, no, no... I felt lightheaded.

"The loss of his land and his divorce might be enough to push Mark over the edge."

The room started to spin. I felt sick. I was going to throw up. I rested my hand on my stomach.

"There's a bathroom right over there," Kathryn said. "Come on."

She guided me to the teachers' bathroom, and I went into a stall and threw up over and over. Kathryn brought me paper towels, including a wet one to wipe my face. She kept her hand on my back, and it was a comfort.

Finally, I had nothing left to throw up. Then I realized the men were out there making plans. I wanted to be part of that. I rinsed my mouth out at the sink, wiped it again, and said, "I need to get out there."

Sure enough, those guys had a whole plan set up, one that didn't include me. "No way," I said, when I heard it. "I'm a searcher and an EMT. I've got the dog. And it's my husband. No way are you searching without me."

To their credit, they yielded immediately.

"Sheriff, if you can get a ping off Scott's iPhone, I'll take a team out and try to find him," I said.

"I'll go with you," Kathryn said.

"And me," Nate chimed in.

"If Mark is involved, I don't want to put my deputies into a position of having to arrest him. Or worse. How about we ask the state police to go with you?"

"Great."

"I've got eight guys," Mike said.

"You should go to the power station, Mike," I suggested. "Because it sounds like Scott may have been right about it being at risk." I was careful not to use the term "ecoterrorist."

He hesitated, conflicted. If Scott was in trouble, he wanted to be there, I could tell.

"I need to check that facility. But let me talk to the troopers and see if we can establish radio contact. Because if Scott's in danger, I want to help."

"Okay. Thanks, Mike."

He started to leave, then turned around, frowning. "What about that tracker thing? Does he have that? Scott?"

The Garmin InReach! I'd forgotten all about it. "Thanks, Mike!" I whipped my phone out of my pocket and opened the app. No signal. "I need to get outside." I looked at Nate. "Get your stuff together. I want to take my Jeep. You can drive if you want, Nate, but I want the Jeep."

Why? Maybe the Jeep is my security blanket. I don't know.

Kathryn slid into her coat. "Don't you want to stay here with the kids?" I asked.

"No. I'm coming with you."

She hardly knew me, but she wanted to support me. "Thank you."

The sheriff called out to me. He had one more thing to say. He pulled out a map. "I don't know exactly where Mark Williams was going to take him, but this is where the power transfer station is." He made an X on the map. "Mark said he'd take him to a place that overlooks the facility. But I don't know beyond that."

"Okay, thanks." I took the map.

"I trusted him, you know?"

People ain't always as they seem.

He walked away, his shoulders slumped. I know he felt betrayed. Responsible. He wasn't. Only Mark Williams was. But I got that feeling.

"See you outside," I said to the others. I couldn't wait to see if I could make contact with the Garmin. I collected Luke and left the building. The snow had completely stopped, and almost all the clouds had disappeared. The sky was an obsidian bowl inverted over the world.

I texted the Garmin but got no response. Disappointment dulled my hope even though signal failure is expected up in the mountains. The terrain is steep, the valleys deep, so what was I thinking? This part of Virginia is a black hole for communications. I guess I hoped for a miracle.

I loaded Luke up in the Jeep. He was somber, mirroring my mood. "We're going to find Scott, okay, buddy?" I said, ruffling his collar. He licked my face, and I closed his crate, then the back of the Jeep.

I admit I was shaking from fear, not cold, although it was cold enough. That's when the miracle came. Garmin has a 24/7 emergency operations center. If you get injured or lost, you can press a button on the unit. The unit alerts the center, and a person tries to contact the Garmin owner and calls emergency services in the area where the Garmin pinged.

Of course, Scott had set it up thinking I'd be using the Garmin. He put his phone number down as the emergency contact. The Garmin people had texted that number several times and had gotten no response. Thankfully, they also identified Highland County, Virginia as the location and called the emergency number.

Deputy Gibson came running out of the building. "Hey, I think I may have Cooper's location!"

"What?"

"Dispatch got a call from Garmin. They got an emergency notification from one of their units. Here's the lat and long!"

Nate, in the driver's seat, started fumbling for his handheld GPS. "Gimme 'em," he said as he powered it on.

Gibson recited the numbers. Then I got a text. The Garmin people had found the other number associated with the inReach. Mine. "I've got them too!" I recited the numbers out loud. They were the same.

"Here!" Nate stepped out of the Jeep and showed me the dot on the map corresponding to the latitude and longitude we'd been given.

The two state troopers left their SUV and came over. "What's going on?" Dave Ward asked.

"We may have a location," I said.

"The sheriff wants me to come with you since I know the county," Gibson said. "If anything goes down with Williams, though, I'll step back." He looked at the troopers. "You okay with that?"

"Yes sir, good," Dave said.

Nate spread the map out on the hood of my Jeep. I knew what he was doing—trying to reconcile the lat and long with the physical map. "Deputy, I could use some help here!" The state troopers went over as well, the four men forming a huddle over the small map. I would have joined them, but I was shaking with excitement or nerves or fear or some combination. Kathryn put her arm around me. I heard her praying, softly, and I relaxed into her words. *Surely, God wouldn't ....*

But I knew well that God often did what I didn't want or expect. So I put that thought aside, and remembered this: *I am not my own, but belong body and soul, both in life and in death, to my faithful Savior, Jesus Christ.* The good old Heidelberg Catechism.

Then I whispered, *and Scott, too, Lord. He is yours, body and soul, in life and death, and I release him to your protection, your care, for your purposes.* Kathryn squeezed my shoulder.

Immediately, the thought flew into my head, *What if he's having chest pains? What if he can't get help What if he's dying?* I gritted my teeth and fought the fear.

"Jess," Nate said, drawing my attention. "Let's doublecheck that lat and long." I pulled up the text I'd received and repeated the numbers to him. He looked at Deputy Gibson and said, "That's right." Then Nate motioned me over. "Those numbers aren't in the direction of the power plant. They're way over here." He pointed to a mark pretty far away. "Was Scott over there earlier?"

"Not that I know of."

"What do you want to do?"

My gut instinct responded. "Follow the lat and long. If Williams lied about one thing, he'll lie about others."

Nate nodded. "Okay. We'll head that direction."

I climbed in the passenger seat of my Jeep, put the lat and long in my phone's GPS, and plugged the phone into the charger. Nate put his handheld on charge too. Maybe between the two of us, we'd get to the right place.

We took the lead. VDOT had gotten the two primary roads we wanted to follow plowed, so it was easier and faster going than we had anticipated. "How you doin'?" Nate asked, glancing over at me.

"Kathryn prayed for me," I said, the surprise still fresh.

He nodded. "I like that girl."

Our next turn took us onto a smaller road. I don't even think you could call it a secondary road. Nate dropped his speed, which was wise but frustrating for me.

Nate glanced in the rearview mirror. "Your dog's sitting up in his crate."

I turned around to look. Sure enough, Luke was sitting up, alert, like he knew something was up. Normally, he's either lying down or moving restlessly, banging his tail against the side, excited and ready to search.

"He's got somethin' on his mind," Nate said. "Maybe picking up on your mood or maybe somethin' else."

"We have a right turn coming up," I said.

"Okay." He glanced at me. "You feelin' okay?"

"Still nauseated. Stress."

"Keep your head."

"I will. Your turn should be beyond those bushes."

He started to turn right, then stopped short. The turn wasn't a road, it was the entrance to a field, and it was gated. My Jeep's headlights glinted off a shiny silver padlock on a rusted chain holding the gate shut. I grabbed my binoculars and walked up to the gate.

Dave and his partner, Trooper Billy Latham, walked up behind me. "What do you see?" Dave asked.

The clouds were gone. A bright white full moon and innumerable stars had the sky to themselves. There was more light than there'd been for days. I scanned the snow-covered field, moonlight glinting off the snow like diamonds scattered on the ground. "I don't see anything," I said.

"These here, they're fresh tracks," Nate said, shining his light on the ground. "They go on beyond the gate."

I followed them with the binoculars. "They lead toward that stand of trees."

"How far away do you figure that is?" Billy asked.

"Half a mile, at least. Maybe three-quarters," Nate said.

"Any livestock in that field?"

"I didn't see any," I responded, "and I don't see animal tracks either." I lowered my binoculars. The two troopers were looking at each other. I imagined they were trying to decide what to do.

"There's no house in sight and no livestock. What reason would a pickup have to drive into a snow-covered field like that in a storm?" Nate said. The two troopers looked at him. "I'm thinkin' y'all got exigent circumstances."

"Yes!" I said quickly.

"Exigent circumstances" means a law-enforcement officer perceives an immediate threat to someone, allowing him or her to enter a property or a house without authorization or a search warrant. Our inability to contact Scott or Mark Williams, the information from Williams's ex, plus the ping the Garmin people got justified it in my eyes.

The troopers thought it over, then agreed. Billy left, came back with some hefty bolt cutters, and in a short couple of minutes, the gate was open. "I'll close it after y'all get through," Deputy Gibson said, "in case there's sheep or cows about."

We got back in our vehicles and drove through the gate. Nate paused while Gibson closed it, then we continued over the field, bouncing over ruts and rocks, our headlights flashing. I did not see any evidence of animals, except for deer tracks and what might have been rabbit trails. Nate drove to the right of the tire track we'd seen, preserving it in case that ended up being evidence.

I think we expected to come upon a house, hidden in the woods, or a barn, or something. Nope, it was just a big empty field. But the red dot from the Garmin people was still ahead.

Nate cracked his window. Seconds later, Luke, who'd been sitting quietly, stood up and whined. He circled in his crate and barked twice.

I sat in the passenger seat, my hands pressed against my temple. "You okay?" Nate asked.

"Scared."

"Of what you're going to find?"

I nodded. Fear had me shaking again.

Nate reached over and squeezed my shoulder.

"Let's stop," I said after Luke barked again. We were close to those trees. To their left was a drop-off of some sort. I'd know better when I could look closer.

"You want to search here?"

"Yes." I was thinking those trees might be hiding a cabin or something. But Luke was getting restless now. Was he already smelling something?

I got out and walked around a little, a plan forming in my head. Get my pack. Put Luke's vest on and his flashing light. Ask him to seek. Let him go. If he started toward what looked to me like a drop-off or cliff, call him back and redirect him. If he went for the trees, follow him.

The guys had gotten out and were looking around, shining their lights on the ground.

Kathryn approached me. "Are you okay?" she asked.

"Sure," I said, hoping she didn't see me trembling. I shouldered my backpack. To this day, I don't know why I did that.

Normally, I'd let Luke out first. It would be easier to put his vest on if I wasn't carrying the backpack.

But I put it on, opened the back of the Jeep, and then Luke's crate. I was about to say something to Kathryn when Luke pushed past me, jumped out of the back, and began casting around for a scent like a mad dog.

"What's he doing?" Kathryn said, fear sharpening her voice.

"He's got something!" My throat went dry.

"Everybody stand still!" Nate thundered. "Give him room."

I'd never seen him act this way, running in circles, whimpering. He stopped and dug furiously in the snow, then raised his head, a patch of white on his nose. I was about to go grab him so I could put the vest and light on, but he took off again. He raced toward the cliff, his head high, his nose working. As I ran toward him, he went back and forth a couple of times, and then I saw him gather himself ... and jump!

37

WHEN I SAW Luke jump off that cliff I swear my heart stopped! I raced for the edge. I heard him yelp when he landed. I peered over the edge, over the rocks, my flashlight shining, trying hard to see his body. Then I saw movement. Luke! He was running off to the right.

Nate grabbed my arm. "What are you doing?" His face looked as close to panicky as I've ever seen him.

I pulled my arm away. "I'm following my dog."

"No! No way. Those rocks are icy. You'll never make it."

I straightened my back. "Nathan Tanner, I ignored my dog once and left you under a pile of rubble for twelve hours. I still regret that. I am not ignoring him again." We heard a burst of barking below. "I'm going."

"It's not safe."

"I'll find a way."

Dave Ward stepped up. "I'll go with her." We both looked at him. "If Williams is there, too, you'll need support."

I nodded. "Thank you."

Nate took a deep breath. I'm sure his exasperation was as

much about his amputated leg and his inability to go with me as it was with my stubbornness. He turned to Deputy Gibson. "Get an ambulance headed this way. Preferably arriving down there."

Why did he do that? Later, when I asked him, he said, "Somebody had to operate out of an abundance of caution."

I turned around to descend down the first drop, about twenty feet. I tried to remember what I'd learned in my ill-fated attempt to learn rock climbing a few years ago. I took off my gloves and stuffed them in my pockets. I turned off my headlamp to force myself to navigate by feel. I leaned into the cliff. I focused on finding the tiny hand- and footholds I needed to descend. Most were full of snow. I shoved my fingers in anyway, ignoring the cold, ignoring the pain, determined to get down that cliff.

I made it down about twelve feet, then slipped and slid down the last eight. "I'm all right!" I yelled when I finally hit bottom. My pack had buffered me. I didn't even hit my head. I just added a few more bruises to the ones I'd gained earlier when the tree fell on me.

Dave Ward had taken a different route. He, too, managed to get most of the way down before he fell. He didn't have a pack, and I heard him cry out as he slammed into the rocks. I wanted to keep going toward Luke. Instead, I turned, went over to him, and helped him up.

"I'm okay," he said. "Man, those rocks are hard."

More barking. "He's this way," I said.

Luke has two main indications that he's found someone. If the person is alive, he comes back to me, pulls the braided cotton tug attached to my belt, and runs back to the person. He keeps doing that until I connect with the person. If the search subject is deceased, he lies down and barks, waiting for me to come to him.

It scared me that he wasn't coming back. Really scared me. Because I was certain he was on Scott's trail. Why else would he be so frantic? Then I remembered I'd taught him a third indication, one for him to use when we were checking a rubble pile, like a collapsed building. In that situation, he was supposed to stand and bark. I didn't want him running back and forth across a pile potentially full of broken glass and jagged metal.

I kept moving toward where I was hearing him, with Dave right behind me. The funny thing was, Luke wasn't just barking, he was whining and yowling. What was that all about?

Finally I saw him. He was in a stand of pines and cedars and other firs, and he was barking at a pile of fallen boughs. Only as I got closer, I saw they weren't fallen. They were cut.

I pulled off my backpack, took away a couple of those boughs, got down on my knees, and pushed my way into the pile. And there, slumped up against a fallen log, was my husband.

Honestly, I thought Scott was dead. His eyes were closed, his skin was blue, he had his knees tucked close to his chest, and his arms crossed in front of him. Worst, he didn't react when I called his name. I froze.

Luke wasn't so reticent. He pushed his way past me and began licking Scott's face. And that's when Scott opened his eyes.

"Scott, hey, Scott. It's me, Jess," I said, my voice cracking with emotion. What my headlamp showed terrified me. He wasn't shivering. That's a bad sign. His right shoulder was covered with snow colored by what? Blood? His face was bruised, bloody, and blue. I saw what looked like a bullet hole in his jacket right in the center of his chest.

My EMT training fought past my fear and clicked in. Warm him up. Stop the bleeding.

Luke, I realized, was trying to handle the first part. He'd pushed his way as close to Scott as he could get, draping himself part way over Scott's lap. Did he know his body heat would help?

How do dogs sense when we're injured or sick or incapacitated? How do they know we need protection? Do they sense a shift in our energy? Do we put off a smell? I don't know. But from the minute Luke and I bonded, he knew when I needed him, sometimes before I did. In fact, that's how Nate first realized I had PTSD. He saw Luke leaning against me, putting his foot on mine, or nudging me when my stress level rose. Now, I was watching Luke do that same thing to Scott. Dogs are amazing.

I could hear the state trooper behind me talking on the radio. I yelled, "Dave, I need the first-aid kit and emergency blanket in my pack!"

"Got it!" he responded, and he shoved them through the boughs. He started to come in, took one look at Scott, and crawled back out. I heard him calling for a medevac helicopter.

My small first-aid kit held one set of gloves, a few rolled bandages, antiseptic wipes, anti-bacterial ointment, gauze, tape, a triangular bandage, one hemostatic gauze pack, small scissors, and some small packs of OTC pain relievers. The hemostatic gauze would stop bleeding. Now, where was he bleeding? Chest? Shoulder?

I felt Scott's face. It was cold to the touch. The pulse in his neck was very slow.

I explored that hole in his jacket. Had he been shot? Was he bleeding? I felt the hole. It went all the way through. Beyond that was ... what?

"I'm going to unzip your jacket, Scott," I said. I tugged on the zipper and the two sides separated. What I saw then made me gasp. "You're wearing your vest!" I said. Not just any vest, his *ballistic* vest. My heart jumped. *Why did he wear his vest?* Was it bloody? No. I loosened it and probed underneath until my hand touched his skin. Cool to the touch, but no blood. I probed the vest more and felt a small, hard object. *Oh, thank God!* "Your vest stopped the bullet!" I said. A shot straight to his center of mass, but he had his vest on. Hot tears filled my eyes.

So he wasn't bleeding from a chest wound. His shoulder was packed with snow. His heart rate was so low I didn't think he was at risk of bleeding out.

He needed to be warmed up. I made that my priority.

I opened the emergency blanket. I gently and carefully moved Scott's legs and positioned Luke between them. My headlamp glinted off something metal—Scott's Glock on the ground near his left hand. I picked it up, made sure that the safety was on, and yelled for Dave.

When he stuck his head in I handed him the gun. "It's Scott's. I don't think it's been fired," I said. That would be evidence. Someone, presumably Williams, would face assault on a federal officer charges.

Then I turned back to Luke, getting him up next to Scott. I told him to stay and covered him as well as Scott with the emergency blanket. I wanted to capture whatever heat Luke could radiate.

Ideally, I would have been the one warming up his chest, his core. But there was nothing ideal about this situation. His ballistic vest would impede heat transfer. I didn't want to move him, to make him lie flat because of his shoulder. So I did the best I could. I unzipped my jacket and my fleece and got close up behind him, under the emergency blanket, hoping I'd radiate heat as well.

AN AMBULANCE ARRIVED before the chopper. When we heard it coming over the field toward us, Dave took down the shelter Scott had made so the EMTs could get to him. Then he helped me get up. I was shivering and stiff.

"The ambulance is here, Scott," I said. I snugged the emergency blanket around him. His eyes were open. His face was regaining some color.

Dave knelt down. "Scott, Dave Ward, state police. Who did this to you?"

One word was all he could get out. "Williams."

"Did you fight?"

Scott didn't answer and Dave didn't push it. The fact that

Scott's gun hadn't been fired was a clue.

"Dave, I think there's a bullet lodged in his ballistic vest."

"I'd like to get that if I can."

"Maybe when the EMTs take that blanket off?"

"I'll wait until he's in the ambulance."

I asked Scott if Luke was hurting him lying over his legs. He shook his head.

The lights of the ambulance reflected on the snow, red and white flashing wildly all around us. The EMTs brought warming blankets and IV fluids with them. When they took Scott's core temperature it was 91 degrees. I wondered how low it had gone.

Hypothermia is defined as a core body temperature under 95 degrees F. When I found him, he was well into moderate, if not severe, hypothermia. He wasn't shivering. His pupils were dilated. His heart beat was slow, his breathing shallow.

How much time did he have left? I wondered. A tremor went through my body when I thought of it.

I had to pull Luke off of Scott. He didn't want to leave his man. Then the EMTs began warming Scott up, using blankets, the IV, and gel packs that they inserted in his clothes. They had to do it slowly, carefully. A jolt of cold blood racing to his core could cause a heart attack.

After they got him situated an EMT began asking me questions about Scott, how long he'd been in the cold, and once she found out I was his wife, some basic medical questions. I was careful to tell her about the chest pains he'd suffered recently.

I heard the male EMT say, "Sir, we're going to move you to a rescue board."

"Wait!" I said.

They both looked at me. "We want to get him into the ambulance."

"I realize that. But before you move him, you need to know he's been shot in the chest and in his right shoulder."

Her eyes widened. She glanced at her partner.

I knew that in all likelihood these were volunteer rescue workers. Which is not to say they weren't well-trained, just that out here they probably saw more car crash cases and tractor accidents than bullet wounds.

I continued. "He's wearing a ballistic vest. I think the shot to his chest didn't penetrate. But the shoulder ... I haven't assessed that."

The male EMT said, "We'll do that in the ambulance."

"But you should raise the head of the board or he'll be in a lot of pain."

He did what I suggested, then said, "Let's go, Kitty."

Gently, they moved him onto the board. It still hurt. I saw him grimace and heard him cry out. He gripped the edge of the board with his left hand. They carried him to the ambulance and put him inside.

"I want to see if I can get the bullet out of his vest," Dave told them. "Let me know when I can get up there."

I stood near the back door, which was open a crack. Kitty did another assessment and commented on his heart rate. It was high, a change from when I took it. All part of the rewarming process.

The male EMT, whose name was Pete, jumped down. "Officer, you can go up in there now." Then he turned to me. "The chopper is ten minutes out. Do you want to go with him?"

"Yes," I answered. "What about his shoulder?"

Pete shook his head. "He's bleeding. We put a hemostatic bandage on it and immobilized his arm. He's beginning to feel pain again, which is good. But he's not out of the woods yet, not by a longshot."

I shivered. "Where will the copter take him?"

"UVA Medical Center. It'll be a quick ride. Maybe forty minutes."

Forty minutes seemed like forever.

Dave climbed back down. "Got it," he said, holding up the

bullet. He put it in a small evidence bag and put that in his breast pocket. "I didn't see any other damage to the vest. I think two shots hit him."

Just two. Two bullets.

"Are you going with him?"

"Yes." What did I need to do? My brain felt frozen. I couldn't think.

"I'm going to set flares out for the chopper." He hesitated. "Do you need to pack up your stuff?"

"Yes, right," I said.

I looked up and saw headlights bouncing over the field. When they got closer, I saw they were from my Jeep.

Nate and Kathryn got out and came running. Nate grabbed me in a bear hug.

"How is he?"

"I thought he was dead!" The reality of it hit me hard. In my mind, I saw Scott sitting frozen, unmoving, his face blue. I choked up. I swallowed hard to get past the lump in my throat. "He's been shot. Twice."

Nate wrapped his arms around me again. He held me close as tears streaked my face. I felt another hand on my back. Kathryn's.

"It's okay. He didn't die. And he ain't gonna. Not yet anyway." Nate pulled a handkerchief out of his pocket. I wiped my face. "God's brought your guy through this. And you too. And I'm thankful for that."

"Yes."

"You scared us both," Kathryn said, "going over that cliff like that."

"I'm okay. Worried about Scott."

"Hey," Nate said, "did Luke hurt himself jumpin' off that cliff?" He nodded toward my dog who was curled up on the emergency blanket I'd used to cover Scott.

"I don't know. I don't think so." Guilt flooded me. "I didn't check him."

"You were busy keeping your husband alive!" Kathryn said, defending me.

I started to follow Nate. "Jessica!" someone called out. I turned to see Dave pointing at the blinking lights of the approaching helicopter. He gestured for me to come. The EMTs were already bringing Scott out of the ambulance.

I looked at Nate, then back at the ambulance, frozen by indecision.

Kathryn put her hand on my arm. "Nate will take good care of him. I'll help him get Luke in your Jeep. You go."

I HAD to go without saying goodbye to Luke. That was much harder than going off that cliff.

I settled into the spare seat in the copter and buckled my seatbelt. Scott looked unconscious, or asleep. He had an IV drip going and blankets covered him. His face looked pale.

The chopper was so loud I couldn't hear what the EMTs were saying, so I silently watched and prayed, and we lifted off. I saw Nate and Kathryn and Luke grow smaller and smaller. Eventually, only the lights of the ambulance showed me their position.

As we banked to turn toward Charlottesville the full moon came into view, a beautiful silver disk in an obsidian sky. And I remembered something Nate said to me once. *The full moon always rises at sunset. Every month. You can count on it.*

At first I was like, *Whaaaat? What does that even mean?* And I wasn't even sure that was true. I looked it up.

He was right. And eventually I got what he was saying. There's an order to our universe, a design created by God— steady, reliable, consistent. And although chaos may seem to take hold for a time, God's order will prevail. He will make things right. And he will make all things beautiful.

I leaned my head back, the airsickness bag gripped in my left hand, and I began to silently repeat these words, "I am not my own, but belong—body and soul, in life and death—to my faithful Savior Jesus Christ."

38

WE WON'T BE able to have Thanksgiving at our house like Scott wanted, I thought, as I sat in the Trauma Care unit at the UVA Medical Center. I was waiting for doctors to examine my husband, but I could tell from the monitors he was doing better. I guess that's why I started thinking forward.

By the time Scott got to trauma care his temperature was up to 96.8. Much better. His color had improved, his breathing was more regular, and his heart rate was steady. Doctors found that in addition to the resolving hypothermia, he had a bullet wound to his right shoulder and an eight-inch diameter bruise in the center of his chest. He also had innumerable cuts and bruises all over his body from the fall he took, plus frostbite on his cheeks. But nothing except his shoulder was broken, not even his patched-together hip.

The bullet wound in his shoulder was not a through-and-through, meaning the bullet was still somewhere in his body. X-rays found it hiding in his trapezius muscle. It had shattered lots of bone but missed the major artery running up his arm and into his chest. I had so much to be thankful for. Who needs a turkey to celebrate?

Both of us slept most of that first day in the hospital, once Scott had a room in the ICU. I looked pretty rough. I hadn't brought my pack with me on the helicopter, so I was still in the clothes I'd worn when I'd fallen down that cliff. All I had on me was my wallet and my phone.

A kind nurse noticed my fingertips, cut on the icy cliff. She brought me soap, antiseptic cream, and bandages. Then she found some clean scrubs and towels and offered to let me shower and change in an employee locker room.

Afterward, I still felt like a mess, but the important thing was Scott was alive and I was with him and everything else would work out.

Late in the day I started receiving updates from Clear Springs. Nate texted to say he'd had Luke checked by a vet up in that area. Nothing was broken, but the vet said she thought Luke had sprained his shoulder and bruised some ribs. She told Nate to keep him quiet for a few days. *He's snorin' like a champ*, Nate texted. *Kathryn's got a steak for him when he wakes up.*

The two young men who hijacked the bus flagged down a deputy and turned themselves in the day after we found the kids. They were cold and hungry and tired and had nowhere to go and no way to get there. Turns out they were from the next county over, two high-school dropouts who had been recruited, as Scott had suggested, to hijack the bus to draw attention away from the plans to attack the power transfer station. The recruiter was Mark Williams, who knew them from his time as deputy in that county.

That attack on the power station was thwarted by Scott's brilliant thinking and Mike's action. Mike got there just in time to interrupt four men and a woman who'd knocked out a guard, cut through the fence, and were planting explosives around the facility. I saw on my phone, though, that the way the news reported it, the state police had interrupted their plan. I didn't know if that was Mike's idea or Washington's. Whatever. The announcement would come later they were associated with Contra2+.

State police and sheriff's deputies went to Mark Williams's home. After a standoff that lasted over two hours, Mark shot himself.

When the police entered his home, they'd found Mark had been in the process of packing up. While he was dying he confessed. He'd cooperated with the organizers of the plan to disable the power transfer station. He was angry the state had taken his land, angry his wife had left, and angry Scott had figured it out before the plan could be executed. "I can't do this anymore," he said, halting between each word. And then he died.

He'd lost his marriage, his kids, and his land, the losses piling up to a level he couldn't cope with.

Later, when I told Scott what had happened, he got really sad. I asked him what he was thinking. "When life starts to go wrong, some cops have no way to cope with it. No one to talk to, no way to deal with their feelings. The job requires you to stuff your feelings and do hard things. But if you can't unstuff them, if you can't sort out what's going on inside, those feelings can turn on you. And cop suicide is often the result." He looked at me. "I feel bad for him. I didn't pick up on the anger or depression. Some profiler I am."

"You hardly knew him!" I said.

"My guess is no one really knew him."

ON THE SECOND DAY, Scott was well enough to move to the step-down unit. Amanda texted me to check on him and see what we needed from home. *Extra clothes, preferably sweats for him and jeans and a sweatshirt for me,* I texted back. She showed up at two o'clock that afternoon with clothes for both of us and a hot cup of coffee for me. Guess who was with her? Ethan.

He wasn't just with her, he was *with* her. You know—arm around her shoulder, standing close, eyes shining with happiness. I could hardly wait to hear that story!

I put the coffee off to the side. The smell was about to make me throw up. They asked how I was doing, and I said okay, except I was still nauseated. "It's been going on for a couple of days," I said. "It's either the stress, or I'm coming down with something, so don't get too close."

We talked a little more. I told them what Scott was dealing with and how long we'd probably be in the hospital. And I told them the whole story of the kids, Mark Williams, and how Scott had managed to survive. I did most of the talking, but Scott filled in some of the details from his end. His voice was still pretty weak.

The whole time, I noticed Amanda kept glancing at the coffee she'd brought me. Finally, she said, "Jess, let's take a break. Ethan can stay with him."

So I followed her out of the room. As soon as we were out of the ICU she turned to me and said, "You're pregnant!"

"What? No! How do you know?"

"Yes, you are. You haven't touched that coffee I brought you. Normally, you'd be guzzling it down and asking for more. And the nausea? You're pregnant."

"No way."

"Yes, you are. I can tell." Her smile was a mile wide. "Come on!" She grabbed my elbow, walked me to the elevators, and took me down to the first floor, where there was a small pharmacy. I followed her lead, dumbstruck, like a lamb being led to the slaughter. Searching the shelves, she found a pregnancy test kit, bought it, and shoved it into my hands. "You don't think you're pregnant? Prove it!" She made no attempt to keep her voice down.

My face was hot with embarrassment. I mean, there were other people in there, staring at us. And Amanda was enjoying every second of it. She turned to the pharmacy clerk. "Can you direct us to a ladies room?"

The clerk and two other women answered the question.

"Right down the hall," they all said, pointing. I was a little surprised they didn't follow us down there.

"Let's go." Amanda grabbed my elbow again. She marched me into the restroom, ripped open the box, pulled out that little stick, handed it to me, and said, "Go!"

And there, in a brown-and-beige public restroom at the UVA hospital in Charlottesville, I found out my prayers, my hundreds of prayers, had been answered. I was pregnant! I emerged from the stall and showed Amanda the test. Then I hugged my crazy stepdaughter and cried and thanked God.

"Do you know what this means?" Amanda said.

"I think so."

"I don't think you do. Listen, it means my child will be a month older than his uncle. Or aunt."

I blinked. "You're still—"

"Pregnant. Yes."

Another good shock. "What happened?"

Amanda waved me off. "I'll tell you later."

"Aw, come on!"

She rolled her eyes. "All right. I was at Nate and Laura's, and I confided in them. Laura showed me pictures of a developing baby in a book. It wasn't a cluster of cells, like I thought. It was a baby. And once I saw that, I couldn't, you know, kill it."

"I'm so excited for you."

"I'm still debating whether to keep it or put it up for adoption. Either way, Dad's gonna be a grandfather a month before he's a father again!"

A grandfather? Scott?

My world spun. I stared at the positive pregnancy test. "How accurate are these?"

"Oh, you're pregnant. Get used to it."

I guessed I would.

. . .

I WAS SO stunned riding back upstairs in the elevator I didn't ask Amanda an important question. What happened with Ethan? I was preoccupied with the new life growing inside me. A boy? A girl? How big was he or she? And when would my due date be?

Right outside the door to Scott's room I made a sudden U-turn and plowed into Amanda. "I don't want to tell him!" I said.

"What do you mean?" she said, laughing.

"It's ... it's such big news. It's going to change everything."

"You are crazy." She turned me around and pushed me. "Get in there."

I did feel a little crazy. After all these months ... after all those prayers ... after all that *grief* ... I was pregnant!

Maybe he'll be asleep, and I can wait a while to tell him. But no. When I stepped inside Scott's room he was half sitting up. He and Ethan were talking about horses. Scott's voice was weak and a little raspy, but he was talking.

He looked at me, then Amanda, then back to me, and he must have seen something in our faces. "What's going on?"

Amanda grinned like the Cheshire cat. "C'mon, Ethan, we gotta go," she said. She gave her dad a quick kiss. "See ya later, old man. You look great." Then she grabbed Ethan's hand and led him out of the room.

"What just happened?" Scott said, stunned.

"Scott, I ..." I couldn't get the words out. Instead, I handed him the pregnancy test.

He frowned, tried to focus on it, then it hit him. His face lit up. "You? You're pregnant?"

I nodded. I leaned over and buried my face on his good shoulder so he wouldn't see my tears.

He put his arm around me and said, "Oh, Jess. I'm so happy!"

THE NEXT THREE days in the hospital gave us lots of time to talk. I discovered how Scott had found the strength to build that shelter, even though he was hurt. "I kept thinking about you and praying," he said. "I didn't want to leave you alone. Not yet."

I asked him why he was wearing the ballistic vest. "I knew before we left I might want to ask Mark to take me down closer to the power transfer station. So I wore it as a precaution."

"Good thing."

Scott asked how I'd found him. I told him about the Garmin getting us close, and then Luke. "He went crazy as soon as I let him out of the car. Running around, smelling you all over the place. He got to the edge of the cliff and began casting back and forth. I saw him leap off, and I knew he had your scent. He acted desperate to find you."

"So you followed him."

I smiled. "Yes."

"Off the cliff."

"Yes."

He shook his head. "Crazy woman."

I shrugged. "What else could I do? But you should have seen Luke. He was going nuts searching for you. He loves you, Scott!"

Doctors said the reconstruction of Scott's shoulder would have to wait until he'd fully recovered from his ordeal. So on the Tuesday before Thanksgiving, they said he could be released.

Ethan and Amanda helped me bring him home. Getting him up the stairs to the bedroom was tough. He had to stop three times to catch his breath, but he finally made it. I helped him get undressed and then he got in bed. I had to pile up pillows behind his back to support his shoulder. He was in a lot of pain, but he didn't want to take meds beyond the over-the-counter stuff.

He slept a lot that first day at home but felt better on Wednesday. Nate brought Luke back. I'd missed my buddy. He greeted me with his goofy grin and wagging tail, then went looking for Scott. When Nate and I followed him upstairs, we found that dog lying on the bed, snuggled up next to Scott, who was not only letting him be on the bed, he was petting him!

"So much for Luke not jumpin' up on anything," Nate said, referring to the vet's orders.

I left the two men talking and went back downstairs to make Scott some breakfast. I still couldn't abide the smell of coffee, but thankfully, Scott couldn't drink it anyway. So I made herbal tea, along with eggs and bacon. Nate came to say goodbye minutes later. He handed me my car keys. That's when I realized Laura must be outside waiting for him. "She didn't want to come in?" I asked.

"No. Not yet. She's struggling. Shame over that pregnancy. Embarrassment over how she treated you. She's doin' what hill people do—hidin'."

When someone sees your scars and loves you anyway, they almost disappear over time.

That old line pushed me into my boots and out the door. Laura was sitting in the driver's seat of her car, waiting for Nate. She did manage to roll down the window partway when I approached.

"Laura, thanks for helping Nate return my car and my dog," I said cheerfully. "I love you guys! Thanks for taking care of Luke!"

A "You're welcome" was all I got, but it was a start. I waved to Nate, turned, and jogged back inside. Man, it was cold! And I had had enough of cold.

By Thursday Scott was ready to come downstairs.

You and Dad better be dressed, Amanda texted. *We'll be there at noon.*

Who was "we," I wondered. Her and Ethan?

I asked Scott if he knew how the two of them got back together, and yes, Ethan had told him in the hospital what happened. Amanda had a problem with one of Nate's horses and called Nate. Nate called Ethan and asked him to go help her. He did. At first she was distant, but they worked together with the horse, resolved the problem, and then, well, they started talking. Ethan built a fire, and they sat on Nate's leather couch and talked all night, the same night we were out hunting for those kids.

He said he loved her. She told him what happened, and that she was pregnant. He said he didn't care. She made it clear she was not aborting that baby. He said good, he'd help her, he'd marry her, he'd raise the baby as his own. And if she didn't want to get married, that was okay. He'd just help her. Whatever she wanted.

And to her, that sounded like a future with hope.

"They're going to wait a few months, at least, to decide what to do," Scott said, "but I'm pretty happy with where they are right now."

Cars began arriving a little before noon. Every time I looked a different vehicle was pulling in the driveway. Amanda's Rogue, Ethan's truck, and then my stepfather's Lexus, my sister's Jeep, and then Mike's SUV ... with Kathryn Grace in the passenger's seat.

The first thing that came in the house was a leather recliner, operated by a remote. "We thought Dad might have trouble sleeping or sitting in a regular chair," Amanda said. "The remote means he can use it while his arm is in a sling."

Very thoughtful.

Next came turkey, mashed potatoes, dressing, sweet potatoes, rolls, salad, hot cider ... the whole, entire Thanksgiving dinner, just like Scott had wanted. And I didn't have to do a thing. Nate had connected Amanda with Kathryn and my mother, and together they conspired to give us this special day.

Scott sat at the end of the table. I sat on his left, my mom chose the seat on his right. Scott asked me to say grace because he didn't have the voice for it. I thanked God for the food, the people gathered, and Scott's survival. For the zillionth time I thanked Him for Luke, and then for the safe recovery of the kids on that bus. I could have gone on, but I knew people were hungry.

When I opened my eyes I saw my mom smile at Scott. "May I help you?" she said. When he nodded, she picked up his knife and began cutting up his food for him. It was almost ... motherly. And I thought she hated him!

That was not the only shocker. At the far end of the table Mike and Ethan started a lively conversation, I suspect about law enforcement. Amanda and Brooke were immersed in talking about Brooke's job and her son. And my stepfather and Kathryn found they knew a lot of the same people in the agency where they both had worked. In fact, he remembered the accident that had killed her parents.

The gentle buzz in our dining room was so normal and yet, for us, so unusual. I sat amazed, inhaling the smell of turkey and gravy and cranberry sauce, listening to the chatter, seeing all these different personalities joined like pieces in a patchwork quilt, a quilt on which someone had written, "Thanksgiving."

Only Nate and Laura were missing. But that was okay. I was learning that love means extending grace. Exercising forbearance. Being patient while love did its work, changing hearts, and forging the spirit of unity in the bond of peace. That was worth waiting for.

Scott made it about halfway through the meal, then he looked at me and said, "I'd better go lie down."

Before I could even scoot my chair back, Mike jumped up. "I got him." He helped Scott to his feet and walked him out to the living room and into the recliner. "He's nodding off already," Mike said to me when he came back.

So we finished dinner. I saved Scott a piece of pumpkin pie, then went into the living room and sat on the couch near my sleeping husband while everybody else cleaned up. Luke jumped up and rested his head on my lap. I stroked him, my heart full of gratitude.

Did we tell our family members and friends our news? Nope. And Amanda didn't spill the beans, either.

They'll have to wait 'til next time to find out about Baby Cooper. Some surprises need to be treasured in private. For a while, anyway.

EPILOGUE

THREE WEEKS later

Our parade of visitors continued after Thanksgiving. Scott's boss, Jeff Bennett, and Marcus Walker, head of CIRG, came out, followed by two agents from a shooting review group, and then two from the Office of Professional Responsibility. Bennett and Walker I considered "friendlies," but I eyed the others with a certain degree of suspicion. First of all, Scott's gun wasn't fired, so how did that need a shooting review? Secondly, who tipped off OPR and what reason did they give? OPR is like internal affairs for police. What did they think he'd done wrong?

I smiled and handed out coffee and muffins while I tried to overhear as much as I could from the kitchen.

My stomach may have been knotted up, but Scott's was not. "I've been through worse," he said, reassuring me afterward. And I knew that he had.

I actually enjoyed the visit we got from Sheriff McCormick and his wife. I made a nice lunch, a new pasta salad I wanted to try and grilled chicken. He told us that the two young men who'd hijacked the bus, Kevin Watters and Anthony Jenkins, had been charged with conspiracy, hijacking, kidnapping, and the second-degree murder of Mr. Nowers. "They'll spend a good deal of time in prison," he said. Thomas "Bean" Jones was facing lesser charges in juvenile court.

On a happier note, Scout Jacobson, Eric Robertson, and Jamie Godwin were going to be honored after the first of the year by the sheriff's office and the community. They'd be showered by gifts donated by town merchants. For their contributions to the rescue of the children, Scout and Eric were getting large college scholarships from the power company.

"We'd like y'all to be there," the sheriff said, and Scott and I said we would be.

Kathryn Grace McCaskill brought the biggest surprise to us. Since Thanksgiving, she'd been coming down, meeting Mike at our place. They'd ride, or clean out the barn, or groom the horses. She'd told Mike outright that she wouldn't date him because, well, their core beliefs didn't match. Apparently, though, meeting at our house wasn't a "date." Okay, then. Whatever.

Just yesterday, though, came the surprise. She brought me one of the paintings we'd found in the attic, the one with the girl sitting on the front porch of a country house, her dog lying at her feet, as a gift. "I thought you'd like it," she said.

And I did.

"The artist is Helen Burns," she explained. "I found out from some older people in town."

My mind tried to connect that name with something.

"She owned the house in the '70s."

"Oh, right!"

"She's also my great aunt, I think."

"Wow," I said, "good work!" I felt so pleased she'd made that family connection.

"That's not all," she said, beaming. "It seems that my father got around. Andrew Gerhardt is my half-brother."

"What?" I felt the shock physically, like a jolt in my spine.

She grinned. "Yes, different mothers, same dad. We've been in touch. We're meeting after Christmas."

I stared at her, wide-eyed. "How do you feel about this?" I managed to ask.

"I'm thrilled. He's eight years older than I am, but if things go well, I may have a little bit of family to relate to. I'm so pleased. Thank you. It's all because of you."

Well, actually, God, I thought. Providence. His hand weaving the tapestry of history.

I set the painting down and hugged her. "I'm so happy for you."

That night, Scott and I sat in front of the fire, tracing all the different threads in this crazy life, all that had brought us together, and all the people we were now connected with. I rested my hand on my belly and thought, *and one more.*

The End

ACKNOWLEDGMENTS

Having just returned from a three-day retreat with some longtime friends, I'm freshly aware of the value of relationships. Being able to share your heart with others, confidentially and constructively, is a priceless gift. Thank you, Terry, Vickie, Kathleen, and Bonnie, for listening to me, for sharing your advice on story ideas and book covers, and especially for wrestling out the things of faith with me in real time and real life. Jess is wiser because of you—and so am I.

For my special friend who shared her story with me so I could write Laura's journey, thank you for your vulnerability and strength. May it encourage others to give long-held shame to Jesus.

My usual suspects helped with the rest: Dru Wells and Sharon Smith on the FBI content, Sharon Johnson on SAR details, and Janet Schutt who read the manuscript early and helped with medical information. My daughter, Becky Chappell, also provided early feedback and later, publishing assistance. My agent, Janet Grant of Books & Such Literary Management supports my work and has helped secure audio- and large-print rights to my books, broadening their availability. Barbara Scott chased commas for me, along with many other details that tend to escape me. June Padgett of Bright Eye Designs created the cover. New to the team is Christian Author Assistant Amanda Geaney, who has been my social media manager and all-around cheerleader this year. Last, my 12-year-old granddaughter, Noelle Chappell, delightfully bounced around story ideas with me, especially regarding the missing school bus. I'm so thankful for all of them!

Most of all, I'm grateful to God, who "drew me up from the pit of destruction, out of the miry bog, and set my feet upon a rock, making my steps secure." (Psalm 40:2) That rock is Jesus Christ. May all I do glorify Him.

SDG

ABOUT THE AUTHOR

Linda J. White has loved dogs and a good dog story since early childhood. Her current buddy is an eleven-year-old Sheltie, Keira, who patiently came out of retirement to do a "nose work" class so Linda could experience the beginnings of training for SAR.

Linda has been a government worker, a mom at home, a Bible study teacher, a freelance writer, and the assistant editorial-page editor of a daily newspaper. Her late husband, Larry, a graduate of the American Film Institute, made training films for the FBI Academy. She has three grown children and five grandchildren and lives in Yorktown, Virginia, where she enjoys watching birds migrate and grandchildren grow.

www.lindajwhite.net

ALSO BY LINDA J. WHITE

The K-9 Search and Rescue Series:

All That I Dread

The Fear That Chases Me

When Evil Finds Us

My Darkest Night

FBI Thrillers:

Bloody Point

Battered Justice

Seeds of Evidence

Sniper!

Words of Conviction

The Tiger's Cage

Made in the USA
Las Vegas, NV
27 December 2023